Dear Tiffani
Enjoy the read !.

The Tempest Bloom

Rise of the Darkling

Book 1

Vernell Chapman

DEDICATION

This book is dedicated to my angels, Chris and Zach.

FOREWORD

Five centuries ago, Garkin and Faeborn lived amongst the humans in peace. They were spread across three prosperous settlements. The town of Luftohk was built within a large valley and surrounded by a forest filled with deerkin and oxen. Jormstad was a workman's town; most of the men were wood carvers or metal benders. Then there was Sjoborg; a coastal town known for its glass blowers and fisherman who spent half their lives at sea.

Each town contributed to the greater good. They traded with each other and insured that everyone lived on an equal footing. All seemed well until a terrible crime occurred. Harmonia Teg, a Faeborn woman, was kidnapped and murdered.

Her husband, Tylwyth held the Garkin responsible. She was taken from her bed chamber and all that remained was a few drops of blood on her pillow and a handful of flowers from the Cebus tree - a tree that grew in the gardens around the Garkin lord's manor.

The humans believed that another being was responsible for the crime. The darkling were a vicious horde of scavengers with no respect for human life or any other life for that matter. They appeared near Luftohk not long before Harmonia disappeared. Their origin was unknown as was most things about them. The humans soon discovered the darkling's one major weakness – intolerance for sunlight.

Because Harmonia was taken after daylight with the sun high overhead, the Faeborn didn't include the darkling as suspects for her disappearance. No darkling could withstand the full weight of the sun, even in a heavy cloak. The humans were ruled out as the perpetrators because none would be powerful enough to stand against a Faeborn. That left only the Garkin.

A motive for the act was never uncovered. Fighting broke out between the Garkin and Faeborn and many lives were lost on both sides. The Garkin have immense strength and the ability to leap to great heights. But the Faeborn are winged creatures with the ability to move objects with their minds. The battle between them carried on for many moons with no clear victor. Ultimately, the Faeborn fled to Tremeria, a land beyond the forest while the Garkin retreated to a mountainous region they called Merovech.

Once the Faeborn and Garkin abandoned their old homes, the darkling were free to ravage the human settlements. They pillaged the town of Luftohk stealing the livestock and slaughtering any man who stood in their way. The town's people tried to defend themselves but how could they? How can you fight an enemy that can appear almost anywhere?

With their sharp claws and narrow muscular bodies, the darkling traveled easily underground. They would appear throughout the town; anywhere there was soft ground. While the darkling appear to be humanoid, their pack-like characteristics are much more animalistic.

After several waves of midnight darkling attacks and numerous human casualties, the town of Luftohk was abandoned all together. The newly formed Faeborn and Garkin kingdoms were each sought out for aide. The human governor, Lad Pierce convinced Queen Nuestria, daughter of Lord Gadot, to sit down with King Tylwyth Teg to discuss a truce. He somehow convinced them to recognize that their fighting had made them both vulnerable to darkling attacks. That very day, a peace treaty was signed.

Lad Pierce also realized that the human realm still needed protection from the darkling. Queen Nuestria and King Tylwyth agreed to share in this responsibility. They sought out every darkling they could find and destroyed it. The few that avoided capture retreated to a patch of underground caverns at the edge of Jormstad.

Queen Nuestria dispatched a small contingent of Garkin to search the caverns but they never returned. It was then decided that the openings to the caves would be sealed. It was too dangerous to travel into the ground where the darkling had the advantage.

With the threat of darkling attacks behind them, the humans carried on with their lives. The Faeborn and Garkin did as well. The truce was intact but only time would tell if lasting peace could exist between the species.

Chapter 1

Anya had known all her life that her father was Garkin born. But she'd never seen a Gargoyle in the flesh until the day her sister changed for the first time. They'd gone for a stroll in the woods when Peter Pierce stepped out from behind a white, oak tree.

"Amy, come closer. I have something for you," Peter teased as he clenched moonflowers wrapped in a silken ribbon. His red hair was overly curly so he kept it cut close to his head. He wore his usual attire of dark pants, a pullover sweater and a vest. He was a carbon copy of his father, freckled face and all.

"What is it, Pete? I need to get home." She pretended to be unimpressed at the cluster of flowers he must have spent all afternoon picking. Ms. Miller's flower bed would certainly show evidence of his visit.

"These are for you." Peter handed Amy the flowers and then pulled her toward his hiding place behind the oak tree.

Anya tried to protest the exchange between Peter and her sister. "Amy, we need to head back. It'll be dark soon." No one had heard of an actual darkling attack in years but everyone still behaved as if they roamed the night unchecked.

"I won't be a moment," Amy said laughing as her long brown hair danced around her shoulders. She moved behind the tree and disappeared from sight.

Anya breathed deeply and sat down hard in the grass. She realized she'd been tricked into another "surprise" rendezvous between her sister and Peter. Amy wasn't allowed to visit him alone but she always managed to run into him when she and Anya were out for an afternoon stroll. *What if they were married* she thought to herself. Peter was Governor Burl Pierce's youngest son so Amy could do a lot worse than to marry him.

Anya leaned back in the grass as she watched the sun hanging in the sky midway between the clouds and the horizon. The forest around her grew quiet – too quiet. She'd just kicked a blade of grass from between her toes when she heard a most horrible sound.

"Oh no, please no!" Peter screamed at the top of his voice. Then Anya saw his shirtless body dart from behind the oak tree. He ran by her so quickly that she couldn't make out the expression on his face. He was terrified, that much was obvious.

Anya stumbled to her feet and went to find her sister. She found Amy lying on the ground in the fetal position. At least she thought it was her sister. Amy was changing into something else.

Her body was becoming harder, more muscular. Her hands and feet became clawed and her ears grew to twice their normal length. She released a throaty groan as her body continued to change.

What Anya found most peculiar was how her skin seemed to blend in with the dark earth she lay upon. Amy's light, brown hair had become darker too. Anya leaned down to touch her sister when she heard a deep voice behind her.

"I wouldn't do that if I were you," said the voice. Within seconds a large form of a man was kneeling down at her side and pulling her away from Amy. "It's not safe."

"Will she be alright?" Anya couldn't look away as her sister's body began to quiver.

"Don't worry, Anya. I'll see that she gets home."

"How do you know my name?" she asked with a shaky voice.

"I am Fredegund, a friend of your family. Hurry home now." He pulled a cloak from his shoulder bag and covered Amy's body. After taking a deep breath, he shifted into his Garkin form. His curly brown hair and close cut beard blended into a mass of chiseled features with animalistic undertones.

Anya turned to see another soldier standing behind them. He watched her closely but he didn't speak. She moved around him and took off running.

Anya reached her family's home much more quickly than normal. "Majka, something's happened…" Anya could barely get the words out. She found her mother in the kitchen and fell to her knees on the floor.

"What is it, Anya?" Her mother kneeled down in front of her. "Where is Amy? What's happened?"

"Amy ch-changed right in front of me." Anya could feel herself shaking as she tried to speak.

"Changed how?" Her mother asked with concern etched in her hazel eyes.

Anya didn't understand the question. "She's Garkin, Majka."

"Of course she is. Let's get you up." Her mother helped her to the sofa and sat down next to her. "Where is your sister now?"

"She's out by the old farmhouse… two Garkin soldiers showed up out of nowhere. The bigger one told me to leave. I didn't want to leave her though."

"It's fine, calm down." Anya's mother started stroking her hair and the side of her face. No matter how badly she felt, her mother could always help her to relax. This was quite an accomplishment considering the guilt she felt over leaving her sister with two strangers.

Before long, there were voices coming from outside. The front door swung open and Anya's father walked in followed by Amy and the two soldiers from the woods. Amy was wearing the cloak and looking like herself again.

"Emma, our daughter has shifted!" Ansoald could hardly contain his pride. He was larger than a normal man with dark features – obviously Garkin. But he had a gentle nature; not something the Garkin held in high regard. "When I saw Pete run into town, I knew right away what had happened. It didn't take long for me to find her either. She'd already changed back to her human form, imagine that!"

"This is wonderful news!" Emma replied steadily. She pushed pass her husband to hug her oldest daughter.

"Mom, it was the strangest thing. I thought it would be painful but it wasn't." Amy sounded so relieved.

"That proves how strong you are," said the larger of the two soldiers. "You should leave with me tonight, if your father permits it."

Ansoald turned toward the soldier wearing a surprised expression. "Fredegund, you would take her untrained?"

"Yes, in fact I insist…" Fredegund stared at Amy in a most peculiar way. She immediately started blushing.

"I consent," said Ansoald. He grasped Fredegund's forearm and put his other hand on his shoulder. "You honor me this day."

"The honor is mine, Ansoald." Fredegund nodded to Emma and then turned to Amy. "Pack only what you'll need for a few days. You'll stay in Merovech until the naming ceremony."

Amy didn't utter a word. She simply turned and started up the stairs with Anya close behind her. She hurried into her bedroom in the back of the house and pulled her clothe sack from under her bed. She filled it with her heaviest clothing.

"You're leaving with him?" Anya asked in a whisper.

"Of course I am. Weren't you listening downstairs?" Amy smiled at her sister as she continued packing.

"Amy, what happened out there?"

"I felt myself shifting and then there he was…" Amy had a distant look in her eyes as if she were reliving the past again. "He told me that he'd been watching me for a long time and now I would be his."

"And you believed him?"

"Yes." Amy picked up her bag and headed toward the bedroom door. She reached for Anya's hand as she went. "Take care of Majka for me. You know how she worries."

"Of course," Anya said with tears in her eyes. She clutched Amy's hand tightly as they descended the stairs.

The mood in the kitchen was jovial to say the least. The two soldiers were sitting at the table drinking ale. When Amy and Anya walked back into the room, Fredegund stood to his feet.

"I'm ready," Amy said brightly.

"Let's go. If we leave now, we'll reach Merovech before dark."

Amy hugged her parents and then turned to her sister. "Don't worry, Anya. I'll see you in a month's time."

"I miss you already," Anya said trying not to cry in front of the soldiers.

THE TEMPEST BLOOM: RISE OF THE DARKLING

Chapter 2

Just beyond the town limits on the north side of Jormstad, there was a jagged path that led to the Garkin city of Merovech. Since the 2nd legion regularly patrolled the city, the path was well used. Anya was relieved that no soldiers happened upon the path this late afternoon. She walked along quietly behind her parents as they made their way toward Merovech.

The city was surrounded by a forty-foot high stone fence and protected by a fortress that stood just beyond the entry gates to the city. As it were, the fortress was the home of the Garkin Queen and all three legions of her soldiers.

The lowest level of the fortress was divided into two sections. The front section included a weapons chamber, an infirmary, a dungeon and a training room. The rear section opened into the Garkin city and housed the 3rd legion of soldiers that protected its inhabitants. The main level held the throne room, the banquet hall and a set of parallel rooms for people waiting for an audience with the Queen.

The next two levels were the quarters for the first and second legions that were tasked with protecting the Queen, the fortress and the human city of Jormstad. The final level was the Queen's quarters which included chambers for her hand maidens and another large chamber for a consort, should the Queen ever take one.

Very few inhabitants of Jormstad had ever laid eyes on the Garkin Queen. She rarely left Merovech. There were rumors that she was very beautiful but what did that mean by Garkin standards?

Today Anya would see inside the fortress for the first time and get a glimpse at her future as well. When Amy married Fredegund, he would give her a new name. Later in that same ceremony, Fredegund's brother would give Anya a new name as well. It was a tradition that had gone on for hundreds of years; brother to brother and sister to sister.

Queen Nuestria, her generals and all of their families would be in attendance at the ceremony. As nervous as Anya felt, she tried to hide it. Her father had mentioned many times that the Garkin viewed displays of emotion as weakness; especially fear.

When they walked through the gates, Anya's legs started to tremble. Standing before her were two soldiers in their Garkin form. They watched her as if they could smell her fear but they didn't speak a word.

Emma turned and grasped Anya's hand. "Don't worry my dear; we are welcome here. This is a great day for the Garkin and our family."

"I'm not afraid," Anya said trying to convince herself more than anyone. She walked shakily along as she watched the guards pacing back and forth along the high stone fence. They began to shift, each one looking more frightful than the last.

When they reached the other end of the courtyard, they moved through the stone archway that formed the entrance to the fortress. Once inside, they walked into a large hallway with several doorways attached to it. The soldier stationed at the main gate pointed straight ahead where the hallway split into two passageways.

"Come this way." Emma took Anya's hand and led her down the left passageway. Ansoald nodded to them and walked to the right.

"Majka, where are we going?"

"We're going to join your sister. You both have a big day today." Emma stopped walking and turned to face Anya. "Your sister will be different. It's best you prepare yourself now."

"What do you mean different?" Anya asked. A month had gone by since she'd seen Amy but how much could she have changed in that time?

"You'll see for yourself." Emma turned and started walking again.

The hallway emptied into a large, dimly lit room. The furniture was old and neglected but it looked sturdy enough. There were painted tapestries on three of the four walls. They added some measure of warmth to the room.

"Hello mother, sister." Amy spoke from behind Anya.

"Amy, you look wonderful!" Anya couldn't believe how much her sister had changed in just one month. Amy's body was leaner with ten pounds of added muscle. She was deeply tan and her light brown hair was pulled back from her face and tied in a knot.

Anya hurried over to hug her but Amy stood rigid.

"You'd better get ready. Your garment hangs in the closet over there." Amy pointed to a wardrobe in the far corner of the room. "You have five minutes."

Amy nodded to her mother and quickly left the room. Anya watched her leave understanding more clearly what her transformation meant. Amy spoke differently, even her countenance had changed. She was Garkin now. There was no mistaking that.

With no time to waste, Anya pulled the dress out of the closet and removed her shepherd coat. Emma helped her youngest daughter into the ill-fitting garment. It looked like a bleached potato sack that had been beaten over a large stone to soften it. Everything the Garkin wore was for convenience and durability. One never knew when hand to hand combat would be in order.

On a round table next to the door, Anya found a small hand mirror. She stared into it realizing how differently she and her sister looked from one another. She still favored her mother with softer facial features and hazel eyes. Amy appeared as if she had been Garkin all her life. The change suited her well.

Anya followed Emma out into the main hall. Everyone was already in place waiting for the procession to start. Queen Nuestria would perform the ceremony and then there would be a feast.

"Hello Anya, your sister asked me to help you find your place." A small Garkin woman approached her wearing the only smile Anya had seen since they arrived. She was quite a bit shorter than Anya but there was a sturdiness about her. She had brown hair that was styled into two braids on either side of her head. "I'm Duran; Fredegund and Aregund are my cousins."

"It's nice to meet you." Anya was still on edge. "Where should I stand?"

"Your place is right behind the bride. Amy will receive a new name in her marriage ceremony. Because of the arrangement between our families, you will receive a new name too."

Anya moved closer to the young Garkin and whispered to her. "What if I don't like my new name?"

Duran laughed much louder than any Garkin should. "No one's ever asked me that before. Your betrothed decides your name so you're stuck with it. Well, you'd better get into place. Your sister is already waiting."

Anya wanted to ask what would happen if she didn't like her betrothed but then she thought better of it. She knew the day would come when she would meet a stranger and she would have to marry that stranger. The day that her sister shifted, she was immediately afraid - not only because of the change in her sister but what that change would mean for her too. Siblings usually shifted around the same time. Anya knew that her turn to change wouldn't be far away.

She found her place in the procession and glanced quickly behind her. Ansoald and Emma were standing proudly in line. Amy, standing just ahead of her made the smallest gesture with her hand.

As the procession moved slowly forward, Anya noticed how full the room was. She couldn't help but feel nervous with everyone watching her and her family. But nothing frightened her more than when the procession came to a standstill at the front of the throne room. She caught a glimpse of Aregund, Fredegund's younger brother. She immediately remembered him from that afternoon in the forest when Amy shifted for the first time.

He didn't address her then nor did he speak to her now. They stood mere inches apart and he hadn't even glanced at her. She would certainly have noticed if he had.

Queen Nuestria called all of the family members into a circle. She linked Amy and Fredegund's hands together for all of the witnesses to see. Then she announced Amy's new name – Basina. Anya saw the beginnings of a smile on Basina's face. But it quickly disappeared.

To Anya's surprise, Basina and Fredegund blended into the circle. Then she and Aregund were ushered in front of Queen Nuestria. It seemed a strange ceremony as Anya and her future husband were not required to speak to each other.

Anya was still able to get a good look at him. His curly brown hair looked almost black and hung down to his ears. He was clean shaven which was odd. Garkin usually loved their facial hair. But she didn't get a look at his eyes. Her father always told her that if you look into any creature's eyes, you'd see their soul.

When the Queen finished the ceremonial pronouncements, she moved on to the only part that Anya cared about – the announcement of her new name.

"You are promised to Aregund and it is his right to give you a new name. You are Anya no more. Your name from this day forward is 'Aisne'."

Aisne couldn't help but smile. She liked the name; in fact she loved it. Her approval wasn't lost on Aregund. It was the first time that evening that he looked at her.

The naming ceremony continued with a feast so everyone migrated into the large banquet hall. Aisne fell into step next to her parents. But instead of finding a table near the other wedding guests, Emma and Ansoald approached Queen Nuestria. She was seated at the head table and surrounded by her generals.

What surprised Aisne most was when the Queen rose from her seat and approached Ansoald with only General Guntram beside her.

"Brother, you look well." The Queen smiled at Ansoald and then moved her gaze to Aisne. "Your daughters have grown well. When do you think this one will shift?"

Aisne felt like a young ox for sale at market but nothing could overshadow the shock she felt at learning that her father was the Queen's brother.

"Very soon majesty." Ansoald bowed slightly toward Queen Nuestria. "We are honored that you have blessed this union."

"On the contrary, General Guntram would have given his life to make sure the agreement was made." She glanced over her shoulder and Guntram stepped forward.

He grasped Ansoald's forearm. "I have waited for this day for a long time."

"As have I," Ansoald replied. "Let us feast together." The men walked off arm in arm. It was a rare display of kinship.

Once everyone started eating and drinking, the mood in the banquet hall became more festive. The musicians played on instruments that looked like they could double as weapons but at least there was music. Aisne knew that the Garkin way would take some getting used to.

After a half pint of ale and very little food, Aisne pulled Emma out of her chair. When Emma declined to dance with her, Aisne took to the floor anyway and danced at the center. She thought her sides would split from laughing at everything and nothing in particular until she turned around and collided with her sister.

Basina wore a disappointed expression. "Everyone is watching you… even the Queen."

"We used to dance this way. Don't you remember?" Aisne sounded out of breath.

"We're not children anymore. Where is your sense of pride, your self-control?" Basina took a deep breath and then walked away leaving Aisne standing in the middle of the floor.

Aisne stared around nervously as she locked eyes with several people in the room; one of which was Aregund. He looked away quickly and pretended to be engrossed in conversation with a soldier named Dax and his twin brother, Roden. Feeling her flight reflex take hold, she hurried out of the room.

When she reached the hall, she pulled at several doors but they were locked. She finally found a doorknob that turned so she opened the door and walked inside. There were cloaks hung along one wall and the other wall had a large trunk against it. Aisne sat down and wiped her face with her sack dress.

She sat there for a few minutes trying to compose herself. Aisne certainly didn't want anyone to see her crying. She stood up and moved her hands down the length of the skirt. The garment was bad enough without being wrinkled and damp. When she walked out of the closet, Emma was standing in the hallway.

"Are you ready to return to the celebration?"

"Do I have a choice?"

"Not really." Emma took her daughter's hand and led her back toward the banquet hall.

Aisne avoided Basina and her new husband which wasn't that hard to do. Basina surrounded herself with her new husband, his father, General Guntram and other soldiers. The only person missing was Aregund. He must have slipped out of the room right after she made her hasty exit.

Aisne didn't expect the walk home to feel so solitary especially since she and her parents were accompanied by a dozen Garkin soldiers. She soon realized that she was the only person feeling less than cheerful. Emma and Ansoald strolled along arm in arm down the path towards Jormstad.

When Aisne arrived home, she said goodnight to her parents and went straight to her room. She still couldn't shake the sadness she felt from the night's events. The close relationship she'd shared with her sister was a distant memory.

And then there was Aregund. He'd left the banquet hall without as much as a word of greeting. It was hard to believe that she'd be marrying a man who didn't care to know her.

Sometime later, there was a knock at her bedroom door. Aisne looked up to see her father filling the doorway. He walked in as quietly as his large frame would allow and sat down at the foot of her bed.

"What is it, Papa?" Aisne sat up slowly.

"Tonight was difficult for you, yes?" Ansoald's uncomfortable posture showed as he struggled to find the words to comfort her. She loved him dearly for his effort.

"Yes," she said quietly.

"It will be easier once you've shifted. You'll see." He reached out to touch Aisne's hand.

"How come you never told us that the Queen was your sister?" Ansoald's face filled with concern. "I chose my path a long time ago. My life is here with my family and that's all I care about."

Aisne always knew that there was more to her father than Garkin strength with a hint of human kindness. "Thank you for checking on me, Papa."

"Well, I'd better let you get some sleep. Aregund will be here tomorrow to start your conditioning." Ansoald stood up to leave.

"Conditioning?" she asked.

"You'll find out tomorrow." He leaned over and kissed the top of her head. Then he quietly left the room.

Chapter 3

Aisne woke with a start but then glanced around at a quiet room. Her last thoughts were of her father's deep calming voice.

"Aisne, are you awake?" There was a sudden knock at her bedroom door.

"Sort of," Aisne grumbled into her pillow. "What it is, Majka?"

"You have a visitor downstairs."

Aisne sat up on her bed. She suddenly remembered her father's words. Without another thought she jumped out of bed, grabbed her dressing gown from the chair and hurried out into the hall. She nearly bumped into Emma on her way to the washroom.

When Aisne got downstairs, Aregund was standing by the window in the front room. Something caught his attention through the window because he didn't turn his attention from it. He was standing so still that he looked like a statue.

"Well, this is a surprise," Aisne said nervously.

"Didn't Ansoald tell you that I was coming?" He asked wearing an expression that gave nothing away. She couldn't tell if he was pleased to see her or just fulfilling a duty.

"I suppose so. I thought maybe I was dreaming... not dreaming about you but dreaming that you were coming here..." Aisne started babbling and she couldn't stop.

"Is that what you're wearing?" Aregund interrupted. He stared at Aisne's prairie dress and sandals giving only a hint of disapproval. "Well, maybe you don't value ankle support." He opened the front door and motioned for her to walk out ahead of him.

Once they reached the paved walking path, Aregund's pace quickly changed. Aisne spent the next few minutes trying to keep up with his long strides. They traveled eastward toward the silver trail. It was the quickest way to reach the edge of town. Once there, Aregund turned north toward the mountains.

"I really should have thought more about my feet." Aisne was stumbling over even the smallest rocks.

"Are your feet bothering you?" Aregund stopped walking and allowed Aisne to catch up to him.

"Yes, they are." She leaned over to pull a rock from the underside of her shoe.

"That's good. It builds character." He started walking again, even faster this time.

Aisne tried harder to keep up with him. Aregund's pace was steady, even after they started climbing the mount toward Merovech. Just when they reached the top of the hill, the large gates slowly opened. Aisne could see the guards pacing across the walkway of the fence.

Once they were inside the gate, it started closing behind them. Aregund started off toward a small doorway in the far right corner of the courtyard. It didn't appear that Aregund could fit through the doorway but he did.

The hallway they entered was dark and winding. The only thing Aisne was sure of was that they were going down. When they walked through the opening, Aisne was surprised at the space. It appeared to be a large hollowed out rock. The floor, the ceiling and the walls were all made of stone. There were lanterns set up along the walls that provided ample lighting.

"Let's see if you're ready to become a Garkin female." Aregund picked up a spear and held it out to her.

"What am I to do with that?" Aisne asked shakily.
"Just take it from my hand." Aregund handed her the spear and then stood with his arms extended straight out from his body. "How would you deal me a death blow?"

Aisne tried to think on her feet. She remembered the war games she used to play with her father so she decided to draw on those memories. Aregund certainly wouldn't expect her to actually come up with a valid strategy. She turned the spear toward him and pointed it at his chest as she spoke. "Well, I might start with the heart, but that would be too obvious. If I cut you at the knees first, that would give me more options later."

A look of surprise flashed across his face. "That's acceptable. If I stood still and let you harm me. Of course that would never happen." He reached for the spear and placed it back against the wall.

"I can be trained you know. I'm not as fragile as I appear." Aisne tried to sound convincing.

"Very well… what do you see?" He turned to face Aisne again with his arms at his side this time.

She stared into his eyes and noticed for the first time that they were light brown with specks of green. There could be kindness in them however he had none to offer her.

"Why are you staring at me like that?"

"I don't know what you mean," she replied in a small voice. He turned away from her and picked up a small rock that was on top of a heap in the corner. "Do you think this is some kind of courting ritual?"

"No, not at all." Aisne could feel her voice shaking but she couldn't stop it. "Why do you have such anger for me?"

"I'm not angry with you…" His voice softened as he moved toward her carrying the rock. "I feel sorry for you. You're small and weak. Your fragility is nothing but a burden for anyone who would risk their life to protect you."

"Well, now that we have that worked out, we can get on with my conditioning." Aisne fought back tears as she pulled the rock from his grip. She refused to look into his eyes again. "What am I to do with this?"

"Hold it straight out in front of you with both hands."

"Is that all?"

"That's it." He returned to the same corner and lifted a much larger rock from the pile. "Just hold it up until I tell you to put it down."

Aisne tried to make conversation to take her mind off the rock she was holding. "So what is this conditioning for?"

"It's so you don't get yourself killed in the courtyard. In a month's time, you will face an opponent."

"Who will it be?"

"You will face Brous. He's the only other whelp in Merovech."

"Whelp?"

"It's what humans are called before they shift." He turned toward Aisne to gauge her facial expression. "You don't have to do it, you know. You can concede before battle."

"Everyone would think me a coward?"

"Yes, that's true," he replied.

Aisne stared around at the dank space. "Who else uses this room? It's pretty awful."

"This room is for early development training. I expect you'll be here for a while." Aregund grunted occasionally as he raised and lowered the large rocks.

"Did my sister train in this room?" Aisne asked cautiously.

Aregund lowered the rock he was holding and turned to face her. "No, she completed her training with Lena and Duran. She was impressive for having shifted so recently."

"When will I shift?" She was straining from holding the rock but she didn't want it to show.

"You know if you stop talking, you can hold the rock for a longer period." Aregund picked up another large rock and held it up over his head. "I don't know when you'll shift. You may not shift at all."

"Is that what you want? If I remain human, you can renege on your promise to my father..."

Aregund let the large rock fall to the ground. It landed with a loud thud. "You will mind your tongue. I have kept my word for both our families' sakes."

"I didn't mean to insult you." Aisne looked away from him. "We don't know each other so..."

Aregund walked over to her and spoke softly in her ear. "Fear not; you will have the husband you desire."

Aisne dropped her rock.

Over the next few days, Aisne's conditioning continued much in the same way. Aregund was trying to make her stronger but by week's end she couldn't lift her arms over her head. The soreness in her torso and arms was unbearable. But she knew if she complained, Aregund would think that much less of her. She waited until she got home at night to cry from the pain.

Her next week of conditioning wasn't much better but at least part of the time was spent outside. Aregund still had her dead lifting rocks in the training room but he also added sprinting. He had her running from one side of the courtyard to the other. She practiced on an incline which wasn't difficult for her. She'd always been light on her feet so she actually enjoyed this part of her training.

She'd overheard Aregund telling Brous that she was quite agile for a human. That was the closest thing to a compliment he'd given her. But Aisne wasn't happy that he shared that information with her opponent. Brous might figure out some way to use that information to his advantage. But deep down Aisne knew why Aregund was being so cavalier about her training. He never thought she had a chance of besting anyone.

After two weeks of training, Aisne realized she wasn't improving. She was supposed to be learning hand to hand combat, but Aregund was only teaching her defensive moves. That wouldn't be nearly good enough. At the end of the training rotation, she would face Brous in the courtyard. Everyone would watch her fail.

When Aisne finished the day's workout, she left the training room feeling defeated. She was walking along the edge of the courtyard, when she heard someone call her name.

"Aisne, up here!" A Garkin soldier leapt off the wall and landed right in front of her. He shifted to his human form but he was still larger than any other man she'd ever seen. "Are you done with Aregund for the day?"

She slowly nodded her head. "I was done before I started."

"I saw you today. You have some natural ability." He leaned against the stone wall and folded his arms across his wide chest.

"If you're here to give me another Garkin pep talk, you can save your breath." She turned and started walking away from him.

"You'd be wise to hear me out little whelp."

Aisne stopped walking but she didn't turn around. "I'm listening…"

"If Aregund doesn't turn you into a fighter, he'll break you. It will happen in this courtyard in front of your aunt, the Queen."

Aisne turned around slowly. "Maybe I'm already broken."

"Self-pity is for the weak. If you want to reduce the odds against you, meet me in the main hall." He flashed a half smile and then strode off down the center of the courtyard.

Aisne hesitated for a moment as she considered her options. Unlike Aregund, this Garkin might actually show her something useful. He might even teach her to fight. She looked around to see if anyone was watching her and then walked back toward Aregund's training room.

Instead of walking through the doorway, she cut across the courtyard closest to the front of the fortress and hurried into the main hall. She caught up to the soldier and followed him up an interior stone staircase that ran parallel to the main corridor. The passage ways on the second level led to a maze of sleeping quarters.

Aisne could easily have gotten lost if she weren't following the Garkin so closely. When they reached the training room, Aisne let out a sigh of relief. The entryway was covered in brown carpet that led into a large open area. There were weapons of varying shapes and sizes lining the walls. But the best part of this training room was the windows in front.

"So he trains you in that dungeon, does he? It's no wonder your conditioning suffers. I am Fyk, legionnaire for the 1st legion. I have not been ordered to train you nor did your father request it so it is not appropriate for meet to do so. You must not tell anyone that I am interfering in your conditioning."

Aisne was pleased that one of the strongest soldiers in Merovech was taking an interest in her training. She didn't know why he was helping her and she didn't quite care. "I understand and I am most grateful to you, Fyk. I don't want to shame my family."

"Don't thank me yet." He stared around the room at the weapons. "Why don't you pick something… something that might suit your small stature?"

Aisne took Fyk's advice and slowly appraised the shelves in front of her. After several minutes, she set her sights on a monkey fist. It was a well-fitted rope connected to a metal ball covered in more rope. She picked it up and started twirling it around her arm.

"Is that your choice?" Fyk asked. "How will you defend yourself with that?"

"You'll see." Aisne turned and walked to the center of the floor. "I heard one of the soldiers say that the element of surprise can often save your life."

"That's true. But once Brous sees your weapon, the surprise is over."

"I know," Aisne said calmly.

"Let's begin, whelp. Your opponent is bigger, stronger and he's being trained by my brother, Grumere. But you are small, agile and a good runner. We can work on your skills and sharpen them."

Aisne slowly nodded her head. "I'm listening," she said calmly.

"But know this; if Brous gets his arms around you, it's over. His specialty is called the bear hug." Fyk's words held a dire warning.

"I understand," she added.

Fyk's combat knowledge was far greater than Aregund's. Or perhaps it was that Fyk was willing to give Aisne the knowledge that is shared with true soldiers. He told Aisne things about herself that could one day save her life. He showed her how her stance gave away what move she was about to make before she made it. Brous had been training longer than Aisne; he would be watching her.

Fyk also showed her the best way to use her weapon of choice. The design of the monkey fist was simple enough. The offender wouldn't know the danger of it until he was feeling the metal ball against his flesh.

When the training session was over, Fyk gave Aisne special pomade for her aching muscles. It was a soothing mixture he usually shared with soldiers who were injured in battle. This would help her train harder than she normally could.

For the first time in weeks, she was able to get a good night sleep and she would need it. For the next two weeks she would do her conditioning with Aregund in the morning. In the afternoon, she would do her combat training with Fyk.

Somehow, she was able to keep her secret training sessions from Aregund. She didn't want to deal with his negativity. Instead of fearing the day she would face Brous in the courtyard, she started looking forward to it. She started feeling like a Garkin woman in spite of everything Aregund said to her.

Chapter 4

On the day of the training summit, Aisne waited in the upstairs training room. She was too nervous to watch the others compete. The stronger matches were scheduled first so of course Aisne's match was one of the last.

Fyk surprised Aisne when he showed up in the training room shortly before her match. "Little whelp, are you ready?"

"I feel like I'm going to be sick…" Aisne held her hand up to her forehead and paced the floor. "What did you do when you were nervous before your first battle?"

"I wasn't nervous," Fyk said seeming to push his chest out further than normal.

"Wonderful," Aisne said as she picked up with pacing the floor.

"I have something for you." Fyk pulled a satchel from over his shoulder and tossed it on the floor at Aisne's feet. "These clothes will offer you some protection. It will make you look like a warrior at least."

"Thank you, Fyk." Aisne felt her eyes becoming misty but she held her emotions inside. Fyk would've been insulted if she cried in front of him. "I will try my best to make you proud."

"So you shall." Fyk nodded to her and walked out of the room. Aisne kneeled down and opened the satchel. She pulled out a metal stringed tunic. It was light weight and sleeveless but it would offer her some protection from a blade that might graze her skin.

There was also a pair of leather boots in the bag that would help protect her feet and ankles. The pants were too long so she wore her own knit pantaloons. She tied her hair back in a tight bun at the nape her neck.

At the last minute, she decided to take off the shirt that she'd put on over the tunic. It would only get in the way. Her chest cover and the tunic would have to be protection enough for her skin. With monkey fist in hand, she headed down the stairs to her destiny.

When Aisne walked out into the courtyard, she could hardly believe her eyes. Not only was Queen Nuestria seated against the south wall of the courtyard but so were her generals. Basina and Fredegund were seated on the right side of the Queen while Aregund and Guntram were seated on her left.

The guards on the wall started shouting as soon as they saw Brous turn to face Aisne. Out of the corner of her eye, Aisne saw the Queen wave her hand to quiet everyone.

"Costumes don't make you a warrior." Brous bellowed using a voice that was cold and hard.

"Where is your weapon whelp?" Aisne spoke in the fighting voice Fyk taught her.

Brous smiled widely. "I don't need a weapon for you little one. My hands are more than enough."

Brous started walking in a sideways motion. Aisne expected this and she started to walk the same way. It was meant to intimidate her but she just kept watching his feet to see what his next move might be.

Suddenly he turned his right foot and lunged toward her. Aisne reacted quickly and moved from his reach. She swung her monkey fist but he ducked out of the way.

Brous acted again sweeping her feet out from under her. She rolled onto her stomach and into a defensive crouch. When he approached to take hold of her, Aisne blew a handful of dirt into his eyes.

While he was wiping the sand away, Aisne used those few seconds to gather all her strength. She planted her left foot and spun around landing a blow with her monkey fist across the left side of Brous' face. He dropped to one knee as several of the onlookers stood to their feet including the Queen.

"Brous, is this little whelp too much for you?" Fredegund yelled excitedly.

Several of the other soldiers started shouting jibes as Brous recovered his footing. He turned away from Aisne who had assumed a defensive stance. She could have tried another move but she wanted to pace herself.

Brous pulled off his shirt and threw it on the ground. Then he cracked his neck to the left side and then the right. When he turned back around his eyes were twinkling. He was actually enjoying this.

"Let's try this again," Brous said. Without warning he lunged toward Aisne. This time he caught her by the leg as she tried to escape. She kicked at him and it seemed like she might get away. But as soon as she righted herself, he was on her again. He grabbed Aisne by the throat and threw her several meters across the courtyard.

This time Basina stood up with concern showing on her face.

Fredegund caught her by the arm. "Don't interfere. She must do this on her own."

Basina snatched her arm away from him but she soon retook her seat. She knew that interfering would do more harm to her sister than good.

Brous slowly approached Aisne who was lying very still on the ground with her eyes closed.

"Well, you haven't conceded to me so I guess the game continues." He grabbed hold of her right leg and dragged her back toward the center of the courtyard. "We can only engage each other in the square."

Brous let go of her leg and walked a few feet away from her. Aisne lay there very still but Brous grew weary of her charade. "Get up, whelp!"

Aisne opened her eyes and slowly staggered to her feet. The only problem was that she stood up facing in the opposite direction from her opponent. Several of the soldiers yelled for Aisne to turn around.

Before she could react, Brous was behind her with his arms wrapped tight. In mere seconds, he could squeeze her rib cage until she lost consciousness or until several of her bones were broken.

"Do you concede whelp?" Brous yelled at her.

"Do you?" Aisne carefully lowered the monkey fist until it dangled from her hands. Using what little mobility she had, Aisne whipped the monkey fist above her head and then down under her body.

The heavy, metal ball caught Brous between his legs. He let out a whimper and crumbled to the ground. If he hadn't lost consciousness then, he wasn't far from it. Whatever the case, he wasn't getting back up. Most everyone in the courtyard was stunned into silence.

The Queen leapt from her seat and moved toward Aisne. "My dear, you have certainly taken your training to heart."

"I am honored by your presence, Queen Nuestria." As beaten down and tired as Aisne was, she went down on one knee out of respect for the queen.

"Stand to your feet, Aisne. You honor me this day." The Queen turned to face the soldiers on the wall. "Let this child remind you that as women, we are still a force to be reckoned with!"

Aregund sat quite still unable to hide the surprise he felt at Aisne's performance. He hadn't trained her to fight that way but he knew that someone had.

When the queen returned to her seat, she gave the signal for the next match to begin. A few of the soldiers standing nearby came into the center of the courtyard to carry Brous to the infirmary. Aisne just turned and stumbled toward the basement training room. All she wanted was to go home and rest.

She'd just finished removing the metal vest when she heard someone knocking on the open door behind her.

"Nicely done," Aregund said. "To which soldier do I owe a debt?"

"I-I can't tell anyone. That was the bargain I made." Aisne held the borrowed vest in her arms nervously. "You aren't angry with me, are you? I just wanted to show you that I could be strong."

Aregund immediately stiffened at her words. "Of course not... just glad its over."

"So, I'll see you at the banquet tonight?"

He nodded to her. "I have to be there; queen's orders."

"I'll see you later then." She half smiled as Aregund left the room.

After a short rest, Aisne made her way up to the courtyard. She was half way to the gate when she noticed Fyk staring down at her. She smiled a thank you to him which for once seemed appropriate. He nodded to her in return and kept walking.

"I have nothing to wear to a fancy banquet." Aisne lay across her parent's bed and covered her face with her arm. "I doubt anyone would notice me if I did."

"Things aren't going well with Aregund?" Emma glanced over her shoulder before turning back to the mass of colored fabric in her wardrobe. She was searching for one garment in particular.

"He has no interest in me." Aisne sat up on the bed so she could watch her mother more closely. "I'm starting to wonder if that would change even if I shifted."

"Aisne, let's see if this fits you." Emma turned around holding up a silver gown that sparkled like nothing Aisne had ever seen. It had a scooped neckline that would flatter anyone and delicate beading that reflected the light flawlessly.

"Majka, where did you get this?" Aisne stood up quickly and moved to her mother's side.

"I was wearing this dress the day I met your father." Emma walked over to the bed and sat down still holding the dress. Aisne could tell that a story was coming so she sat at her mother's side. "Ansoald was the most handsome soldier I had ever seen. But they are trained to be so formal that I didn't know if he would speak to me. Later that night, I stepped out into the courtyard and he followed me."

"What happened next?" Aisne moved closer to her mother. "What did he say to you?"

"He said that I was very beautiful. Then he asked me if I was promised to anyone." Emma started blushing which was nothing new. The flush in her cheeks always made her light brown hair appear lighter. "I told him that I didn't have a husband so he made a promise to me that very night."

"Your parents allowed you to marry a soldier?" Aisne had never heard this story about her parents so of course she was curious.

"No, they didn't. Your father and I made that decision for ourselves… and you my daughter are wasting time." Emma stood up and laid the gown on Aisne's lap. "Now it's your turn to carve out your destiny.

"Very well," she replied as she lumbered off to her room.

When Aisne came downstairs fully dressed, her parents were already waiting for her. Ansoald took her hand and kissed it. "You look lovely my daughter and congratulations on your victory today. I wish I could've seen it with my own eyes."

"Thank you, papa." Aisne stared lovingly at her father. She knew that her days of living in her parent's house were numbered. Once she shifted, everything would change. Her fears about becoming Garkin seemed to be falling away. The banquet tonight would bring her one step closer to her new life.

The sun was about to set when Aisne and her parents reached the gates of Merovech. They could hear the festive music coming from inside. This would be the last Garkin banquet before the Protectorate Assembly so they knew it would be special.

When they walked into the banquet hall, Queen Nuestria was making an announcement to those in attendance. Aisne and her parents were ushered to a table so they could listen in.

"This is a great opportunity for us to reflect on our duty, our lives and our kinsman. Very soon, we will be hosting the Faeborn delegation for the Protectorate Assembly. This gathering will mark the beginning of King Tylwyth's century long duty of authority and protection over the humans. We wish him well."

While Aisne was listening to the Queen's speech, she'd noticed several Garkin soldiers watching her from across the room; one of whom was Brous. He didn't seem angry at her which was good. After the crushing blow he'd received to his private parts, she assumed he'd be recuperating most of the night. He must have used some of Fyk's pomade just as she had.

When the Queen's speech was over, everyone started mulling around the room. Aisne was surprised when her sister Basina approached her.

"Hello Aisne, I hardly expected to see you here after your rigorous match today." Basina stood in front of her sister leaving some distance between them. "You were impressive."

"Thank you, Basina. I had a very good teacher." Aisne was still adjusting to her sister's disposition. She just tried to mirror Basina's cool demeanor.

"One that you aren't reporting, I hear…" Basina actually smiled.

"I promised." Aisne added kindly. "You look well, Basina."

"As do you," Basina said matter-of-factly. "How is Majka?"

"She is quite well as you can see." Aisne glanced over her shoulder to where their parents were dancing. When she turned back around, she noticed that Basina was staring at them too. "Are you allowed to visit us?"

Before Basina could respond, Duran interrupted them. "Aisne, you must come quickly… Brous and I are trying to settle an argument about your match."

"Why don't you go with your friends?" Basina started backing away from Aisne. "We'll talk later."

Aisne reluctantly nodded her head as Duran led her over to the table where she and Brous were sitting.

"Now Brous, tell Aisne what you just told me." Duran belted out.

"I won't hold my tongue. If I'd had two trainers as she did, maybe things would've gone differently."

"For your information Brous, I only had one trainer." Aisne announced proudly not realizing that Aregund had walked up behind her.

"So am I mincemeat pie?" Aregund asked.

Aisne turned around to meet Aregund's lighthearted expression. "What exactly is mincemeat pie?"

"It's what the soldiers are fed when they're at war," he replied. "Would you care to dance?"

"…I'd be delighted." Aisne was surprised by the invitation but she tried not to seem too impressed. Garkin weren't known for their dancing but she wouldn't miss the chance to learn more about her future husband. He put one of his hands on her waist and the other hand, he held in the air. They were dancing arm's length apart but Aisne still considered it an improvement over every other encounter they'd had.

They danced around as others looked on. Even Duran and Brous watched them. Aisne remained calm on the outside but inside her heart was all aflutter. Could she finally be breaking through Aregund's tough exterior and finding the lovely Garkin within? She couldn't be sure.

Even though they were dancing together, they had little to say to each other. Aisne could barely stand the silence. "So why the sudden invitation?" she asked.

"What do you mean?"

"Well, when we attended my naming ceremony, you wouldn't even look at me. Tonight you've asked me to dance. I'm not complaining but I'm certainly curious."

Aregund shrugged his shoulders. "I suppose you deserve the truth. The reason I asked you to dance was completely selfish."

"I don't mind, Aregund." Aisne could feel herself blushing.

"You don't understand… there are a number of soldiers here who were impressed with your showing in the courtyard. With you being dressed like a Sally seller and all, I didn't want to be challenged for you. Garkin soldiers still do that, you know."

Aisne pulled away from him abruptly. "Sally seller?"

"You know, a Sally seller is a…"

"I know what it means…" Aisne replied shakily. "I don't feel like dancing anymore." She glanced at him one last time before pushing her way through the couples who were dancing nearby.

She wanted to scream or cry but doing either in a room full of Garkin would give Aregund the confirmation he wanted of just how unsuitable Aisne was. She couldn't remember the last time she'd been as angry with someone as she was with Aregund at that moment.

Chapter 5

When Aisne reached the doorway to the banquet hall, she almost collided with the soldier standing outside the door. She found herself back in the broom closet again. She wasn't in there for more than five minutes when she heard a tap on the door.

"Who is it?" She asked quietly.

"It's me and my two friends." A moment later she saw a small hand in the doorway holding a pint of ale. "May I join you?"

"…if you wish." Aisne pulled the door open a little more to find Duran standing there. "How did you know I was here?"

"I followed you." Duran handed Aisne the pint in her right hand and drank from the bottle in her left. She sat down next to Aisne on the large trunk. "Do you mind if I sit down?"

Aisne took a big gulp of ale. "You're already sitting down." Duran looked down at the floor and said, "So I am. Why are you here, Aisne?" Duran asked and then hiccupped.

"Aregund hates me." Aisne took another gulp of ale and then closed her eyes. "I just don't know why."

"I know the feeling. Brous has sworn to join the 1ˢᵗ legion when he shifts. That means that he can never marry."

"You like him?" Aisne asked trying to keep a straight face. Brous was tall with dark, spiky hair and a bushy beard. His nose was crooked from being broken so many times and he had a severe rash on his forehead.

"I know what you're thinking but I like him. I more than like him and I'm running out of time to convince him not to join the 1ˢᵗ."

"Who am I to judge?" Aisne took another large gulp of ale. "My husband-to-be can't go five minutes without insulting me."

"What do you expect? He's good at what he does." Duran's words were starting to slur.

"Come again?"

Duran tried to focus before she said anything else. "Aregund is trying to make you angry..."

"But why?"

"He thinks that if you get angry enough, you'll shift." Duran let out a round of giggles. "I'm sorry. I don't know where that came from."

Aisne stood up quickly surprising Duran and herself. Having only drank ale occasionally – and never a whole pint - she struggled to stay on her feet. She leaned her head back and drank the last bit of her ale before walking clumsily out of the closet. Duran walked out behind her in a similar condition.

"Aisne, where are you going?" Duran was still sipping from her pint.

"I'm going back to the dining hall to find Aregund." She started walking in the direction of the music.

"Well, there's one problem with your plan," Duran said slowly. "He left the room soon after you did… I can show you to his chambers if you like."

"Lead the way," Aisne said trying to whisper. Even in her current condition, she knew that going to Aregund's chambers wasn't proper. She tipped her pint back realizing for the third time that it was empty. With a huff, she followed Duran toward the stone staircase.

When she and Duran reached Aregund's bed chamber, she felt surprisingly nervous. She stood outside his door speaking in a loud whisper.

"Duran, I've never been alone with a man before."

"You haven't?" Duran asked.

"No!"

"You really haven't?"

"I already said no!"

"Neither have I," Duran answered falling into another fit of laughter.

"I can hear you both." Aregund yelled through the door. Aisne attempted to whisper through an inebriated grin. "Duran, you'd better go now." Aisne cleared her throat and set the empty pint bottle on the floor. She smoothed her dress with her hands and then knocked on the door.

"Okay, I'll play along. '*Who is it?*'" he replied sounding slightly irritated.

"It's Aisne. May I come in?"

"You don't have any weapons, do you?"

Aisne walked inside the room and found Aregund lying on his bed reading a pamphlet. The shirt he'd worn earlier in the evening was folded neatly on a chest at the foot of his bed.

Aisne noticed his bare chest, smooth and hairless. Aregund seemed different from the Garkin in some ways but more Garkin in others. The more she knew of him, the more he confused her. "If you don't care for humans, then why are you reading about them?"

"I was actually having a bit of a laugh." He put the pamphlet down and looked over at Aisne. "What are you doing here? Did you come to humiliate me again?"

"You're not humiliated," she said remembering the few moments they'd spent dancing together.

"Okay, are you here to *try* and humiliate me again?"

"I want to talk to you about what you've been doing. You're trying to make me angry so I'll shift."

Aregund suddenly looked uncomfortable. "What are you talking about?"

"Don't try to deny it. I'm not all that upset anymore." Aisne stared around at the fabric on the walls. "You're just going about it all wrong."

"How so?"

"My sister wasn't angry when she shifted. She was kissing a boy." Even intoxicated, Aisne couldn't bring herself to say more. The realization of what Aisne was admitting washed over him. Aregund got up off the bed and walked over to her. He stood so close that Aisne could feel his breath on her face.

"Look at me," he said.

Aisne stared up into his eyes and noticed the green flecks in a sea of brown.

Aregund leaned toward her until his lips were right in front of hers. When their lips finally touched, Aregund's body went rigid. Aisne tried to ignore the fact that he might not be enjoying their kiss. But after a few uncomfortable moments, Aisne moved off of her tip toes and stepped away from him.

"What's the matter?" Aregund asked.

"I don't think this is going to work. I'm pretty sure Pete wanted to kiss my sister as much as she wanted to be kissed." Aisne felt tears threatening to break free of her eyelashes.

"So you presume to blame me for why you're still human?"

"It's nobody's fault, Aregund. It's what I am. Is it so horrible that I'm human?"

"I don't know what you mean." He was having trouble looking at her now.

"Until I shift, I don't belong here. I don't belong with you. We both know that."

"I don't know what you expect." Aregund turned away from her. "This is difficult for me as well."

Aisne backed into the door and started turning the knob from behind her. "I'd better get back to the celebration. My mother is probably looking for me."

"Of course." Aregund kept his back to her. "Goodnight, Aisne."

"Goodnight," Aisne replied and left the room with a heavy heart and no ale to keep her company.

She returned to the banquet hall to find that most everyone was enjoying themselves. Duran had even convinced Brous to dance with her. As sad as she was, Aisne couldn't help but smile at them.

A little while later, Emma joined Aisne at the table. She hadn't missed the fact that something was wrong with her youngest daughter. "Aisne, what's troubling you?"

"I'm just tired, Majka... really tired."

On the way home, Aisne stared up at the stars in the sky. She made a wish on the brightest star she could find. She wanted to let go of the confusion that plagued her thoughts. Going forward, she'd stop waiting for her body to change. She would accept who she was and demand that those around her did the same.

The next morning, Aisne woke earlier than usual. She got dressed in work clothes and went downstairs.

"You're up early, my dear." Emma was making breakfast and tidying the kitchen all at once.

Even her father was surprised to see Aisne out of bed. "Are you feeling well?" he asked with a mouth full of humus bread.

"I feel fine. Why do you ask?" Aisne answered calmly.

"Aisne, you usually don't get up until Majka's called for you several times."

"I want to go to the shop with you today." Aisne started eating the eggs her mother put on a plate in front of her. "Remember how you used to say that I needed to be more productive?"

"Aisne that was before…" Ansoald hesitated wanting to choose his words carefully.

"Papa, nothing has changed for me. I'm still Anya."

"I knew this was coming." Ansoald turned his body completely around to face his daughter. "What about Aregund? Are you forgetting about him?"

"I haven't forgotten him. I'm just tired of everyone watching me like a hoekenbird about to hatch." Aisne pushed her chair back from the table and walked outside.

Ansoald knew that there was nothing he could say to change her mind. Aisne was accepting what might be her reality even if he didn't agree with her.

"She's right, you know." Emma spoke up from washing dishes. "We have no idea what her future holds. She needs to know that we support her."

Ansoald stood up and released a deep breath. "We'll be at the shop."

Chapter 6

Aisne walked slightly behind her father as they traversed the streets of Jormstad. Ansoald was always kind to the neighbors and the other shop keepers even though they sometimes feared him. He was an excellent carpenter who'd even sold furniture to the governor. But to some, he would never be anything more than a monster hiding in human skin.

Her mother usually worked the front counter during the day but with Aisne there, she could take a well deserved break. Aisne could organize the furniture screws and sweep the work room floor. There was always plenty to be done.

The little carpentry shop consisted of four rooms. A work room for Ansoald, a storage room for his finished work, a small washroom and the front counter where customers came in. When Aisne occasionally showed up at the shop, she helped the customers at the front counter. There was little chance she could break something out there.

Aisne had just kicked over a small can of furniture paint when she heard a familiar voice behind her. "Same old Anya, clumsy as ever," Peter said with a laugh.

Aisne turned around to see Peter's sun tanned face. She suddenly had a memory of the last time she saw him running for dear life from her sister. "How are you?" She had a genuine look of concern on her face.

"I'm fine; better than fine actually. I've just come from visiting with my older brother in Sjoborg."

"Well, I should have guessed by how tan you are. How are Kimbra and your nephews?"

"They're doing well. Williams says he might even visit Jormstad after the fishing season is over." Peter leaned in closer to the counter. "Is your sister... feeling better?"

Aisne nodded her head quickly. "She's fine too."

"Will you tell her that I said hello?"

"Of course I will." Aisne smiled at Peter and watched him walk from the shop. He must have assumed that Amy was disappointed by his sudden disappearance. She didn't dare tell him that her sister was now married and living at Merovech.

Aisne bent town to clean up the spilled paint when she heard someone walk into the shop. "Did you forget something, Pete?" She yelled over her shoulder.

"Who's Pete?" Aregund asked.

Aisne stood up and turned around. Aregund was staring at her with a confused look on his face.

"He's a friend of mine. What are you doing here?"

"Your mother told me where to find you." He started looking around the room. It was obvious he wasn't comfortable there.

"Is something the matter?" Aisne moved toward the counter and started organizing the screws again.

"I wanted to invite you back to Merovech."

"That's very kind of you but I'm helping my father now." Aisne was pretending to be hard at work.

"So how long will you be helping him?"

"...until I find another job. I figure I'll help Ms. Miller in the orchards when I'm done here."

"Are you planning to just avoid me from now on?" Aregund moved closer to the counter waiting for her to look up. He realized rather quickly that he was being ignored.

"Aregund, I need to start doing human things; not running around in a stone fortress with someone who can barely stand the sight of me." Aisne looked up at him this time.

"Well, that's unfortunate." Aregund started walking around the room touching various pieces of wood furniture. "I was going on an adventure and I wanted to take you with me."

Aisne couldn't hide the fact that she was intrigued. She wanted to know more about where he was going without seeming overly concerned. "What kind of adventure?" She tried to focus on the screws again which was a lost cause.

"I'm going into the mountains on a secret mission. It's the queen's business. " He flashed a crooked smile which didn't suit him. "But I understand if you're afraid."

"I'm not afraid." He had Aisne's full attention now. "Why would you want me to go with you?"

"Why not?" He asked matter-of-factly.

"I don't know, Aregund. My father needs me here."

"Well, let's ask him…" Aregund said as if he already knew what the outcome would be. Of course he was right.

"Aisne, you should be by your husband's side." Of course Aregund wasn't officially her husband yet but Ansoald already considered him a part of the family.

Emma agreed with her husband as well. She wanted Aisne and Aregund to spend more time together to bond. But Aisne wasn't convinced. What good would it do to spend time with Aregund if he wouldn't accept her as a human?

With her knapsack packed and thrown over her shoulder, Aisne followed Aregund through Jormstad and toward the mountains. They didn't say much to each other until they were just outside the gates of Merovech.

"So, here I am again." Aisne said almost under her breath.

"Aisne, are you really so sad to be here?" Aregund sounded almost wounded.

Though she would never admit it, Aisne loved to hear him say her name. It meant if only in name, she belonged to him. "I guess being here is better than counting nails at my father's shop."

They walked through the large gates and Aisne immediately noticed the Garkin soldiers standing on the stone fence. Several of them had shifted and appeared to be an extension of the fence itself. Aisne was still in awe of just how much of their human features were retained after they shifted. Even as stone-like figures, she immediately recognized Fyk and Grumere.

As she and Aregund walked through the courtyard, Aisne saw the young soldiers practicing their fighting skills. Brous and three of his friends were fighting with javelins. And in the far corner, Duran stood watching the young fighters. When she noticed Aisne, she hurried over to say hello.

"I didn't expect to see you back here." Duran said lightly. "Aregund looked like a lost lamb after you left."

Aregund pretended not to hear his cousin's supposed admission. Instead he greeted her kindly. "Are you feeling fit little Duran?"

"I feel fine, just taking in the view." She glanced over in Brous' direction. "So how did you convince Aisne to return?"

"I'm taking her into the mountains. We're going on a little adventure." Aregund had a playful look on his face. "But you can't tell anyone."

"I wouldn't dream of it." Duran winked her eye at Aregund and picked up her spear. It looked like a child's toy but Duran knew how to use it. She took off in Brous' direction with her spear at her side. Aregund motioned for Aisne to follow him. They walked through the main hall of the fortress acknowledging the occasional soldier as they went.

Once they reached the border gate that led into the Garkin city, Aregund turned toward Aisne and gave her his best effort at a reassuring smile. "Just remember, we don't live like the humans."

There were a few guards scattered about the city but most of them patrolled the borders not unlike the soldiers at the fortress. But there was a noticeable difference in these soldiers; they were female. They were about ten paces inside the city when a guard leapt from the wall landing directly in front of them. "What is your business here, soldier?" the female asked remaining in her Garkin form.

"I am Aregund, half legionnaire for the 2nd and this is my companion. We seek to cross at the South wall."

"I am Lena, half legionnaire for the 3rd." She glanced at Aisne before shifting into her human form. She was only an inch or two shorter than Aregund but she had narrow shoulders and a face that still had roundness to it. Her moss colored hair was cut just above her jaw line and her eyes were roughly the same color. "No one alerted our legionnaire that you were coming. Should we alert Basina now?"

"I am on the Queen's business, her secret business."

"What is this business you speak of?" She realized that Aregund outranked her but she wouldn't completely back down.

"Since it is the Queen's business, I certainly cannot discuss it with you. Will you let me pass or should I tell the Queen that a city guard held me up?"

She thought for a moment before nodding her head. "Be off with you."

Once Aisne entered the Garkin city, she found herself staring around in a childlike daze. It was so different from Jormstad. The houses were small and plain with no real way to distinguish between them. There were no fancy curtains or other unnecessary decorations hanging about. Everyone lived on the same footing in Merovech.

About halfway through the city, Aisne noticed a group of Garkin children playing war near a vegetable garden. Their mothers were in their human forms picking vegetables and taking turns watching Aisne with a careful curiosity. She'd never felt as unwelcome in Merovech as she did at that moment.

Aisne found herself almost captivated by the children. She tried to look away from them but she couldn't. "Do they understand what they are?" she asked.

"Of course they do. Why do you ask?" Aregund replied.

"I envy them." Aisne continued to stare back at the children even though they were almost out of view.

The stone fence at this end of the city was just as high as the fence that surrounded the fortress. It must have taken years to build the gate around the entire city.

"There is one thing I forgot to mention…" Aregund was cautious then. "I'll need to carry you over the fence."

"I understand," she answered before realizing what that meant. He could only carry her over the fence after first jumping to the top. In order to reach the top, he would need to shift.

"Are you ready?" he asked quickly.

"Yes." Aisne wasn't sure if he heard her voice or not. But moments later, Aregund removed his shoes and tucked them into his knapsack. He turned toward the stone fence and placed both of his hands against it.

His body quivered for a few moments and then Aisne heard a low groan from within his chest. It reminded her of the day her sister shifted for the first time.

Aregund's body swelled under his skin; muscle and bone expanding in unison. His chiseled features hardened as his skin blended with the stone wall he touched. His brow grew larger, with longer ears and darkened eyes. His hands and feet became like claws.

With his transformation complete, Aregund grabbed Aisne around the waist and hoisted her up onto the stone fence with ease.

She didn't have time to prepare herself for the huge leap. Just as quickly, they were on the ground on the other side of the fence.

Aregund started walking away from the fence as he shifted back to his resting form. "Are you injured?"

"No, I'm fine." Aisne wasn't quite telling the truth. She'd never seen Aregund in his Garkin form before.

She struggled to replace the image of his transformation with thoughts of the sloping terrain that lay before them. After hiking for just over two hours, they approached a small cabin which was just out of view from the city below. Aisne stood in front of the structure too afraid to go inside. She and Aregund were completely alone and she still didn't know why they were there.

"Are you planning to stay outside all night?" Aregund opened the door and motioned for Aisne to follow him inside.

The little cabin was nicer than anything she'd seen in Merovech city. The walls were made of bleached wood with a mole hair carpet on the floor of the living room. The wooden arm chairs appeared barely used.

The kitchen had a wood burning stove and a sink in the corner next to a wooden hutch. The rest of the kitchen was furnished with a drop leaf table and two side chairs. It was almost cozy.

Aisne stood between the kitchen and living room which allowed her to see into every room in the cabin. Next to the washroom was a small bedroom. It had a four poster bed inside dressed with a white coverlet. The night table was crafted of Cebus wood and painted in a warm honey tone. There was another small piece of carpet on the floor and a painting of a young woman Aisne didn't recognize.

"This isn't what I was expecting." Aisne walked back into the living room and sat down on the chair by the window. "So are you going to tell me what we're doing here?"

"Yes, but first I want to tell you where we are." He sat down in the chair across from Aisne and stared around the room. "This cabin has been in my family for centuries and it is the last structure that remains of the old Garkin city. My people didn't always live behind a giant wall of stone."

"I didn't know there was another Garkin city."

"Well technically, it wasn't an entire city. There were a few dozen families who chose to live separate from the humans. It seemed to be an easier way of life. My mother's family was one of those families."

"Is that her picture in the bedroom?"

"Yes, it is." As Aregund spoke of his mother, Aisne saw more emotion in his face then she had at any other moment since they'd met. "She died in a hunting accident when I was very young. My father was tasked with raising two spirited boys on his own. Our training helped. We were two of the youngest to join the legions."

"Basina and I always wondered if we'd have what it takes to become soldiers. I always feared becoming Garkin…"

"So how do you feel now?" Aregund watched her intently.

"Now I'm more afraid of not becoming Garkin." She looked away from him, too afraid to see his reaction.

"You'll shift when you're body is ready," he added sounding sure of himself.

"How old were you when you shifted for the first time?"

"It's hard to say in human years. I'd just reached puberty."

"Was it painful?"

"No, not at all. You'd think with all of the changes in the body that there would be some discomfort but there wasn't. It just felt natural."

Aisne had relaxed considerably from when they'd first arrived. "Thank you for bringing me here. It's nice."

Aregund nodded and made his best attempt at a smile.

"How long can we stay?" she asked.

"I requested two days leave. I had to clear it with Fredegund since he's legionnaire for the 2nd and my commander."

"So what reason did you give for needing time away?" she asked lightly.

"I'm glad you asked that." Aregund got up and walked into the little bedroom. He came back a few moments later holding Aisne's monkey fist in his hand. "If you show me how to use this, I'll show you how to use an axe."

"You want to do more training?" Aisne could hardly believe her ears. "That's why you brought me here?"

Aregund looked stunned by the question. "What else is there?"

Aisne suddenly had a vision of Aregund shirtless and sweaty swinging an axe over his head. "I can't think if a thing… well there is one thing," She added gingerly.

"And what might that be?" Aregund wasn't concerned but he pretended to be.

"Before we start training, you have to take me to the top of that mountain over there." Aisne pointed out the window at a large mountain range not far from the cabin.

Aregund stared out at where she was pointing. "You want to go to Elbrus Peak?"

"Is that a problem?"

"It's almost a vertical climb. I'd be carrying you for part of the journey. I may have to shift…" Aregund remembered how frightened she looked the last time he changed into his Garkin form in front of her.

"Do we have a deal?" She reached her hand out to him.

"We do." Aregund grabbed her hand and shook it firmly. "Well, if we're going to climb Elbrus, we'd better get some rest."
He yawned slowly pulling off his shirt. He noticed Aisne watching him so he motioned toward the bedroom. "You can take the bed."

"Yes, of course." Aisne stood up quickly and hurried into the bedroom. She changed into her pajamas and lay across the bed. She didn't know how much rest she would get under the circumstances. Her future husband, whom she barely knew, was sleeping in the next room.

She couldn't hear any animals outside; not even an owl which seemed strange. However, she did hear Aregund moving around a bit. As she waited for him to settle down, the quiet calmed her mind. She finally drifted off to sleep imagining his shirtless body holding an axe.

Chapter 7

Aisne woke to the sight of Aregund standing over her. She had no idea of the hour but it was still dark outside. And by the look on Aregund's face, something was wrong.

"Get up, we have to leave." Aregund was almost whispering.

"What is it?" Aisne could feel her fear mounting.

"We're not alone." Aregund pulled the covers back and helped Aisne off the bed. "Get your knapsack and follow me quietly. They may not know that we're here."

Aisne suddenly felt sick. There was only one thing that could make Aregund react this way – darklings. "Aregund, I'm afraid."

"I know. Come quickly now." Aregund took her hand as they moved toward the front door of the cabin.

Aisne suddenly noticed how Aregund was dressed. His chest and feet were bare which Aisne thought unusual unless he was planning to shift.

When Aregund opened the front door of the cabin, Aisne smelled a most horrible odor. She put her hand over her nose as her eyes started to water.

"Its sulfur and the smell will only get worse as they get closer. Now run!" Aregund yelled to Aisne as he took off running toward the hills. Whatever they were running from was between the cabin and Merovech.

Aregund was surprised at how fast she was and relieved. They would need to move as quickly as possible. Luckily for them, the moon was high overhead. They could see their way through the hilly terrain.

Aregund saw Aisne glance behind them a time or two. "Don't turn around. It will only slow you down."

"Are they gaining on us?" Aisne asked breathlessly.

"I'm not sure." He replied quickly.

"How many are there?"

"I don't know! Stop talking… save… your… breath…"

They reached the base of Elbrus and Aregund immediately started climbing. "Come on, Aisne. Climb as fast as you can."

Elbrus was a mountain with several ridges jetting out from it but its base was an almost vertical incline. They had to climb several stories before they reached the first landing. They had just reached the third ridge when Aisne saw one of the darkling. It was heavily cloaked but she could see the figure moving toward them.

"Aregund, I can see it." Aisne felt almost paralyzed.

"Aisne, keep moving!" He yelled to her but she wasn't listening.

"There are so many of them. What do they want?" Aisne stepped away from the ledge and moved into a crouch near the wall. Aregund leaned over and saw the darkling approaching. They had mere seconds before they would be over run. He counted a dozen of them but he knew there were more out there.

"Aisne, I want you to keep climbing. The sun will be up soon and they'll have to retreat." Aregund walked over to her and knelt down at her side. "I'll give you a head start."

"What about you?" Aisne stared back at him intently. "I can't just leave you here."

"If I remain here in my human form, they'll focus on me. You can still get away." Aregund stood up and pulled Aisne to her feet.

"I won't leave you here, I won't leave…" Aisne repeated the words as if she were in a trance.

At that very moment, the first of the darkling reached the ridge they sat upon. It watched them for a moment, and then it focused its attention on Aregund. He must have sensed that Aregund was Garkin but he didn't understand why Aregund simply sat there holding onto a frail human.

Soon there were more of them. Aregund told Aisne some time ago that they attacked in numbers and now they had them. Deep inside of Aisne, she felt a spark began to grow. Something at her innermost core was springing to life.

Aisne's fear somehow disappeared. She felt another emotion much more strongly – regret. The man who now protected her had done the very thing he feared. Her weakness would cost them both their lives.

Aregund stood to his feet and moved in front of Aisne. The darkling reacted to his movement forming a line across the ridge. There was nowhere for Aregund and Aisne to go.

Aisne knew that at any moment, they would attack Aregund. But she just couldn't stand there and watch him die. Without realizing where the strength came from, Aisne pushed Aregund lightly but he flew back against the wall of the ridge.

Then she stepped toward the darkling and raised her hands above her head. "If you want the Garkin, you will have to take him!"

Aisne's entire body became illuminated in bright, blinding light. Her hair turned flaxen and her eyes glowed white. The back of her night shirt began to pull away as large wings emerged from her spine. She now hovered slightly above the ground.

The darkling moaned as if in pain from the light she projected but they still lumbered forward. They moved in toward Aisne as she blocked their path to Aregund. As if nothing more than a reflex, Aisne glowed more brightly as they approached.

The darkling moved closer still. In a final show of anger, Aisne let out a piercing shriek and white, hot light exploded from her body in the direction of the darkling. Then everything went dark.

Aisne awoke on the bed in the cabin. She felt rested but something inside her was different. She suddenly remembered being on the ridge with Aregund and the darkling!

"Aregund!" She sat up quickly. "Aregund, where are you?"

He hurried into the room and sat down on the bed beside her.

"I'm here. How are you feeling?"

"I feel fine. What happened? How did I get back here?"

"I brought you back."

"What happened to the darkling?"

"The few that survived ran away." Aregund half smiled. He was trying to help Aisne relax. "You saved us, Aisne. I was so wrong about everything."

"What do you mean?"

"I thought that your emotions were a weakness but that's your strength. You were worried about them harming me and that triggered your transformation."

Aisne suddenly remembered more of what happened. "What am I, Aregund?"

"You are Faeborn, Aisne. Today was your first bloom." His face was a mix of pride and sadness.

Aisne felt warm tears touch her face and she didn't care what Aregund thought of her. She knew exactly what it meant for her to be Faeborn. Even though she'd saved their lives, they wouldn't be allowed to be together.

"Calm yourself. I'll get you some food and then you'll rest." Aregund stood up to leave. When he reached the doorway, he stopped. "I don't want you to worry about any of this. You just need to get your strength back."

Aisne ate the rye bread and humus that he brought her. As much as she protested, she did need more rest. Aregund went up on the roof to make sure they didn't have any more visitors. In his Garkin form, he could detect darkling from miles away.

He could also detect a stubborn woman walking around the cabin. He shifted back to his human form and walked into the cabin. Aisne was sitting at the table drinking tea.

"So that means that my mother is also Faeborn…" Aisne didn't say it as a question but Aregund responded.

"Yes, she would have to be." Aregund pulled on his shirt and sat down at the table with her. "It is very important that you don't tell anyone your true form. Your parents would be in violation of Garkin law."

"How could she have kept her secret all these years?"

"I don't know. But you must learn to temper your energy as well, Aisne." Aregund seemed to be choosing his words carefully. "When you faced the darkling, you used a tremendous amount of energy. That can be dangerous for you."

"What happened to them?"

"The darkling closest to you were incinerated and the others fled. They won't stay away forever so we'll leave in the morning."

"Did I harm you, Aregund?"

"I was burned a little but I heal quickly in my Garkin form. I shifted when I saw you turning up the heat." Aregund laughed to himself.

"How did you know what would happen?"

"I've heard of it. There was one other fairy that could burn like the sun – Queen Harmonia."

Aisne suddenly felt the blood rush from her face. "What if I can't control it? What if I simply burn up?"

"Don't be ridiculous. You won't burn up." Aregund was smiling until he saw the look on her face. "Aisne, I will help you all I can."

Aisne slowly rose from the table. She had so many thoughts running through her mind. She felt like screaming. "If you don't mind, I'd like a few minutes to myself."

"I'll go back on the roof to check the area again." Aregund stood up and watched her walk out of the room.

Aisne went into the washroom and picked up the torn shirt that she was wearing before. She examined the back of the night shirt where her wings had torn through. Her transformation was just as Aregund said it would be. There was no pain. The only discomfort she felt was the fear she had for Aregund's safety.

She went back to the bedroom with one thought in mind. Could she control her transformation? There was only one way to find out. Aisne pushed the bedroom door shut and removed her clothes.

She lay across the bed and tried to calm her mind. Drawing on the strength she used to bloom the first time, she focused on Aregund and how she felt when she thought the darkling would harm him. Slowly her body responded to her mental command. She watched her arms and legs as her body began to glow. She felt her wings expand from behind her.

Her body became engulfed in a gentle radiance. She stretched her arms above her head and extended her wings once more. It was an intoxicating feeling.

Aisne turned around and noticed that Aregund was in the doorway watching her. She reached for a blanket to cover her body but of course he'd already seen her. Their eyes met for a moment before he closed the door behind him.

As she pulled her shirt over her head, she heard the front door of the cabin open and close. Then she heard a thump on the roof as Aregund retook his place of protection. She wanted to go to him but she didn't know what to say.

Nightfall rolled in and Aisne waited for Aregund to come down from the roof. Standing like a statue for hours on end had to make him hungry. When he walked inside the door, he had trouble meeting her gaze.

"Did you get more rest?" he asked.

"Yes, I did. Thank you." She watched him as he washed his hands at the sink. "There's more humus left. Are you hungry?"

"Yes." He sat down at the table. "We leave in the morning; first light."

"Very well." She put the rye bread on the table in front of him and sat down. She found herself eating slowly and taking occasional glances in his direction.

"If you have something to say Aisne, then just say it." Aregund seemed agitated as he took a large bite of the bread. He knew what she would ask him and he didn't want to answer her.

"Why were you watching me before?"

He took a deep breath. "I thought you needed me. I could smell your fear."

"I'm sorry. I was trying to… bloom. But I felt the strangest sensations. On the ridge, I felt anger, confusion and rage. But just then, I felt caring and warmth."

"Your emotions are out of control. You'll get used to it." He got up from the table and walked over to the arm chair. "I'm tired. I'll sleep a few hours and then go back on the roof."

Aisne sat there for a moment before getting up to clear the table. It seemed that the old Aregund had returned. Cold and distant were his specialty.

As she lay in bed that night, she wondered what would happen when they returned to Merovech. They would have to tell the queen that the darkling had returned. The peace that had engulfed the known world for the last few centuries was gone.

Chapter 8

When Aisne woke the next morning, she heard only quiet. She figured that Aregund was still on the rooftop watching out for darkling. Soon he would come and collect her so they could return to Merovech.

There was just one thing she wanted to do before they left and that was to fly. And why not? Once they left this place, she would have to keep her nature a secret. There would be no opportunities to test her wings in Jormstad or Merovech.

There was nothing in her bag that catered to her desire to fly. Dressed in her knit pantaloons, she pulled a shirt from her bag. But then she thought about what would happen if she bloomed in her normal clothes.

She decided to retrieve her torn night shirt and to make it into something useful. She fastened it into a halter top of sorts. She tied two pieces of fabric at the top around her neck and the other two pieces around her waist. That left her back completely exposed for when she sprouted wings.

Once outside, Aisne stared up at the rooftop. Aregund was there standing as still as a statue. With his eyes closed, he appeared to be sleeping.

Aisne crept around to the back of the house and tried to find a soft spot to practice on. There wasn't much grass behind the little cottage so this would take some planning.

She took several running leaps and tried flapping her wings to no avail. She never made it more than a few inches off the ground. On her fourth attempt, she took a tumble and landed on her knees. She shifted back to her human form, a sure sign of defeat.

"If you were going to practice flying, you should have asked for my help." Aregund spoke behind her. He was still in his Garkin form.

"I didn't want to bother you." Aisne tried to appear unfazed by his presence. Their run in with the darkling had left her a little skittish.

"If you don't want my help, I can leave…" Aregund turned to walk away.

"I do… I have no idea what I'm doing."
He turned back around and walked over to Aisne. "You'll need to bloom so I can look at you."

Aisne looked over at him and stifled a laugh. When he caught her expression he immediately became agitated. "Be serious, Aisne. You know what my intentions are. I have to look at your wings. I've never spoken to a fairy and asked them how they fly before."

"I'm sorry," she said shyly. Then she kneeled down and touched the ground around at her feet. She felt her skin glowing as her transformation took hold.

"So… we have two choices," Aregund said flatly. "You can either take a running leap off the roof or I can throw you into the air. Either way, you should have the lift you need to take flight."

"I'll try the second option." Aisne walked over to Aregund and nervously put her hands at her sides. "Ok, now what?"
He leaned down and picked her. Once he was cradling her in his arms, he stared down at her face. "Are you ready?"

"I'm ready!"

With that, he hurled Aisne straight up into the air. She started flapping her arms and moving her wings in a mismatched pattern. Needless to say, it didn't work. Aisne dropped out of the sky like a piece of lead.

Aregund caught her in his arms and then fell back on the ground. She heard his Garkin laughter as he rolled her onto the ground. Then he shifted into his human form.

"What is so funny, gargoyle? You could have killed me!" Aisne didn't know why she was so angry but she was.

"You have wings fairy, use them!" Aregund's voice was barely recognizable through his laughter.

"I'm pleased to entertain you so fully." Aisne was trying to stay angry but it wasn't working. She'd never seen Aregund in such a light mood. "What is so amusing?"

"You are and you don't realize it." Aregund was finally gaining his composure. His face and stomach ached from laughing so hard.

Before he could protest, Aisne lay next to him on the ground. "So what happens when we return to Merovech?"

"What do you mean?"

"How will you explain why you're avoiding me? I am after all a hated Faeborn."

"Aisne, I don't hate you or anyone else for that matter." He sat up trying to put some space between them. "We'll just go on as if nothing's changed. We came up here together and we were attacked – end of story."

"But we can't go on pretending forever. Will you wait a few months and then find an excuse to end our engagement? You'll want to find yourself a proper Garkin wife, I'm sure." Aisne stood up and walked a few paces away from him.

"Aisne, this isn't the time to discuss such things. Have you forgotten about the darkling?"

"Of course not…" Aisne threw her hands up in the air. "I can't get the thought of them out of my mind."

Aregund stood up and looked around. "We should head back now."

"Indeed." Aisne replied flatly.

"Are you certain of what you saw, Aregund?" The queen didn't seem afraid but nor was she her usual cavalier self. "It's a miracle that you escaped with your lives."

"We were very lucky, Queen Nuestria. I smelled them from a distance and I was able to get to high ground just as the sun came up." Aisne hadn't realized until that moment what a masterful story teller Aregund was.

"Whatever were you doing so far north of Merovech?" she asked.

Aregund was suddenly short on words. No doubt his story about a quest for the queen had been his own invention. Aisne decided to help him but he knew she would have questions later.

"We were training, my queen. He'll make a Garkin woman of me yet," she added for emphasis.

"I doubt that you need much help in that area." The queen stared at both of them cautiously. "Keep in mind that you can't marry until after you shift. And they'll be no other remote training exercises until after that time. Am I clear?"

"Yes, Queen Nuestria." Aisne responded lightly. Aregund just nodded his head.

The queen dismissed them from the throne room and turned her attention toward her most trusted general. "Guntram, the time has come for us to set our plan in motion."

"Yes, it is indeed."

As Aisne walked out of the throne room, she couldn't help but be curious about what the queen's plan was for dealing with the darkling. What plan could she have when everyone thought that the darkling were gone for good?

When Aregund and Aisne were out of the throne room and away from the listening ears of any guards, Aregund took her by the arm. "Come, I'm taking you home."

She pulled away from him. "I can find my own way." Aisne felt as if the time she'd spent with Aregund over the last two days didn't matter. Her transformation ruled over everything. Even if the darkling were defeated, she was still Faeborn.

"Why won't you let me see you home safely? I can gather a dozen 2nd legion soldiers in a matter of minutes."

"Isn't it ironic that you would bring me a dozen soldiers when there is only one that I want?" Aisne slung her bag over her shoulder and walked off down the corridor. She didn't wait for his answer. She didn't want to talk about the darkling threat or the queen's orders or anything else that he would undoubtedly spout off about.

By the time she reached the front gate, Aregund had caught up to her. He had gone to collect his shirt of armor and his battle axe. "One soldier as you requested…" He motioned for Aisne to walk out ahead of him.

Just inside the town limits of Jormstad, the first patch of white oak trees became visible from the path. Their conversation was limited to simple questions like, "are you thirsty?" or "do you need to take a rest?" It seemed that the trip to Aisne's home would happen without incident. But once she stopped walking and leaned against a white oak tree, Aregund knew that wouldn't be the case.

"Aisne, what are you doing?" he started toward her.
"If this is the last time I'm going to see you, I have a question." When he continued frowning at her, she kept talking. "I want to know if there was ever a time that you thought of me as your wife."

"That's a silly question. It's not like I had a choice in the matter."

"Did you ever want to me my husband?"

"I won't answer that."

"How do you feel about me now?"

"...not that either. None of this matters when we're about to face another darkling attack. We have no idea what we're up against." Aregund folded his arms over his chest and turned away from her.

"Will you at least kiss me goodbye?" Aisne had nothing to lose at that moment. She might as well ask for what she wanted.

She watched Aregund as he thought about her question. He still had his back to her. When he finally turned around, she tried to guess at what he was feeling. He might as well have been in his Garkin form, his expression was unreadable. Surprise covered her face when he slowly nodded his head.

He took two long strides toward her covering the distance between them. Then he held her face in his hands. Aisne closed her eyes just as his lips reached hers. His body was rigid at first but he soon relaxed his posture moving his mouth against hers.

She knew that he hadn't intended to kiss her that way. If it was up to him, they would have grabbed each other's forearm and growled at one another. But Aregund couldn't deny that he felt something for her. They shared a passionate moment; a moment that ended when Aregund abruptly pulled away from her.

"You're glowing," he said flatly. "Make it stop before someone sees you."

"What are you doing home so soon?" Emma met her daughter at the front door. She reached for Aisne's face sensing that something was bothering her.

"I need to speak with you, Majka." Aisne sat down on the couch and stared up at her mother.

"What's the matter, Aisne?" She sat down wearing a concerned expression.

"I'm not going to ask questions about the past because I can guess at your motives. But I've changed Majka and I think you know how."

"What are you saying, child?" Emma looked more nervous than before.

"I'm Faeborn and so are you."

Aisne had spent the last few days working in the apple orchard under Ms. Miller's watchful eye. At her mother's suggestion, she tried to return to a normal life but how could she? She discovered that her mother was Faeborn through her own transformation, her marriage to Aregund was off and worst yet, the darkling had returned

No one in Jormstad was allowed out after dark, governor's orders. The 2nd legion stepped up patrols of Jormstad and the queen added more soldiers from the 1st legion to assist. Everyone seemed to be gearing up for a war that couldn't be won.

The darkling were fine tuning their own tactics. They would only strike in groups and never the same place twice. So far no one had been killed but it was only a matter of time.

Whenever Aisne saw soldiers about, she always looked to see if one of them was Aregund. With everything that was going on, she still struggled to put him out of her mind. She longed to see him again, if only for a short while.

She was just about to fill another apple barrel when Jenny Wright came running toward her. "Aisne, I have to speak with you." She was out of breath having run from the center of town.

"Jenny, what is it?" Aisne asked.

"It's your mother. She's been arrested. The queen has collected your parents from the shop!"

Without hearing another word, Aisne took off toward Merovech. The orchard was in northern Jormstad which made her journey to Merovech a simple one. She ran most of the way to the stone fortress unsure of what would happen when she arrived.

They opened the gate when she approached but nothing felt the same. It was as if the guards knew her secret. As the gates closed behind her, she wondered if she would be allowed to leave.

Fyk leapt from the wall and landed a few feet in front of her. "Your parents are in the throne room. You know they way."

Aisne looked at him for a moment and then hurried across the courtyard.

The queen rose from her throne when she saw Aisne enter the room. "Come in, Aisne. You must be so confused."

When Aisne saw her parents shackled at the queen's feet she hurried over to them. "Queen Nuestria, what is this? Why are you holding my parents?"

Aisne couldn't believe her eyes. Her father was locked in a metal cage too small for a man his size. Her mother was in shackles with a metal vest attached to her torso.

Queen Nuestria turned her attention toward Ansoald. Her expression changed to one of anger and disgust. "My own brother has broken our most sacred law. He must be punished." She motioned toward Emma and Ansoald.

Aisne stared around the room at the extra guard that stood watch. When she found Aregund in the crowd, she had trouble looking at him. Had he exposed her secret to the queen? If so, why wasn't she shackled at her mother's side?

Either way, it didn't matter. She couldn't watch her parents being treated this way. With nothing left but her anger, Aisne removed her cloak.

"Well, I suppose you'll need to shackle me too." Aisne bloomed as everyone in the throne room watched. The two guards closest to her tried to act but she quickly pushed them aside.

With one swipe of her hand, she pulled apart the shackles on her mother's wrists and removed the metal vest she wore. By the time Aisne turned her attention back to her father, a dozen of the queen's guard were surrounding her.

Aregund moved in quickly to shield her from the onslaught of brute force that came next. Even in his Garkin form, he was no match for even a handful of the queen's seasoned guard. The room erupted into chaos.

When Aisne awoke, she was laying on a cot in a cell that was smaller than her bedroom at home. She stared around realizing that she was in the dungeon beneath Merovech and she was the only guest.

Suddenly a light came on in the corridor. Someone was approaching. Aisne stood up quickly and pressed her back against the rear of the cell so she could face what was coming.

"Hello sister." Basina sat down in a chair just outside of Aisne's cell. "It pains me to see you this way."

"Then why don't you let me go?" Aisne folded her arms over her body refusing to look in Basina's direction.

Basina hardly noticed her sister's demeanor. She was too busy struggling with her own emotions. "I'm here on behalf of the queen. She wanted me to speak with you about a very important matter."

"Why doesn't she speak to me herself?"

"She thought that I could persuade you. We are sisters after all."

Aisne laughed to herself. "Are we really? Because the sister I knew would never allow our parents to be shackled like animals!"

"Will you hear the queen's offer or not?" Basina was losing her temper more so that she would've liked.

"I don't care what the queen wants anymore than I did five minutes ago…"

"What if you could free our parents? Would you do it then?" Aisne suddenly became interested. "I'm listening," she added.

"While the queen is heartbroken by the realization of your true nature, she has discovered what could be a positive outcome."

"Go on…"

"As you know, the Garkin and Faeborn have struggled to solidify a lasting peace. A royal wedding would go a long way in strengthening a relationship that has been broken for centuries."

"A royal wedding?" Aisne was slowly realizing what her role would be but she didn't want to admit it to herself.

"Queen Nuestria will offer you to wed King Tylwyth's eldest son." Basina hesitated for a moment. "If you agree, our parents will be pardoned and released."

Aisne finally looked at her sister. "What of my marriage to Aregund?"

Basina stood to her feet. "You cannot marry a Garkin. A new wife will be chosen for him."

"I see." Aisne slowly turned toward the cell wall. She didn't want Basina to see the tears that ran from her eyes.

"I'll give you some time to think it over." Basina turned to walk away when Aisne moved toward the front of the cell.

"I'll do it," she said flatly.

Basina turned back toward the cell. "I think you've made a wise decision. The queen will be quite pleased." Basina turned to leave.

"What of Aregund?"

Basina softened for a moment. "He hasn't been punished if that is your concern. Queen Nuestria proclaimed that he was bewitched by you and that is why he defended you in her presence. After a thorough evaluation, he will be returned to his duty."

"Thank you, Basina." Aisne was relieved to learn that Aregund wasn't harmed. After all, he'd risked himself defending her.

"Now I have a question for you…" Basina seemed thoughtful then. "Did you know that Emma was Faeborn?"

"I didn't know until I experienced my own transformation. That's the truth." Aisne answered solemnly.

But as she thought to herself, it made perfect sense. She remembered her mother's gentle touch, her calming voice that was almost angelic at times. Her father's sacrifice became completely clear now. He gave up his life as a Garkin because he loved a Faeborn.

Aisne suddenly thought of Aregund and it made her heart ache. She wanted to live the life her parents had. She'd never seen two people more in love than they were.

The next morning, Aisne awoke to the sound of a familiar voice. "Aisne, are you sleeping?"

"Duran, what are you doing here?" Aisne stared around the cell and noticed there were two guards standing on either side of her.

"I've come to take you someplace nice. Would you like that?" Duran was trying to make it seem like an invitation although Aisne knew better.

"I'd like that," Aisne replied cautiously. "Where are my parents?"

"They are back in Jormstad. The queen released them after you agreed to marry Prince Rigunth." She motioned for Aisne to follow her out of the cell.

"So when do I get to meet this prince?" Aisne tried to keep her voice even. She didn't know if she could trust Duran anymore but she might part with some useful information.

"If the queen's offer is viewed favorably, you'll meet him in about a week." Duran led Aisne up a set of winding stairs onto the main level and toward another staircase. "If not, well let's just hope King Tylwyth accepts."

After climbing the last set of stairs, they reach a short hallway with one door on it. The door had a fancy pattern etched in the wood. "Go ahead, open it." Duran smiled widely.

The room was full of such niceties. It's hard to believe that mere moments ago, Aisne was in the dungeon. She stared at the tapestries along the wall opposite the door. She also noticed the set of windows with frosted etchings of maidens dancing together.

On the right side wall was a painting of Queen Nuestria that hung over the bed. The bed itself was a work of art with an elaborate, wood-carved headboard that almost reached the ceiling.

"Whose room is this?" Aisne asked.

"This is where you'll be staying until the prince arrives… a room fit for a princess."

"It's very nice. I just don't feel like I belong here." Aisne pulled at the neckline of her shirt.

"Dax, Roden, can you wait in the hall?" Duran waited for the guards to leave and then turned her attention toward Aisne. "I know that you're confused and wondering why all of this is happening. But I want you to know that I think you're doing the right thing. Your actions have saved your parents; I wish I could have done the same for my own."

"What happened to your parents?" Aisne realized at that moment that she knew very little about Duran other than her being related to Aregund.

"They were killed in a raid so my uncle Guntram took me in." Duran knitted her hands together. "When I was a child, I imagined being born in a different family. The life of a Garkin female is a difficult one. But I've adjusted to my life and now that's what you must do."

Aisne smiled at her. "I know there is truth to your words. I will do everything I can to keep my parents safe and to abide by the queen's wishes."

"I'm glad to hear it. Well, I will take my leave of you so that you can rest properly. Dax will be right outside that door in case you need anything."

Aisne nodded and took a step away from Duran. She was almost tempted to hug her but that wouldn't have been proper.

As soon as Duran walked out the door, Aisne started searching the room. She checked the large chest of drawers. Then she opened the door to a large wardrobe near the window. Inside were a host of pastel colored dresses and floor length gowns. There were several shades of pantaloons and knit jumpers. She had a sneaking suspicion that the clothes would fit her perfectly.

The whole of it confounded Aisne. Had the queen been plotting this arrangement with King Tylwyth since she bloomed? The fancy sleeping quarters, the wardrobe full of clothes, some part of this arrangement with the queen seemed misguided.

After a well needed bath, Aisne got dressed. She couldn't shake the feeling that more was going on with the queen than she knew. She needed answers and she wasn't going to get them hold up in her chambers.

With two guards outside her door, Aisne decided that the window was a better option for escape. After a quick look out of the window to assess the distance to the ground, Aisne bloomed.

There was a sudden knock at the door.

"I just need another minute," she said quickly.

"What's going on in there?" Dax shouted through the door.

Aisne stepped back from the window and with a flick of her wrist, plucked the panes of glass away. She stepped out onto the window ledge and glanced down at the ground. "Listen up wings... it's about a fifty foot drop to the ground. If you don't work we're certainly going to die."

Just as she let herself fall from the window, the guards burst into her room.

Chapter 9

Aisne's landing wasn't pretty but at least she landed on two feet. She hurried through the main corridor of the fortress toward the courtyard. The two guards from her room weren't far behind her. It was obvious that they were tasked with babysitting her until she could be handed off to the Faeborn.

The courtyard was full of soldiers performing some sort of training exercise. Fyk and Grumere had divided them into two teams. They seemed to all be chasing something but Aisne couldn't see what it was. When she finally moved around the Garkin soldier blocking her view, she saw a small creature tied to a post on the ground.

It had been terribly beaten and painted gold from head to toe. The soldiers had even glued feathers to its back. It was a darkling they'd made up to look like a fairy. There wasn't anything she'd seen in her life more horrible than what they were doing to the creature.

The soldiers were all laughing and cheering until she stepped forward and addressed them.

"Why don't you pick on a real fairy?" She yelled at them as she slowly bloomed in the center of the courtyard.

The soldiers were nearly silent as they watched her kneel down next to the broken creature. She was too afraid to touch it but when it looked up at her with fear in its eyes, she felt compelled. She stroked the creature's head very gently and then the area above its black eyes. The creature took one final breath and closed its eyes for good.

Several moments passed and no one made a sound. Aisne finally stood up and walked toward her two handlers.

To everyone's surprise, Brous leapt off the wall and landed in front of Aisne. He'd finally shifted to his Garkin form and would now seek retribution for the beating Aisne had given him not long ago.

"I'll take your challenge fairy. You dare to enter this courtyard so boldly!" He slapped Aisne with a powerful backhand that sent her flying into the group of soldiers behind her.

The soldiers cleared the center of the courtyard as Aisne stumbled to her feet. "So, you're looking for a rematch?"

"Yes!" Using the element of surprise, Brous charged forward. Just as he reached her, she rolled back on her wings and kicked him twice in the face.

The blow sent him flying back against the stone wall of the courtyard. Brous got up quickly and moved towards the center of the courtyard. Just when he was about to attack again, Aisne flicked her wrist and struck Brous hard with a shelf of heavy, metal shields.

He stumbled to his feet and blinked his eyes several times. Aisne was a little afraid that she'd actually hurt him but she didn't want it to show.

"I'm tired of this." Aisne once again started off toward the main hall of the fortress.

Without warning, Brous jumped across the courtyard and landed on Aisne's back. She wasn't harmed by the blow but it did knock the wind out of her. "I didn't say we were finished fairy." Brous whispered in her ear. Then he smashed her face into the ground. She'd almost lost consciousness.

In a final move, Brous picked Aisne up and clutched her in his arms. "I could crush you to death right now and no one would care."

"Or we could die together gargoyle!" Aisne closed her eyes tightly and focused on her core. Her body glowed with white light and released scorching heat that would have killed a normal man in such close proximity. Everyone watched in horror as Brous began to scream.

"Aisne stop!" Aregund shouted to her from the gateway to the fortress. He'd just returned to Merovech with his brother Fredegund and two others who didn't appear to be Garkin.

Once Brous lost consciousness, Aisne pushed him off her back and watched him fall to the ground. She turned to walk away but then came back and kicked him once in the face for good measure.

Fredegund leaned over to Aregund and spoke under his breath. "Are you sure she isn't half Garkin?"

Aregund stared at his brother for a moment before starting off toward the fortress. The two visitors followed quietly.

"That's enough… the spectacle is over." Fyk addressed the rest of the soldiers. "Dax, Roden, take Brous to the medical ward."

"We have orders to stay with the Fa-… to stay with Aisne," Roden replied.

"Now your orders have changed." Fyk growled his words more so than spoke them.

"Yes sir," Dax said as he picked up Brous' legs. Roden grabbed Brous's arms and they carried him off to the infirmary.

"The rest of you, it's back to training." Grumere yelled to the soldiers.

When Aisne returned to her chambers, her window had already been repaired. She walked inside and plopped down on the bed. She knew she'd be scolded for her fight with Brous but she was surprised to see who would be delivering the queen's message of disappointment.

"Aregund, what are you doing here?" she said as she sat up on the bed.

"I came to check on you."

"I knew the queen would send someone to speak to me. How long do we have?"

"About five minutes…" Aregund had a sheepish look on his face.

"I'm fine. Don't I look fine?"

"Well, you almost killed someone today…" His tone was sarcastic.

"Someone did die today. Or didn't you notice?" Aisne replied.

"The darkling? Aisne for all we know, that could've been one of the creatures that attacked us near Elbrus peak."

"I saw the fear in its eyes right before it died… I felt it. You can't know what that's like."

Aregund sat at the foot of her bed. "Aisne, you have to be careful whose feelings you let in. It can be dangerous to expose yourself to the emotions of others."

"It's a little late for that warning, don't you think?"

Aregund just stared at her for a moment. Before he could think of something noble to say, there was a knock at the door.

"Aisne, its Nuestria. May I have a word?"

Aregund walked over and opened the door. "Remember what I said, Aisne." He bowed to the queen and then walked out of the room.

"I didn't want to risk another soldier being burned alive but sending Aregund may not have been beneficial either." Queen Nuestria shut the door and then sat down on the bed next to Aisne.

"Your timing is perfect aunt. I was just about to lose my virginity."

"Come now, Aisne. You're not a child. You have some understanding of how the world works. This union between you and Prince Rigunth will benefit both of our people."

"What would be the benefit of forcing Garkin and Faeborn into a stronger alliance? You hate each other."

"But we have a common enemy," Queen Nuestria interjected. "We don't know enough about our enemy to lose this opportunity to work together. Who knows how many darkling are out there? They could have the numbers to overrun our defenses and destroy us. We need an ironclad alliance with the Faeborn to defeat them. I knew this day would come… it was only a matter of when."

"I suppose it was lucky for you that your brother fell in love with a Faeborn woman."

"I don't believe in luck my dear; only prudent planning." Aisne was surprised by the queen's admission. She needed to know more. "So why the charade? Why pretend that you were so shocked and horrified by their union?"

"That is what the Garkin need to believe; that a fairy and a gargoyle aren't meant to be together. But the opposite is true. We have reason to believe that a being of immense power will be born from that union and I need to ensure that their loyalty lies with me."

"So you were hoping that Basina or I would be that mythical creature?"

"The Tempest Bloom is not a myth my dear. It's not whether or not the creature will be born but when. In the meantime, I must make sure that our world has some stability. I will align myself with the Faeborn King if that is what is needed to ensure our survival."

"That sounds noble for someone who has lost nothing in this arrangement." Aisne spoke boldly. She no longer feared punishment. The queen needed her.

"We have all made sacrifices, my dear. Of that you can be sure." Queen Nuestria took a deep breath. "I understand your discontent. Aregund is a fine soldier and you care for him. But he is not a part of your destiny."

"I will do as you ask, Queen Nuestria." Aisne was suddenly reminded of the promise she made to ensure her parent's freedom.

"Excellent. King Tylwyth has sent representatives to greet you on behalf of his son. If they approve of you, Tylwyth will accept you to wed Prince Rigunth." Queen Nuestria walked over to the door of Aisne's chambers and opened the door wide. "There is one matter that must be handled first."

One of her guards walked into the room carrying a strong box covered in a magenta fabric and traced with gold filigree. He placed it on the vanity table and steppe back toward the window. General Guntram walked in next carrying a rolled parchment of paper with a red ribbon around it. After greeting Aisne with a quick nod of his head, he unrolled the parchment and turned to face Nuestria.

"Aisne, daughter of Ansoald, I name you as my heir and the sole Princess of Merovech from this day forth." She leaned over the scroll and signed it in her own hand. She then motioned for Aisne to do the same.

Aisne didn't bother trying to read the document. All she cared about was making sure her parents were safe from harm. She signed the doctrine as Princess Aisne and handed the pen to General Guntram.

"Excellent," Nuestria said as she handed the document to Guntram. The general bowed to her and quickly left the room with the soldier behind him.

Queen Nuestria motioned toward the large wardrobe in the corner of the room. "Now you must dress yourself in one of those lovely gowns and come down for the introduction."

"What if they don't like me?" Aisne replied.

Queen Nuestria reached out to touch Aisne's hair but then thought better of it. "They will love you, my dear. But just to be sure, let's stay out of the courtyard until they're gone. It was quite difficult explaining the training exercise you were involved in today."

Aisne smiled and nodded her head. She suddenly remembered the two men who arrived with Aregund. They must have been the Faeborn visitors Nuestria was speaking about.

When Nuestria was gone, Aisne opened the strong box. Inside was a beautiful diamond and aquamarine tiara. She took a deep breath and lifted it from the box. She walked over to the mirror and set the tiara in place on her head. "What would my mother think of me now?"

"You look so beautiful!" Duran was standing next to Aisne as she stood in front of the mirror of her wardrobe. "The visitors will want to fly home and give the news to their King." She giggled more feverishly than any Garkin should; male or female.

"I don't look like myself." Aisne could hardly believe her own reflection. Duran insisted on picking out the gown she wore. It was a floor length halter style gown made of silk and layer after layer of organza that gave the dress a unique flow. The powder blue gown was finished off with a thin gold belt.

"Will you wear the crown now?"

"I suppose I should." Aisne sat down at the vanity so that Duran could fix it into her hair. "It feels strange that I've been made a princess and my sister hasn't."

"When a soldier becomes a legionnaire, they forfeit any royal claim. Your father followed the same path which is why Nuestria became Queen."

"I didn't know that." Aisne replied softly. "There's a whole world full of things I don't know."

"You'll be fine. We should get you downstairs now." Duran clapped her hands and giggled again.

Aisne walked to the doorway and then turned to face the small Garkin. "Take a good long look at me. This is the last time I will be myself."

Duran grabbed Aisne's left hand and squeezed it gently. "You will always be you, Aisne. You are brave, fiercely loyal and kind. No one can take that away from you."

Nodding her head, Aisne quickly left from the room. She was touched by Duran's words. She only hoped that she would be able to return the kindness that Duran always showed her.

Aisne walked down the stairs with Dax and Roden close behind her. She was still adjusting to having guards that followed her every minute of the day but she thought it best to play along especially with Faeborn guests at Merovech.

In a moment of selfishness, she tried to imagine how she might benefit from the marriage to Prince Rigunth. If nothing else, she'd escape a life of trying unsuccessfully to fit into the Garkin world. She'd also avoid the pain of seeing Aregund but not being close to him. That was probably the best part of all.

When Aisne reached the Queen's private dining room, there were four Garkin soldiers standing guard. She practiced her curtsy for the first time in front of them. The soldiers didn't quite know what to make of her. They simply nodded to Dax and Roden and stepped aside.

Aisne moved into the room and approached the large table where Queen Nuestria, her three generals and the Faeborn visitors were seated. All of the men stood to their feet. She slowly curtsied again and waited for her aunt to make the introductions.

"Princess Aisne, I'd like to introduce you to Toben Marro and Burnish Haraday of the Faeborn High Council." Both men bowed as Queen Nuestria mentioned their names.

"It's an honor to meet you both," Aisne replied kindly. Her two hours of etiquette training with Duran were paying off.

"The honor is ours," Toben said softly. He was tall and thin with blonde hair that was almost white. His kind blue eyes locked on Aisne then moved to Nuestria. "Queen Nuestria, I must say your niece is simply breathtaking. Prince Rigunth will be quite pleased."

"I agree completely," Burnish added. His blue eyes were larger than Toben's but he had a round face and belly to match. "This is a great day, indeed."

"You both honor us with your kind words. Let us now enjoy the feast." Queen Nuestria was her most blissful self yet. She had just received the confirmation she was so hoping for. Toben's approval of Aisne was practically the same as King Tylwyth's.

Aisne glanced around the table at everyone dressed in their finery. Even the Garkin soldiers standing in the corners of the room wore their dress uniforms. Their navy blue suits with gold embellishments were the same style of Garkin uniform worn for over a thousand years.

What she hadn't noticed before was her sister Basina and Fredegund sitting across from her at the other end of the table. Seated to their right was Aregund. She tried not to stare in his direction but now that she knew where he was, she couldn't divert her attention from him for very long.

A meal of roasted oxen was prepared for the evening and a rare treat of sea bass. Of course the meal was in honor of the Faeborn visitors who enjoyed a diet rich in sea fowl. As the meal progressed, Aisne found herself captivated by Queen Nuestria's tales of her early days as queen. But somehow the conversation found its way back to Aisne.

"Well Princess Aisne, if all goes well, you'll be recounting your own tales as a young Queen..." Toben remarked after a few too many sips of ale.

"That would be something indeed..." Aisne laughed and most everyone joined in with her.

Queen Nuestria was practically bursting with delight as the evening progressed. Aisne was doing her best to play the part of Princess and the Faeborn were obviously taken with her. Standing up and raising her arms, Nuestria called for everyone's attention. "Now that we have enjoyed a most wonderful meal together, I welcome you all to join me in the banquet hall."

She led the group out into the main hall and down to the main dining area. Most of the other soldiers were there having dinner. They all stood up as Nuestria led her group to her table on the raised platform.

As soon as Queen Nuestria sat down, she turned her attention to the two Faeborn visitors seated to her right. "Gentleman, we are so honored to have you with us. But now we are moving into a less formal part of the evening. You are welcome to have some more ale, some tea or even to dance if you so choose."

Burnish Haraday was the first to speak up. "Queen Nuestria, we would enjoy some more of your wonderful ale."

Just as the drink bearers descended on the main table, Aisne noticed her sister leaving the room. Basina never joined the group on the raised platform. While she realized the importance of Aisne's possible marriage to Prince Rigunth, it was obvious that she had no desire to watch her sister being put on display.

But Aisne needed to speak with her sister. She needed to clear the air between them. Of all of the relationships Aisne was losing, she wasn't willing to allow the relationship with her sister to fall away without a fight.

Aisne smiled widely and excused herself from the table. She intended to follow Basina but Brous caught up to her before she could reach the doorway.

"Aisne, may I have a word?" Brous was trying to be pleasant which was difficult for him. "I wanted to explain my behavior from today." He was attempting some form of apology but Aisne refused to let him suffer through it.

"It's fine Brous. I could have been kinder to you as well." As Aisne was talking she noticed Aregund get up from the table. He was coming toward her.

"It was I who challenged you in the first place…" Brous continued his painful apology.

"But I did hit you with a shelf of weapons and I burned your flesh." Aisne started walking towards Aregund. "And I should apologize for kicking you in the face."

"What? When did you kick me in the face?"

Aisne hadn't heard Brous. She was watching Aregund as he approached her wearing half a smile. He was quite handsome in his navy blue legionnaire's uniform.

"Will you dance with me, Aisne?" Aregund took her hand and led her to the center of the floor. The music playing wasn't really suitable for slow dancing but the musicians quickly changed the tempo when they noticed Aregund and Aisne.

"You didn't even wait for my answer. That's a different Aregund, simply taking what you want."

"I've always been a gentleman with you. That's who I am."

"And now?"

"Now I want to dance." He smiled down at her. "I don't have the words to describe how beautiful you are."

Aisne could barely look at him. "Why flatter me now? We're no longer engaged."

"Is that such a disappointment for you?" Aregund asked softly. Burnish Haraday suddenly tapped Aregund on his shoulder. "May I cut in?"

Aregund reluctantly let go of Aisne and returned to his table. But it wasn't long before General Guntram and Queen Nuestria were hovering over him. Aisne knew exactly what they were saying. They wanted him to stay away from her so she wouldn't become confused about the promise to Prince Rigunth.

Even though they were in the same fortress, she didn't see Aregund again for almost a week. Unfortunately, it was the same day that she saw Prince Rigunth for the very first time.

Chapter 10

The day the Faeborn royal family was set to arrive, everyone was on edge. Queen Nuestria went to great lengths and agonized over the smallest details in her preparations. Of course, it was all a show. Everyone knew of the distain that Queen Nuestria and King Tylwyth had for one another but their alliance was necessary for the survival of both kingdoms.

Aisne knew that as well as anyone. So when Queen Nuestria sent half a dozen women to her room to help her get dressed for the assembly, she didn't complain. They were the Queen's own dressers and they came prepared to work on Aisne from head to toe. The final piece was a special gown that Queen Nuestria kept hidden in her own chambers. The only souls who'd laid eyes on it were Nuestria and the woman who made it. When the gown was brought in, all of the other ladies were excused from the room.

Queen Nuestria held the gown under a drape until the last person left the room. Then she closed the door and helped Aisne step into the garment. The ivory gown was made of pure silk that flowed down to the floor. Aisne couldn't tell which part of the dress she found most striking. The front of the gown came up over her chest just enough to hide her cleavage but the only thing holding the dress up was a gold wreath that went around her neck. Her back was completely exposed.

"You will captivate every man in the room." Queen Nuestria smiled widely as she circled around Aisne.

"It's so beautiful." Aisne stared into the mirror at herself.

"Yes, my dear. You look like a Faeborn Queen and that is exactly what you will become." Queen Nuestria walked over to the bedroom door and opened it. "I have another surprise for you."

When Aisne turned around, Emma was standing in the doorway. "Majka!"

Emma rushed into the room. She went to hug her daughter when Queen Nuestria stepped between them. "Please hold your emotional tirade for now Emmaluna. The gown must not be soiled."

"…of course Queen Nuestria." Emma had tears in her eyes as she grasped Aisne's hands. "You are so beautiful my darling. But that is only a small part of your gifts. With your strength and self-sacrifice, you will help to save us all!"

"Thank you, Majka. I will remember your words always." Aisne was holding back her own tears.

Queen Nuestria walked over to the door and opened it wide. "The moment has come. Let's get you downstairs."

Emma walked into the hallway still holding Aisne's hand. Queen Nuestria was leading the way with a victory smile on her face. Down in the throne room everyone would be taking their positions. The Garkin soldiers of note would be lined up across the back of the throne room. Nuestria's generals would be standing in front of them.

For this one ceremony, Aisne's parents would have a place next to Queen Nuestria on her raised platform. When Nuestria, Emma and Aisne reached the hallway outside the throne room, they were joined by Ansoald and Basina.

Aisne quickly noticed the contrast between what she and her sister were wearing. Basina wore a plain blue gown that covered her from her neck to just below her knees. It was shapeless but it didn't completely hide the natural beauty that she'd inherited from her Faeborn mother.

"Hello Basina," Aisne said kindly.

Basina nodded to her and to Queen Nuestria before taking a step back.

"Welcome, Queen Nuestria." The guard at the door of the throne room bowed before opening the door. Queen Nuestria walked into the room followed by Aisne, Basina and their parents. They walked along the red velvet carpet until they reached their places on the raised platform at the head of the room.

Aisne took one step back and turned to face the throng of soldiers.

She felt as if every one of them was watching her. It didn't take long for her to find Aregund standing among them. She quickly turned her attention to her father who came to stand next to her.

Moments later, the music started announcing the arrival of the

Faeborn delegation. Tradition dictated that Queen Nuestria would be greeted first, followed by Emma and finally Aisne. Ansoald and Basina were standing behind Nuestria and would be greeted later in the ceremony.

As it happened, King Tylwyth Teg was the first to enter the throne room. He greeted Queen Nuestria hastily and then turned his attention to Emma.

"Emmaluna, it is certainly a pleasure to see you again."

"It is my pleasure as well, King Tylwyth." Emma bowed before him.

When King Tylwyth glanced over at Aisne, the smile on his face grew wider. "Princess Aisne, you are everything I've heard and more. Prince Rigunth will be most pleased."

"You are very kind, majesty." Aisne bowed slowly.

"Let us hope that a pretty face is enough to bond our people together." Princess Respa, King Tylwyth's eldest daughter, stood next to him.

"We'll find out soon enough, won't we?" King Tylwyth responded wryly to his daughter's rudeness. Aisne could see the embarrassment on his face.

As King Tylwyth's other children greeted her, Aisne could feel her heart racing. As the oldest child, Respa walked in first. She was followed by Rhain, Owain and Dain. Then Patia and his youngest daughter Raven strolled in looking pleased to be there. Aisne tried to keep her attention on each of the Faeborn royals as they greeted her.

After a few terrifying moments passed, Aisne saw Prince Rigunth approaching. She was too afraid to look in his direction so she kept her head down. He kissed Queen Nuestria's hand and bowed to her. When he greeted Emma, he kissed her hand as well. When he reached Aisne, his countenance suddenly changed. He was about to kiss her hand but instead, he leaned over and kissed her cheek.

Across the room, Aregund clinched his fists together; he was close to shifting.

"Easy brother..." Fredegund tried to calm him. "This isn't the time to make war. But you'll get your chance, don't worry."

There was elevated chatter throughout the room. Prince Rigunth's breach of protocol wasn't lost on anyone, least of all the

Queen. "Prince Rigunth, perhaps you should save your zeal for your wedding night."

"My apologies, Queen Nuestria. I fear your niece has bewitched me." Rigunth didn't take his eyes off of Aisne. "From this moment on, I will be counting the days."

Aisne wanted to look away from him but she couldn't. He was the most beautiful man she'd ever seen. His eyes were the truest shade of green. His sun bleached hair hung well below his shoulders. He had a playful look in his eyes and a confidence that Aisne found captivating.

"You are most kind," Aisne said as she bowed to Prince Rigunth.

As the introductions came to a close, the formalities were concluded. King Tylwyth happily signed a contract with Queen Nuestria regarding the marriage between Rigunth and Aisne. The only question that remained was when the ceremony would take place.

The monarchs along with their trusted advisors spoke of renewed commitments while the Teg children talked mostly amongst themselves. Aisne was somehow able to capture Rigunth's attention. She coaxed him away from his family and out of the room.

If she was going to marry him, she figured she should get to know him better. Aisne led him out to the center of the courtyard leaving her guards behind. They could finally speak to each other and be free of any prying ears.

"Are you sure you want to marry me, Prince Rigunth?"

"I wasn't sure before I met you but I am now." He continued to watch her closely.

"It just seems strange to marry someone that you don't love."

"I suppose I shouldn't be surprised that you're asking me this. You could certainly have your pick from that room."

"I don't know what you mean?"

"Let's just say you have a few admirers in Merovech." Rigunth laughed out loud. "Most Faeborn are empaths and very good ones. I can teach you to use your gifts."

Aisne was having trouble holding his gaze. Rigunth was very attractive but she barely knew him. He spoke to her in such a provocative way. She struggled to find her voice. "Why did you kiss me?"

"I wanted to see if I'd get a reaction."

"…from me or from someone else?"

"Both actually…" Rigunth's smile had returned with a vengeance. "I wanted to know if I had any competition for your affections."

"What have you decided?" She replied in the same small voice.

"Let's just say I'd rather not chance it. I want you to leave with me tomorrow."

"Tomorrow? But that's so soon."

"Aisne, you've been here too long already. It's time you were with your own people." His expression suddenly turned serious. "Will you come with me?"

Aisne knew that Rigunth was right. The longer she waited to leave Merovech, the harder it would be. "Yes, I'll go."

Aisne and Rigunth returned to the throne room and a much smaller gathering than before. Many of the soldiers were excused so that they could return to their posts or whatever other duties that might need their attention.

Aisne was sure that Aregund would've left the room by then but he was still there. He and his brother were at their father's side as he held audience with Queen Nuestria and King Tylwyth. Aisne wanted to greet her parents but Rigunth insisted that they join the Queen's company.

As soon as they reached Queen Nuestria and her group, Aisne felt as if someone had taken all of the air out of the room. She could barely breathe. She tried to ignore the sensation but it kept getting stronger.

"Aisne, are you feeling well?" Rigunth blurted out in a way that made everyone take notice.

"I'm fine." Aisne stared down at her feet realizing that everyone was watching her.

"If you're sure… we have a long journey to Tremeria tomorrow. I want you travel ready." Rigunth's concern seemed sincere but Aisne knew he was making a point to mention their plans in front of the group.

"…leaving so soon?" Queen Nuestria cooed. "I thought you all might stay on for a few days at least."

King Tylwyth, who normally appeared so at ease, suddenly took on a troubled expression. "We are honored by your invitation Queen

Nuestria, but we really must be returning home. The latest attacks on the humans have made our people restless. It's only a matter of time before the darkling turn their attention to one of us."

"What human attacks?" Aisne couldn't hide her surprise at this revelation. What bothered her most was that no one else in the group seemed surprised by this information.

"Nothing you should trouble yourself with, princess." Rigunth chimed in. "The darkling wouldn't be foolish enough to challenge Faeborn or Garkin now."

"Maybe someone should tell them that," Aregund said flatly. "They attacked me and my companion near Elbrus peak not long ago. That area is much closer to Merovech than Jormstad."

"I suppose we should be grateful that you survived your ordeal. Would the two of you like to review your strategy with us later this evening?"

Aregund glanced at Aisne but then turned his attention back to Rigunth. "There really isn't much to tell. We were lucky."

Out of the corner of her eye, Aisne could see the queen watching her. She knew that Aisne was the companion Aregund spoke about. But that detail wouldn't be mentioned now. All of the time Aisne spent with Aregund would be swept out of Garkin history. But Aisne would remember and so would her heart.

Aisne wanted to run full speed from the throne room but she couldn't. She had to stand there and play princess with little more than a piece of silk covering her most intimate parts. Having so much of her skin exposed was something Aisne wasn't accustomed to.

Emma and Ansoald came over and joined in on the queen's conversation. Thankfully, it had taken a much lighter tone. King Tylwyth was inquiring on the construction work going on in the courtyard. The queen made up some excuse about reinforcing a section of the stone fence to add a guard tower. Of course, she couldn't mention that the real reason the improvements were needed was because of Aisne's skirmish with Brous.

Aisne could barely contain her amusement watching the queen dance around the subject. There weren't many occasions when Queen Nuestria wasn't in complete control. She seemed almost relieved when the meal for the evening was served.

Instead of a sit down dinner, Queen Nuestria requested that the cooks prepare light hors d'oeuvres. Small goblets of wine were set up on tables lining the south wall. This was the way the Faeborn entertained and Queen Nuestria wanted to honor their traditions.

Aisne was finally able to break away from Rigunth long enough to spend time with her family. It was uneasy at first. Basina was still adapting to the fact that her mother and sister were Faeborn. But after some wine and therus bread, Basina actually managed to smile. She seemed to relax for the first time in weeks. Unfortunately, it wouldn't last.

"Can I borrow my wife, Ansoald?" Fredegund seemed to come out of nowhere.

"Of course," Ansoald replied quickly.

Basina looked a little disappointed but she didn't protest. "Safe travels to you Aisne. Mother, father, be well." She walked off with Fredegund at her side.

Aisne wished that they had longer to talk. After all, she didn't know when she would see her sister again.

"I suppose I should turn in for the night as well. I have a long journey tomorrow." Aisne hugged her mother tightly and then her father. She said goodnight to Queen Nuestria and King Tylwyth before leaving the throne room for the night.

When she reached her chambers, she shut the door and collapsed on her bed. She was more exhausted than she realized. She didn't notice Aregund sitting at her vanity until he spoke to her from across the darkened room.

"Are you really leaving tomorrow?" he asked.

"What are you doing here?" she whispered. "Dax and Roden are right outside my door."

"I was waiting for you." His voice faltered. He suddenly stood up and walked over to the window. Aisne thought he might open the window and jump to the ground below.

She sat up slowly realizing this might be their last opportunity to speak to each other alone. "Is something the matter?"

"Yes, but…"

There was a sudden knock at the door. Aregund put his finger over his lips. Then he stepped into the wardrobe closing the door behind him.

Aisne hesitated for a moment and then walked over to the door. She opened it wide to find Rigunth standing there with Roden at his side.

"I wanted to make sure you were resting comfortably." He glanced over at Roden and then turned back toward her. "May I speak with you privately?"

"Prince Rigunth, I'm truly exhausted." She pretended to yawn. "I'll see you in the morning…"

"Are you sure I can't come in?"

"That wouldn't be appropriate, now would it?" Aisne gave him a weary smile.

"I suppose you're right." Rigunth smiled at her and then walked back toward the stairs. He didn't seem completely convinced of her demeanor but there wasn't much he could do.

Aisne closed the door and locked it. When she turned around, Aregund was standing behind her.

"I wanted to tell you something before you left…" He leaned over her and stared into her eyes. "Do you remember when we were on Elbrus peak?"

"Yes," she replied nervously.

"The emotions you were sensing didn't belong to you." He hesitated before continuing. "When you felt coldness and rage on the cliff, those feelings came from the darkling. The emotions you felt in the cabin were coming from me."

Aisne didn't know what to make of his words but somehow she knew he was telling the truth. "Why are you telling me this now?" Aisne took a step back trying to put some distance between them.

"I didn't want you to leave thinking that I never cared for you."

"Those are fine words, Aregund. I would have loved to hear them long before now." Aisne moved closer to the window.

"I don't want to upset you but I would like to ask something of you…" He joined her near the window.

"What is it?" she asked nervously.

He reached for her hand and pulled her closer to him. Before she could protest, he pressed his lips against her cheek. He knew he was taking a risk being so close to her. There was a chance she'd reject him.

But pushing Aregund away was the last thing on her mind. Aisne put her arms around his neck and leaned into him. She could feel the warmth of his hands on her bare back and it caused her to shiver. He kissed her as gently as he could, not wanting to ruin the moment. But his efforts were virtually in vain.

Every emotion he'd kept hidden from her came pouring out in those few moments. Aisne was so overwhelmed by his longing for her that she reflexively bloomed. Aregund barely noticed her change. He held her to him as her large wings wrapped them in an embrace only a fairy could create. Her entire body glowed like a beacon of light in the darkness.

Chapter 11

Aisne woke slowly as sunlight spilled into her bedroom window. Her mind was filled with thoughts of Aregund and the words they exchanged.

Hearing the way he felt about her from his own mouth made leaving Merovech that much more difficult. She would help rebuild the trust between Faeborn and Garkin but she would also leave the man she loved behind.

As she lay emerged in her thoughts, she heard a knock at the door. "Who is it?" she asked.

"It's Nuestria."

"Please come in." Aisne sat up quickly in bed.

Queen Nuestria glanced around expecting that someone else might be in the room. "So today you leave us."

"Yes." Aisne nodded her head. "Duran is coming to help me prepare."

"That's excellent news." Nuestria went over and stood by the window. "You might not realize this but you aren't the first member of our family to sacrifice your own love."

"How so?"

"I was in love once myself." She turned to face Aisne.

"What happened?" Aisne couldn't help being curious. She had so few opportunities to learn who her aunt was other than a queen.

"When my father named me as his successor, I was newly engaged. But I knew that I couldn't be both a queen and a wife. Calderon took the news well or at least that's what I believed. He left Merovech a short while later."

"What happened to him?"

"He took a post guarding the governor's family in Jormstad. It wasn't long before he met someone."

"A human?" Aisne asked softly.

"She was Faeborn." Nuestria suddenly looked uncomfortable.

Aisne could only imagine what fate Calderon and his Faeborn lover were met with. She had no desire to hear more of the story. "You don't have to talk about him if it bothers you."

Nuestria seemed somewhat relieved. "I didn't plan to revive old ghosts. I just wanted you to know that I understand that you and Aregund have feelings for each other. Those feelings brought him to this room last night."

"Nothing happened between us, if that's your concern." It was Aisne's turn to be uncomfortable. "We talked for a while and then he left." Aisne thought to herself for a moment. She didn't really recall when Aregund left her room but she wasn't about to make that confession.

"Well, whatever you said to him must have made an impact. No one's seen him since last night."

"I don't know where he could be but I hope he will turn up soon."

"As do I." Queen Nuestria smiled at Aisne before walking over to the door. "Safe travels to you."

She waited to hear the queen's footfalls on the stairs before closing her bedroom door and locking it. Aisne went to the closet and opened the door wide. Some part of her expected Aregund to be smiling back at her but he wasn't there.

Selecting the dress with the least amount of ruffles seemed a wise choice for the day. She knew that Duran would protest but her decision was made. She'd at least be comfortable during her travels.

Aisne walked out into the courtyard surrounded by at least ten Garkin soldiers. She wasn't sure what the escort was for. Perhaps Queen Nuestria thought she might make a run for it at the last minute. Of course she had no intention of changing her mind. Her marriage to Rigunth was too important to both their people.

Aisne had crossed half the distance to where Queen Nuestria and a small contingent of dignitaries waited. She'd managed to paste a smile on her face until she noticed Rigunth and Aregund talking amongst themselves. They seemed cordial enough, so she decided to join them. But once she moved closer, she realized the conversation wasn't as light as she'd thought.

"Just make sure nothing happens to her." Aregund was barely

composed wearing his best armor.

"You presume to give me orders, soldier?" Rigunth was maintaining his calm demeanor as usual. "I don't have to guess that you're the one she's leaving behind."

"There are things at play here that are bigger than she and I." Aregund kept his eyes locked on Rigunth even though Aisne was standing right across from him.

"Yes, there are." Rigunth turned to Aisne and reached out to her. "Come along, princess. I've grown weary of this place."

Aisne took Rigunth's hand as Aregund stood watching them. She didn't look back at him but she could feel his sadness. It made her want to cry. Or perhaps it was her own sadness; she wasn't completely sure.

Rigunth led Aisne over to where his father and Queen Nuestria were standing. He touched his father's shoulder and Tylwyth slowly nodded his head.

"This was a most pleasant visit Queen Nuestria. I welcome the strengthening of our bond through this marriage," King Tylwyth announced proudly.

"As do I," Queen Nuestria replied happily.

The large gates opened wide and the Faeborn delegation headed down to the horse drawn carriages waiting at the base of the hill. Rigunth was still holding Aisne's hand as they followed behind the king. The gates closed with a loud bang and Aisne could feel the sense of loss almost immediately.

"I can feel how tense you are," Rigunth told her in a kind voice.

"I'm fine… just a little nervous about the journey." Aisne glanced over her shoulder and noticed Aregund standing on the stone gate. He didn't move a muscle as he watched her move farther away.

"You needn't worry, Princess. There are many wonders in Tremeria, to the likes of which you've never seen. You may feel gloomy now, but you won't stay that way for long."

Just as Aisne and Rigunth reached the base of the hill, a strange sound filled the air. It was a mix of a lion's roar and laughter resonating into the ground around them.

"Rigunth, what is that sound?" Aisne asked nervously.

"Not what, but who." He pointed to a large mare standing just beyond Aisne's field of view. "His name is Mra."

Aisne moved cautiously onto the dirt road and found herself face to face with a large, white stallion. He was larger than any horse she'd ever seen, not that she'd seen many in her life. Only the richest families in Jormstad owned horses and hers wasn't one of them.

"He's beautiful, Rigunth." Aisne reached up to stroke his mane.

"They roam freely in the plains of Tremeria. You can catch a glimpse of them almost any time of day." Rigunth stood on the other side of the horse stroking his snout. "Let's go home, princess."

Aisne nodded her head and watched Rigunth mount the gentle giant. When he was comfortably in the saddle, he reached down and pulled Aisne up by one arm.

"Easy Mra," Rigunth tallied with the reigns until the horse calmed down.

"What's wrong with him?" Aisne grew nervous.

"He can sense that we've been around Garkin kind." Rigunth spoke over his shoulder. "He'll be fine in a little while. It seems that horses enjoy gargoyles as much as fairies do."

Having recovered from his bout of fear, Mra trotted past the king's carriage. Aisne didn't get a good look at King Tylwyth's expression but she was sure he'd be concerned that his heir was riding recklessly on a horse. With Rigunth's prodding, Mra was running full stride away from Merovech and into the hills above Jormstad.

Aisne held onto Rigunth for dear life. She wrapped her arms around his waist and locked her hands together. She had a suspicion that Rigunth enjoyed her show of panic. They rode that way for some time slowing down only when the horse needed to rest.

Just before nightfall, they reached the River of Sorrow. There were parts of the riding path that were quite narrow so Rigunth slowed the horse to a trot. He held the reigns in his left hand and patted the horse with his right. "Easy Mra..."

"Is this where they found the strands of her hair?" Aisne asked.

"Yes, it is." Rigunth spoke quietly.

"My mother told me about this river but I've never seen it for myself." Aisne was immediately affected by the murky water. She felt a heavy weight pressing against her chest.

"I used to come here as a child but I don't know why. Being here always frightened me," Rigunth said wearing a blank expression. "Many Tremerian women come here to release their sorrows."

Aisne wanted nothing more than to leave the river. She didn't need to be an empath to know how much the river bothered Rigunth. He was usually so light and carefree. This was a side to him that Aisne didn't know existed. "Is it much farther to Tremeria? I'd like to rest."

"We have a short distance to cover. Tremeria is over that hill and through the forest." Rigunth gave a quick tug to the reigns and Mra moved into a gallop.

Once they reached the forest, Aisne was able to relax. The redwood trees seemed to extend up into the clouds. They completely surrounded Tremeria making them an important landmark for all Faeborn.

Just inside the forest, the trees were some distance apart. But as they moved deeper into the forest, the trees were much closer together. By the time they reached the edge of the forest, the higher branches were intertwined. Mra carried them across the plain and slowed down just as they reached the main entrance to the palace.

Aisne stared up at the elegant structure that was now her home. Moonlight danced against the narrow panes of glass that speckled the front of the palace. There were no bars on any of the windows and no guards standing at the front doors. This was very different than the fortress at Merovech.

"This palace looks like something out of a dream," she exclaimed.

"I assure you, it's quite real. Would you like to get a look inside?" Rigunth leapt from the horse and then turned to pull her from the saddle.

He set her comfortably on her feet but didn't move his hands from around her waist. "I'm so delighted that you're here, princess."

Aisne could only smile at him. She didn't want to be rude but she didn't want to lie about her feelings either. "I hope we will all be well."

"You sound like your aunt… always searching for the right words to say." Rigunth swatted Mra on his hind quarter and the horse darted off toward the plains.

"Is that so wrong?" she asked.

"You don't have to put on airs here. Just relax and be yourself." He reached for her hand and led her up the marble stairs to the palace doors.

Once inside, the sound of music filled the air. There were four flute players on the mezzanine above the entry doors. When Aisne turned to watch them play, they bowed to her. Rigunth took her hand again and led her through the grand entrance and up a curved staircase.

"Where are you taking me?" Aisne asked.

"I'm going to show you to your chambers before the king arrives. He'll want to give me another lecture about my riding ahead of the caravan."

"I have a feeling you do that a lot."

"And he complains every time." Rigunth laughed to himself.

When they reached the landing, Aisne stared down an incredibly long hallway. There were a number of doors lining the hall and next to each door was a decorative pattern that bore the Faeborn symbol for each of Tylwyth's heirs.

Aisne feared that someone might see them tearing down the hall and protest their childish acts but no one came. There were no guards standing on a giant wall to make them feel insignificant. There were no guards to follow them around at every turn.

"You'll be staying here in my chambers. I'll be moving to the other corridor… for now." He motioned for Aisne to walk into the room behind him. "Is the space acceptable for you?"

"Yes, thank you." Aisne was surprised at how elaborate Rigunth's chambers were.

The first thing she noticed was the sheer size of the room. Her family's home in Jormstad could have easily fit into the space. The walls were painted ivory with gold filigree in the trim of the chair molding. The ceiling in the center of the room was covered by a stucco allegory of Lady Harmonia holding Rigunth as a newborn. It was a stunning representation.

The large, canopy bed fit into an alcove on the longest wall in the room. The bed was positioned east-west in the palace to face the rising sun. The furnishings were more elaborate than those in Queen Nuestria's own chamber. He was truly treated like a king.

"They'll bring your belongings shortly. Can I get you anything?" Rigunth moved behind Aisne in a casual movement. He untied her cloak and pulled it off her shoulders. "You won't need this."

"Thank you." Aisne wasn't sure how to respond to him. He was standing so close to her that it made her uncomfortable.

With one hand and then two, Rigunth gently massage her shoulders. "You're so tense. I can help you to relax, if you like..."

The door suddenly swung open and a Faeborn woman came in carrying Aisne's garment bags. "My apologies Prince Rigunth, I didn't mean to interrupt you."

"Its fine, Laila." He dropped his hands to his side and stepped away from Aisne. He kept watching her though. "I should leave you to get settled in, princess."

"Thank you, Rigunth. You've been most helpful." Aisne still found it difficult to be so close to him. She wondered how long it would take for her to be comfortable in his company. After all, they'd soon be married.

Once he left the room, Aisne breathed a sigh of relief. She almost forgot that she wasn't alone.

"He's very fond of you, Princess Aisne. I hope you'll be happy here." Laila smiled and turned back to the bed.

"I hope so. I just don't know what he wants from me."

Laila gave her a strange look but she didn't say anything. She continued putting away Aisne's clothes.

"I know what males want, I just feel that there's something else. There's something more to this arrangement than what I know." Aisne didn't know why she felt so comfortable speaking to Laila. They'd only just met.

"We all have a part to play in this. Just have faith."

Aisne turned so that she could watch Laila for a moment. "Who are you?" she asked cautiously.

"I'm Faeborn, like you."

"I figured as much but where is your family? How did you come to work in the palace?"

"I was a dress maker for Queen Harmonia... after she was gone; I was able to stay on here. My son works in the arena." Laila seemed almost proud for a moment. "He trains the soldier candidates."

"That sounds exciting," Aisne replied. "I should like to meet him."

"That would be lovely." Laila smile warmly at her.

"Do you enjoy working here?"

"It is an honor to serve King Tylwyth."

"Is he a just king?"

"Yes, he is." Laila put the last of Aisne's clothes in the armoire across from the door. "I'll leave you to rest now, princess."

"Will you visit me again?" Aisne asked.

"Of course, I will." Laila smiled as she backed out the door and closed it behind her.

The room grew eerily quiet which Aisne wasn't accustomed to. She didn't remember one quiet place in all of Merovech. She turned to face the balcony and stared out at the night sky. As she stood there, she thought about everyone she'd left behind in the Garkin city. She could only wonder what they were doing now.

Chapter 12

Aisne spent the morning being dressed by Laila and two other Faeborn women. She had no idea why they were making such a big deal about her breakfast with Rigunth but she figured their efforts were on his orders. She spent the time smiling at them and pretending to be excited. After all, if she couldn't convince them of her mood, she certainly couldn't convince her intended.

"Laila, you don't think this dress is too much?" Aisne stood up and covered her exposed cleavage with her hands.

"That's the perfect dress, princess." Mira chimed in. She smiled as she watched Aisne's reflection in the mirror. She was the taller of the two girls that joined Laila. She was showing a fair amount of cleavage herself that was partially hidden by her long dark hair.

The other girl, Brie had dark hair as well but it only reached her shoulders. She didn't seem as enthusiastic about helping Aisne but she kept a smile pasted on her face. She was dressed much more modestly which made Aisne more curious about her.

"Do you enjoy working in the palace?" Aisne asked her.

Brie nodded her head and nervously glanced at Laila.

Laila smiled at Brie before turning her attention back to Aisne. "It's time to put on your crown." Laila placed the jeweled halo on Aisne's head. "You're ready for your prince now, yes?"

"I suppose so." Aisne smiled as she walked out the door. She noticed Rigunth waiting for her at the end of the hall so she hurried to join him.

He was wearing a huge grin and looking somewhat uncomfortable.

"I could hardly wait to see you this morning. I barely slept at all." Rigunth bowed to her.

"I had trouble sleeping as well," Aisne admitted. "I hope the people of Tremeria will accept me."

"You have nothing to fear, princess. They'll love you. If nothing else, they will be inspired by your beauty."

"You're very kind, Prince Rigunth." Aisne tried to sound her most sincere. In truth, what Aisne feared most was a life with Rigunth. He was beautiful for a man but with the disposition of a lynx that had just swallowed a dove. She knew that even in marriage, she'd never know all of his secrets.

"And now we go." Rigunth led her down the circular staircase into the main hall. "I want to show you Tremeria. Once you've seen it, you'll never want to leave."

"I've heard of how beautiful it is." Aisne admitted only half of what she'd been told. *"The Faeborn are a self-indulgent and petty people,"* she remembered one Garkin soldier tell her. At least she'd find out for herself what Tremeria was really like.

The main hall was lined with paintings of Faeborn royalty but nothing captured Aisne's attention quite as much as the great room at the rear of the palace. The ceiling was over twenty feet high with gold filigree sculptures in every corner of the room. The sculptures were in the shape of the noble lynx perched on a daise of stone and ice. If not for their color, they looked as if they might spring to life at any moment.

Aisne drifted aimlessly around the room wondering if she would ever feel at home in a palace. It was certainly beautiful but she didn't feel the warmth that she felt at Merovech – not that Merovech was warm on its own. There was a certain soldier whose kindness made any other place in the world feel somewhat less than desirable. Not even the most exotic palace could replace that.

She turned to see Rigunth watching her closely. She saw what looked like hope in his eyes but she had none to offer. She felt loneliness in spite of him standing right next to her. She wanted to move his focus to something else; anything but her.

"What's out there?" Aisne motioned toward the arch shaped doorway at the back of the room.

"Why don't you see for yourself?" Rigunth clasped his hands behind him and walked through the door.

Aisne followed him onto a stone patio that was decorated with an intricate flower mosaic. The mosaic was a painted blend of petals from the apricotta and the wild rose julep. She'd never seen such intricate stone work before but the wonderment didn't end there.

Beyond the patio was a finely manicured garden surrounded by rows of shrubs that grew taller as they moved away from the palace.

Aisne searched for the entrance to the garden as she knew she'd need a possible escape if Rigunth ever decided to read her true emotions.

"There is the opening to the garden that leads to the bath houses." He pointed to a stone structure that was submerged within the garden. Aisne had overlooked it completely. Once he had her attention, he continued with an overview of the landscape. "Over there is the arena and the meeting house for visitors." He glanced over his right shoulder at a building that was partially visible from the patio.

"And there?" Aisne looked beyond the garden and out onto the single layer structures that peppered the landscape

"That is Tremeria. Your people are there." Rigunth started walking down the stairs toward the garden but he stopped about midway. "What shall I show you first?" he said holding his hand out to her.

"The arena of course," she said excitedly.

"Of course," he replied.

When they reached the floor of the arena, Aisne imagined what it would be like to meet an opponent there with her monkey fist in hand. She felt completely at home. It wasn't the courtyard at Merovech but it would certainly due.

Aisne heard someone shout a battle cry so she turned her attention toward a group of young male Faeborn. They were practicing their fighting techniques in pairs along the right side of the arena. Young Faeborn maidens were sitting in the observation areas nearby. Brie and Mira were among them.

The luxury of the arena surprised her. It looked less like a training arena and more like a respite for the wealthy with its cushioned seating and paved walkways. There were numerous flags around the edge of the arena that seemed to serve no purpose. She didn't understand why the Faeborn had wasted such resources to build a structure that wasn't focused on more rigorous training.

"It's not what you think," said a strange voice from behind her. Aisne turned to find a man with thick curly hair and a full beard staring down at her.

"Oh? You know my thoughts?" she asked reflexively.

"You were thinking that our arena needs more flags… I am Soren." He smiled slyly before turning to Rigunth and bowing. "…Majesty."

"Hello Soren." Rigunth placed Aisne's hand on his forearm. "This is Princess Aisne, my betrothed."

"Princess, this is an honor." Instead of bowing Soren went down on one knee. Aisne stifled a laugh. It was obvious he was mocking them but Rigunth was none the wiser. He was so accustomed to people fawning over him that he couldn't tell when he was being mocked.

"Have you readied our new candidates?" Rigunth asked.

"I certainly have. They're preparing for their sparring ceremony." He glanced in Aisne's direction again. "This will be their last youth drill before Thoran gets his hands on them."

"What is a sparring ceremony?" Aisne asked.

"It's how we determine who will be a fighter," Rigunth replied proudly.

"I see," she said glancing back at the young ones in the arena. She was trying to make sense of Rigunth's words. How could they pick and choose who would fight to defend Tremeria? In Merovech, everyone fought including the women. That was just a reality of being Garkin.

When Aisne turned her attention back to Soren, she noticed him watching her closely. Perhaps he was as curious about her as she was about him. For a Faeborn, his look was all wrong. His facial hair and larger stature made him stand out from the others. He even wore a strange marking of a broken wing on his right forearm.

"Is there anything else I can show the princess?" Soren folded his arms over his chest covering the mark.

"No, Soren. I think we've seen enough of this arena." Rigunth smiled but it only lasted a moment. He took Aisne's hand and led her toward the arena's arched entryway.

Once they exited the arena, Rigunth glanced over his shoulder. He almost appeared to expect someone to be following them. "A word of caution, princess. I recommend that you stay away from the arena. Soren is quite strange at times. I've even seen him watching my sisters."

Aisne was surprised by the princes' admission. "He seemed quite harmless to me."

"Looks can be deceiving… believe me." Rigunth's words were well-intentioned but Aisne knew there was more to it. Rigunth didn't care for Soren and it was obvious that the feeling was mutual.

Prince Rigunth had an air of calmness about him as he led Aisne the short distance from the plains that surrounded the arena to the cobblestone walkway that led into the Faeborn village.

Aisne had never seen such serenity, not even in Jormstad. The smell of mint filled the air as several small cottages came into view. They were similar in size but with doors and window shutters of varying pastel shades.

Aisne walked warily along the cobblestone road as the Faeborn villagers started to emerge from their homes. They were curious about the Garkin Princess who would one day lead them at Prince Rigunth's side. Some of the women were accompanied by their young ones but all came wearing smiles on their faces.

Aisne could feel their kindness and well wishes. It was a pleasant departure from the mistrust and challenges she faced at Merovech. But there was still one thing that bothered her. She hadn't seen one soldier patrol since she arrived in Tremeria.

"Where are the soldiers?" Aisne asked trying to keep her tone even. "Don't you fear a darkling attack?"

"There are no darkling here, princess."

"But what if they did come? These people would be virtually defenseless."

"Have you ever seen one of them?" Rigunth asked as he guided her toward the main road that led to the center of the village.

"I have." Aisne suddenly remembered the creatures that chased her and Aregund up the mountain side. But she had no intention of mentioning that event. "I saw one at Merovech. The soldiers found it on one of their raids. They tried to study it."

"Catching one won't do any good. They have a hive mentality. We need to find their nest."

"There's a nest?"

Rigunth nodded his head as he walked slowly ahead of her.

"Does Queen Nuestria know this?"

"I don't know what information my father shares with her." Something in his voice didn't ring true. "Not long ago, we were at war with the Garkin. Now we're supposed to be allies?"

"That's exactly what we are," Aisne answered quickly.

Rigunth laughed under his breath before turning toward her. "So whose side are you on, princess?"

"Whatever do you mean?" Aisne asked nervously.

"I want to know if you're loyal to me and the Faeborn. You are one of us after all."

Aisne suddenly remembered a similar promise she'd made to her aunt. "You will be my husband, Rigunth. What other promise of loyalty do you need?"

"Well spoken," he said smiling. "Come this way. I want to show you something."

Rigunth led Aisne through the rest of the village and back toward the gardens behind the palace. They maneuvered through a labyrinth of neatly trimmed shrubberies until they arrived at a stone formation partially hidden by the foliage.

The structure was created as a single rectangular room that was fifteen feet wide and twenty-one feet long. It was composed primarily of a pale grey limestone with a simple granite floor. The three windows on the north facing side of the room were covered in vines of jasmine that connected between them.

The wall opposite the windows was where two wooden benches were positioned. There was also a fire pit at the center of the room that appeared to have been recently lit.

Until that moment, Aisne hadn't noticed what was the focal point of the room. An opening in the ceiling allowed the sun to flow into the room and rest on a statue of Queen Harmonia made of the purest nephrite. Although Aisne had never met the queen in life, the rendition of her was so striking that it almost moved her to tears.

"She was beautiful," Aisne said softly.

"Yes, she was." Rigunth replied. "My father built this memorial to her not long after she died but he's found it too painful to visit himself."

"He must have loved her very much…"

"Yes, he did and so did I." Rigunth suddenly turned to Aisne wearing a pained expression. "That is why I will not rest until I find out the truth of who murdered her!"

"Do you still believe it was a Garkin?"

"Yes, I do. In fact, I'm sure of it."

Aisne didn't delve any further. She realized that he carried a great deal of resentment for the Garkin. She didn't know if she could change his mind but as his wife and a Garkin princess, she would try.

"Good evening." Aisne greeted everyone as she sat down at the dining table. Having arrived after the rest of the family, Aisne hoped the king wouldn't be offended.

The palace's main dining room was intimate by Garkin standards. There was room enough for a large dining table, twenty high back chairs and a side table that ran the length of the room.

Rigunth watched her for a moment before taking his seat again. "You are lovely."

"Thank you," she replied kindly. Being the center of attention was still difficult for her. She found it difficult to stare back at the kind faces around the table including the king.

But there was one exception to the well wishers. Rigunth's eldest sister, Respa was wearing an expression that didn't exactly match the emotions she felt. Aisne didn't need to be Faeborn to know that the woman didn't care for her. What she didn't know at the time was why.

"Princess, I must tell you how delighted we are to have you here." King Tylwyth waived away the wine bearer and leaned closer to the left side of the table where Rigunth and Aisne were closest to him. "I trust that the prince has shown you some of our beautiful land."

"It is beautiful here, King Tylwyth. I must admit my surprise at how well the Faeborn live."

"I thought you might, princess. We conduct ourselves quite differently than the Garkin. We do not engage our women or our young ones in battle. Soldiers are selected not forced to protect Tremeria."

Aisne raised her eyebrows. "What if a woman wishes to fight? Is she not allowed?"

Rigunth took Aisne's hand and stroked it gently. "There are many things for women to engage in and battle is not one of them."

"I'm sure." Aisne lowered her head slightly. She was in Tremeria now. She would need to adapt to life here if she wanted to help keep the peace between the Faeborn and Garkin. After all, that was why she agreed to leave Merovech.

During dinner, Aisne interacted with all of Rigunth's siblings. She struggled with the fact that there were so many of them and even a set of twins that she couldn't tell apart from one another. Her only comfort for now was the knowledge that she'd have time to learn them all individually. After all, Tremeria was her home now.

Rigunth's brother Dain invited everyone around the table to tea on the patio. To her relief, Rigunth insisted that they already had plans that evening. Rigunth grasped her hand and led her off the patio and into the gardens.

"If you don't hurry, you're going to miss it," he said as he moved through the manicured bushes just ahead of Aisne.

"What am I going to miss?" Just as Aisne rounded the last ficus bush, she heard the sound of a stampede just beyond her field of view.

"Look there…" Rigunth lifted her chin gently with his hand.

Before Aisne could protest his gesture, she noticed more than two dozen horses running full speed across the plain. She thought that Mra might be among them but she couldn't be sure. Aisne took a few steps forward imagining herself as one of them. She envied their freedom.

"Where are they going?" she asked not expecting Rigunth to answer her.

"As much as I can guess, they're racing. It's a show of power… they want to show the females who's strongest."

"So who's winning?" Aisne wondered if Rigunth was really talking about the horses.

"It depends on the night, I suppose." he replied before smiling.

"This was a nice surprise…"

"There are many wonders here if you give it a chance." He stroked Aisne's arm and then took a step back from her. He must have sensed her apprehension.

"I'm just trying to find my way. This is all so new." Aisne stared out at where the horses had just passed by only moments ago. "Maybe we should say goodnight," she added.

Rigunth's calm demeanor slipped for a moment. "I don't want to take my leave of you; not yet anyway."

Aisne smiled and said, "Goodnight Prince Rigunth." She turned and walked toward the entrance to the garden. When she glanced over her shoulder, she saw that Rigunth hadn't moved from where he stood.

"Can you sense my emotions?" he asked over his shoulder.

"I can't," Aisne replied although she hadn't even tried.

"Maybe you've spent too much time in Merovech." Rigunth closed his eyes tightly and took a deep breath. "Goodnight Princess."

As Aisne stood there watching him, she began to feel his disappointment. But that wasn't all. She wondered if he was testing her… testing the level of commitment she had to their engagement. She needed to know him better and that would only happen if she spent time alone with him. "How many guesses do I get?" she asked.

He turned toward and smiled. "How many do you want?"

Chapter 13

"Aisne, are you going to join me or not?" Rigunth was hovering just beyond Aisne's balcony with his huge wings gently stroking the air.

"I don't think this is a good idea… what if I fall?" Aisne had bloomed and was crouched on the ledge of her balcony. "Why don't we go and watch the stallions? Then we can come back and finish up training."

"Trust me, princess. I won't let you come to harm." Rigunth stared at her intently and reached his hand out to her. With her eyes closed, Aisne jumped off the ledge.

Rigunth caught her in his arms that were stronger than she thought they would be. He held her close to him as he drifted slowly down to the ground below her balcony. "You didn't even try," Rigunth said softly.

"I am trying," she replied as she struggled to relax her breathing. Rigunth clung to her even after they were safely on the ground. The way he held her was an instant reminder of what Rigunth had shared with her the night before. She found her consciousness being bombarded with his attraction for her.

"Am I making you uncomfortable?" he asked.

"Of course not." Aisne smiled up at him. "Every woman wants to be desired by her intended."

"I know exactly what you mean." Rigunth kissed her gently on her forehead. "I pray to the heavens for the time when you will desire me."

Aisne took a step back from him deciding it was a good time to change the conversation. "Have you ever flown to Merovech from here?"

Rigunth laughed under his breath. "Aisne, we are winged creatures but we aren't birds. The distance to Merovech is too far to fly at once. You'd need to make several stops to rest. And if you were carrying food or supplies your flying time would be reduced further."

"Interesting…" Aisne turned her back to Rigunth and stared out at the plains.

"Do you miss Merovech that much?" Rigunth asked moving closer to her. "Don't answer that. I already know the answer."

"Rigunth, I…" Before Aisne could find more words to stumble over, Dain suddenly appeared from behind her with his wings spread.

"Rigunth, father needs you. There's a visitor he'd like you to meet." Dain leapt off the ground and disappeared in a flash of wind and wings.

"Princess, why don't you go for a stroll in the gardens? I'll check on you later." Rigunth smiled at her and took off after his younger brother.

Over the next few weeks, Aisne worked hard to fit into her new position as the future Queen of Tremeria. She spent her days learning to be more Faeborn and her nights watching the stallions roam free across the plains. She longed to run with them and disappear into the forest.

But she remembered the promise she made to her aunt. She knew how important it was for the Faeborn and Garkin to be at peace, especially with the rise of the darkling. She just wished she knew what was going on.

The Faeborn didn't believe their females should be involved in protecting Tremeria and that included Aisne. Even though she was quite active in the courtyard at Merovech, Rigunth had no interest in her battle skills. In fact, he discouraged her from visiting the fighting arena without him.

So the first opportunity Aisne had to inspect the arena alone, she used it. Rigunth escorted her to the arena for final preparation of the sparring ceremony but less than an hour later, he'd left her unattended to speak with some of the soldier candidates. He asked her to wait for him in the stands but she drifted off toward the entrance to the arena instead.

Aisne was about to walk out of the entrance when two Faeborn soldiers walked in. She didn't know where they were going so she decided to watch them. They moved near the center of the arena and the smaller of the two pulled at a trap door that Aisne didn't realize was there.

They both disappeared into the hole closing the trap door behind them. Aisne knew that if she tried to follow them, Rigunth was sure to see her. She needed to find another way down to the lower level.

After a few minutes, she noticed a narrow stairwell behind the main level of seating. She looked over her shoulder to make sure she wasn't being watched and then hurried down the stairs. The basement floor opened onto a long hallway that was lit by a single lantern.

She approached the door to the right and listened for sounds of movement. When she didn't hear anything, she slowly turned the knob. There were four large holding cells in the room that looked as if they'd never been used. This was another stark difference from Merovech; its dungeons had a constant flow of guests. She herself had been one of them.

Aisne continued down the hall to the last remaining door. When she reached for the knob, she could hear a number of voices coming from inside the room. She could hear metal clanking against metal and the sound of objects being hurled across the room and crashing to the floor. It reminded her of Merovech.

After waiting as long as her curiosity would allow, she stepped inside the door. The room was deceptively large with a twenty-five foot high ceiling. Its u-shape allowed for weapons play on the back side and hand to hand combat closest to the entrance.

The two soldiers she'd seen come through the trap door had blended in with more than three dozen other soldiers. Several of them had bloomed and were hovering above the floor. Thoran was among them but he was too busy sparring to notice her. Unfortunately, her presence hadn't gone completely unnoticed.

"Are you lost, princess?" Soren had just entered the room behind her.

She turned around to face him. "Not at all, I was looking for you."

"Looking for me? But why?"

"I was wondering why my tour didn't include this part of the arena." Aisne found it difficult to take her eyes off the soldiers. She watched as they used their Faeborn abilities against each other. The soldier closest to Thoran launched a spear into the air. His opponent redirected it into the floor with a flick of his wrist. Their spears and swords seemed almost useless against each other.

"I don't usually come down here," Soren replied sternly. "You shouldn't be down here either. Prince Rigunth would be loathed to find you in such a dangerous environment.

"I've never seen Faeborn fighting this way before... They are more powerful than I realized."

"Isn't your mother Faeborn?" He moved closer to her so that others wouldn't hear his words. "I thought it strange myself but I assumed she taught you to fight as a Faeborn..."

Aisne suddenly felt defensive. "I didn't discover her true nature until recently. This is all quite new to me."

"Is that so?" Soren's usually carefree expression turned serious. "And now you think we're kindred spirits, is that it?"

"I don't understand," she said.

"Come with me, please." He opened the door that led into the hallway.

Aisne followed him down the hall and into the other room. He walked inside and leaned against the bars of the first cell.

"You're not going to lock me up, are you?" Aisne asked as she slowly entered the room.

"That wasn't my original plan but now I'm not sure."

"I'm not ashamed of who my parents are." Aisne raised her chin slightly. "It turns out that the queen knew they were in love. She actually encouraged it."

"I can't say the same about my parents." Soren looked uncomfortable again. "My mother raised me by herself. I've never met my father."

"Was he killed in the war?"

"My mother doesn't speak of him. I only know that he was Garkin."

"Really?" Aisne had never encountered anyone else born of both Faeborn and Garkin blood. "Have you tried to find your father?"

"Why would I? I know all I need to know about him."

"You can't believe that. Knowing your family gives you a sense of belonging."

Soren hesitated before speaking. He seemed to be choosing his words carefully. "I'm part Faeborn and part Garkin so I don't truly belong anywhere. Unlike you, I don't have a queen for an aunt."

"That is true but that doesn't make you any less valuable. My aunt would certainly be interested in speaking with you."

"That's not going to happen." Soren shifted his weight from one leg to the other. "Tylwyth doesn't allow me to leave Tremeria. He's worried what others would think if they saw my true form."

"What form is that?" Aisne asked nervously.

"Let's just say it's different than anything you've witnessed before."

"Will you show me?" Aisne asked almost under her breath.

"I don't think so!" Soren shot back.

"Why not?" she asked sounding almost confused.

Soren watched her for a few moments. "I'll make you a deal," he said. "When you show me your fighting skills in the arena, then I'll show you my true self."

"…but Rigunth has asked that I not…"

"I understand." Soren replied calmly raising his hands in surrender. "You'd better get back up to the arena floor. Your prince will be searching for you."

"So I'll see you a little later?" Aisne climbed the stairs with Soren close behind her.

"But of course, princess." He answered bowing slightly.

"I'm so glad you came." Rigunth led Aisne into his chambers and shut the door behind her. "I searched for you at the arena today."

"I decided to go for a stroll. It's so peaceful here." Aisne pulled at the collar of her gown. The ruffles were nice to look at but not as easy to wear. Since she'd been in Tremeria, she was developing into a softer, milder version of her former self. She hadn't swung a sword or punched anyone in weeks. She wondered if she would forget all she learned in Merovech. If Rigunth had his way, that's exactly what would happen.

"Yes, it is." Rigunth didn't make a secret of watching Aisne's every move. "You look lovely but then that's nothing new."

"You look handsome as well." For once Aisne didn't feel uncomfortable giving Rigunth a compliment. He looked quite appealing in grey fitted trousers and a white shirt. He smelled as if he'd just come in out of the wind.

"I have something for you." Rigunth picked up a small box from the top drawer of his armoire. He opened it and pulled out a silver bracelet that was shaped like a vine. Once he put the bracelet on Aisne's wrist, she noticed the heart shaped stone that was the warmest shade of green she'd ever seen.

"What a peculiar looking stone," Aisne remarked.

"It's nephrite. Do you like it?" he asked.

"I've never seen anything as beautiful as this." Aisne stared at her wrist with quiet admiration.

"I have." Rigunth smiled widely. He took her hand and kissed it gently. It reminded Aisne of the day he kissed her cheek in Queen Nuestria's throne room. Before Aisne could inquire on this latest gesture, Rigunth started leading her toward the door. "We should be on our way to the arena."

As they climbed the stairs to the royal family's platform, Aisne stared out over the high railing at the mass of Faeborn in attendance. The stands were filled with delighted onlookers who welcomed any opportunity to see the king and his family. The sparring ceremony was the most anticipated Faeborn event of the year.

King Tylwyth stood at the podium and addressed the soldier candidates with pride in his voice. "Today, many of you will join the soldiers in defense of our land. We face a dangerous enemy we thought was destroyed. Once again we must join the Garkin and now our bond will be stronger than ever." King Tylwyth turned and smiled at Aisne. "It is with great pleasure that I formally introduce you to the future Queen of Tremeria, Princess Aisne of Merovech!"

There was rousing applause from the arena. Aisne glanced over at Rigunth and saw the warmth in his eyes. Rigunth was pleased by the king's announcement. He was ready to marry her.

The king continued his speech by providing a brief history on the sparring ceremonies. He remarked of the first ceremony that took place more than four hundred years ago. Tremeria was still quite new but the need for a security force became a paramount concern. The selection of soldiers and their training protocol hadn't changed in all those years.

The candidates were paired off for the sparring matches. Each candidate would show their skill in three specific areas; hand to hand combat, control in flight and kinetic ability. The Faeborn didn't value weapons training as much as their Garkin counterparts because a Faeborn with developed abilities was far more value than someone who knew how to wield an axe. But a complete soldier would be well versed in weapons use all the same.

Aisne hadn't anticipated how excited she would be at attending these events. She watched as many of the matches as she could paying close attention to the younger and smaller recruits. Their victories were much more meaningful to her because they reminded her of her own battles in Merovech.

Once the sparring sessions were completed, the successful candidates were selected to become soldiers. Those selected were called by name and moved to a standing position behind Thoran at the other end of the arena.

Of the fifty recruits Soren trained, forty-one of them were selected as soldiers. King Tylwyth was quite pleased with this outcome. He even went down to the floor of the arena to greet each of the new soldiers individually.

For the next part of the ceremony, a wreath of honor was given to Soren and Thoran for their support of the Tremerian guard. They were called to the podium so that Prince Rigunth could greet them. Aisne stood next to her Rigunth and smiled graciously.

Thoran was the first to approach the podium. He shook Rigunth's hand firmly and then Aisne handed the wreath to him. As Soren approached the podium, he wore the same expression of indifference he'd worn the first time she saw him.

Aisne handed the second wreath to Soren and waited to see what gesture he would make. After accepting the wreath from her, he bowed in dramatic fashion. For once, Rigunth was paying close enough attention to be bothered by Soren's display.

Rigunth was obviously displeased by the gesture. He didn't think that Soren was as respectful of the royal family as he should be. Aisne tried to quiet Rigunth's anger by taking his hand and squeezing it gently. Almost immediately, he was more concerned with the touch of her hand than Soren's antics.

When the ceremony ended, Aisne assumed that Rigunth would escort her to her chambers. He'd used every opportunity he could to spend a few minutes alone with her and she assumed tonight wouldn't be any different. But instead, he kissed her hand and asked her to accompany his sisters back to the palace.

Before Aisne could show the disappointment she felt, Respa was leading her down the stairs from the platform. "It's now time for the men to talk war," Respa added smiling. She hadn't completely lost the coldness she showed towards Aisne but it was lessoned somehow. Perhaps she now considered Aisne to be a member of the family. Of course her father's announcement tonight made it official. In ten days time, Aisne and Rigunth would be married.

As Aisne lay in her bed that night, she thought about what her life would be like once she married Rigunth. A few months ago she was the daughter of a shop keep; nothing special. Now she was a princess; how quickly her fortunes had changed.

She finally felt herself getting sleepy when she heard a faint scraping sound outside her window. She thought she might have dreamt it until she heard the sound again. She slowly got up off the bed and walked out onto the patio. She stared over the balcony and down at Mra. He started scraping more rapidly when he saw her.

"Mra, what are you doing?" Aisne tried to whisper to him but then felt ridiculous speaking to a horse as if he'd understand her. She decided to go down and try to calm him. But once she reached the stairwell, she noticed a single guard in the hallway below. She didn't want anyone to see her roaming around outside so she hurried back into her chambers.

She stepped out onto the balcony again and noticed that Mra was still in the same place. Without giving it another thought, she bloomed and gently floated down to the ground. Mra seemed quite please by her decision to join him but she still approached him with caution.

She moved toward him with her arms outstretched. "Beautiful Mra… what are you doing here?" Aisne moved closer to stroke his mane but he lowered his head and took a step back.

"What's the matter, Mra?" Aisne approached the horse again but this time he didn't move away from her. He turned around as if he was offering her a place to sit. "Are we going for a ride, boy?"

Aisne pulled her dressing gown up to her knees and quickly mounted the horse. As soon as she was steady, Mra shot off toward the meadow. Aisne held on for dear life wondering what convinced her to mount him in the first place.

After a few minutes, Mra started slowing down. He fell into a trot as he neared the forest which Aisne found odd. Moments later, he came to a complete stop in front of a hooded figure. Aisne held her breath as the person removed their hood and stepped closer to

Mra. It was Rigunth.

Aisne tried to hide her surprise at seeing him. "That's a nice trick. Do you usually send Mra to pick up women for you?"

"Only the one that I'm to marry..." Rigunth seemed short of words for once. He stood quietly holding Mra in place as Aisne dismounted. "I wanted to speak with you alone."

"Very well..." Aisne suddenly felt the need to adjust the neckline of her dressing gown.

"My father has announced our wedding date as I knew he would. A part of me is content in that knowledge but another part of me is... worried."

"Worried? What do you have to be worried about?"

"I want to know your true feelings. Sometimes what I detect from you confounds me. I suspect that my own feelings get in the way." He took a step toward her. "I have grown to care for you, princess and I'd hate to think that I was alone in my affections."

Aisne stared down at her trembling hands. "Rigunth, I care for you as well. I will marry you."

"Then kiss me..." Rigunth moved closer still.

Aisne was relieved to learn that Rigunth struggled to read her emotions clearly. She was certainly intrigued by him but her heart belonged to another. That knowledge wouldn't please Rigunth and would only cause harm to their relationship.

But what would please him, is a show of affection from her. She could certainly manage that in the environment he'd created. With nothing between them but a dance of air, Aisne placed her hands against his chest and leaned forward.

As soon as their lips met, Aisne felt a spark of excitement between them. Rigunth wrapped his arms firmly around her waist. She didn't know which of their hearts was beating faster as they held each other tightly.

Aisne felt Rigunth bloom against her which was the catalyst for her own transformation. With nothing to keep them in place, they began to float a few feet above the ground. The light they gave off was soft and warm in the dark forest.

There was a measure of comfort in being with Rigunth. He was her own kind – Faeborn. Maybe this was a lesson she had to learn.

She would never be allowed to marry a Garkin. That much was clear. Her relationship with Rigunth was more than just a promise she'd made. For the first time, she actually imagined finding some measure of happiness with the Faeborn prince.

Chapter 14

Aregund stood atop the stone fence at Merovech staring off into the distance. He'd been standing in the same position for almost an hour when he heard someone calling his name.

"Aregund, come and join me. Brous will take your post!" Fredegund motioned to Brous who quickly shifted and leapt onto the wall.

Aregund landed on the ground with a thud. He shifted to his human form and turned to face his brother. "What is it?" Aregund asked flatly.

"The queen requests your presence in the throne room."

"Understood," Aregund replied before starting off toward the entrance to the fortress.

"There's more…" Fredegund started. "There's word from Tremeria. Aisne will marry Rigunth in eight days." Fredegund spoke in a deliberate tone as he moved toward his brother. "You must not concern yourself with Aisne any longer."

"I don't want to discuss this, Fredegund."

Fredegund glanced at his brother as they entered the main hall of the fortress. "Since she left, you've been sulking like a human child and it hasn't gone unnoticed. Do you want to be challenged for your position in the guard?"

"This wouldn't be a good time for anyone to challenge me including you, Fredegund." Aregund's fists swelled at his side.

"It's not me you have to worry about." Fredegund stopped outside the queen's throne room. "Be well, brother."

Fredegund walked back down the hall toward the courtyard. Aregund reluctantly knocked on the throne room door. He was surprised when the door swung open and the guard stepped aside.

"I've been waiting for you." Nuestria waved her guard out of the room leaving them completely alone. Aregund walked over and stood in front of the queen's throne. He bowed slightly waiting for her to give him his orders.

"I'm sure you're wondering why I've sent for you." Queen Nuestria stared at the arm rest to her chair before placing her arm upon it.

"Your wish is my command," he replied.

"Peter Pierce has gone missing. Do you remember him?" Nuestria was paying too much attention to her arm rest again.

"He's Burl Pierce's son." Aregund remembered the human who'd run off when Basina shifted for the first time.

"The governor has asked for my help in finding his youngest son." Nuestria finally looked at Aregund. He was the best tracker she had. If anyone could find the boy, he could. "This matter is of the utmost importance."

"How long has he been missing?" Aregund asked.

"He disappeared from Jormstad a few days ago. I want you to begin your search at once."

"As you wish." Aregund bowed quickly and turned to leave the throne room.

"Aregund…" Queen Nuestria called to him calmly. "The governor has given his permission for you to use whatever methods you see fit. You may interview anyone in Jormstad."

"Very good." Aregund bowed once more and walked out of the throne room door. When he reached the main hall, Duran was waiting for him.

"What did the queen want with you?" She fell into step next to Aregund.

"You know I can't tell you that." Aregund walked out into the courtyard and headed toward his small training room.

"Are you going on a mission?" Duran asked. "Can I go with you?"

Aregund stopped walking and turned to face her. "Absolutely not."

"Why can't I come? You might get lost or hurt… you need someone to shadow you."

"If I needed a shadow, I wouldn't use someone of your stature." Aregund frowned at her as he disappeared down the stairs to his training room.

He grabbed his hooded travel cloak and slipped it over his head. Then he picked up his favorite axe and slid it into the holster over his shoulder. Duran watched as he moved across the courtyard and out the front gates.

By the time Aregund reached Jormstad, he was filled with angst over being surrounded by so many the humans. He had travelled the settlement many times but never in the light of day and never in the most densely populated areas. He found himself imagining what Ansoald must have felt being surrounded by the humans for so long.

He greeted the governor who was kind enough but he never felt completely at ease. He wasn't making a social call. Humans may have played a part in Peter's disappearance and he was tasked with eliminating that as a possibility.

Aregund was shown to a meeting area on the lower level of the governor's mansion. He was given free rein to question anyone he wished to but privacy in his methods was necessary. He didn't want anyone in town to hear what others informed him of.

After several interrogations, a young human named Lyle Dollery directed Aregund to Jenny Wright. Lyle swore that she was the last person to see Peter before his disappearance. As soon as he started questioning her, he knew that she was hiding something.

"Why don't you start over…"Aregund sat with his arms crossed over his chest as several of the governor's staff watched from across the meeting room.

Jenny stared nervously in their direction and then closed her eyes. She seemed afraid of something or someone.

"Gentlemen, may I speak with Jenny alone?" Aregund asked.

"We were told to be present for all of the interviews," Kenbridge replied. He was the governor's trusted advisor.

"As you can see, we're not getting very far," Aregund grumbled. "Peter's been gone for three days. If you truly want to find him, I need your cooperation."

"Very well," Kenbridge replied and then motioned for the other two men to follow him out of the room.

Aregund turned his attention back to Jenny. "I don't know what you're hiding. If Peter truly is a friend of yours, you need to tell me the truth. Where did you see him last?"

Jenny looked at him with tears in her eyes. "A few of us gathered on the north side of town. It was harmless enough…"

"What was harmless?" Aregund moved closer to her.

"Someone in the group teased Peter that he wouldn't collect

water from the River of Sorrow. That was the last time I saw him."

"Don't you know that area is forbidden for humans?" He tried not to appear angry.

"I told him that but he wouldn't listen."

"Thank you, Jenny. That's what I needed to know." Aregund hurried from the room. He told Kenbridge that he had the information he needed and that he'd report back to him in a few days.

Aregund new the journey to the river would be dangerous because it was Faeborn territory. But he'd given his promise to search for Peter even if that included risking his own life. The Garkin never traveled near Tremeria and certainly not unannounced. In the interest of time, Aregund would have to make an exception.

As soon as he reached the river, he started searching for clues that Peter had been there. Having visited Peter's chambers, he was sure to pick up the boy's scent. He shifted to his Garkin form and made a sweep of the river's edge.

Just when he'd caught Peter's scent, he realized that he was surrounded. He turned away from the river and saw a dozen or so Faeborn guard descending from the trees around him. The largest of them, a red haired Faeborn called Lorax, stepped forward. "Are you lost gargoyle or just foolish?"

Aregund ignored the Faeborn's tone somehow managing to hold his composure. The way the Faeborn soldiers surrounded him made it obvious that an attack was imminent. His only possible chance at survival was to cooperate with them. "I'm here on a mission from my queen. There was a human boy who went missing in this area two days ago. Have you seen him?"

"We'll ask the questions Garkin," said the largest of the group. "You'll answer to Prince Rigunth now. Start moving…"

The Faeborn soldiers formed a circle around Aregund and marched him through the forest surrounding Tremeria. Even in his human form, they didn't trust him. They tied his hands together behind his back and shackled his feet.

Aregund had never seen the palace at Tremeria before and he had to admit to himself that it was striking in its design and form. From the outside, the reflective material it was composed of made it difficult for anyone to scale its outer walls. It was designed to resist a direct attack not that the Garkin would be foolish enough to meet the Faeborn in their territory.

The closer Aregund moved toward the palace, they less he worried about his own safety. If the Faeborn were going to kill him, they would've done it by now. He just hoped that Peter was still alive and unharmed. With the humans currently under Garkin protection, any deaths at the hands of the Faeborn would cause further tension.

As Aregund sat in the meeting house adjacent to the arena, he found himself thinking of Aisne. This was the closest he'd been to her in weeks. He wondered if she knew he was in there.

The door to the meeting room unexpectedly swung open and Aisne walked into the room. The princess crown and pale pink gown she wore made her almost unrecognizable to him. None the less, Aregund was pleased to see her. He sat smiling until he saw Prince Rigunth saunter into the room behind her.

"Well, isn't this a surprise. Aregund is it?" Rigunth grinned at the Garkin soldier but it wasn't meant to show kindness.

"Prince Rigunth." Aregund bowed slightly.

"You're a long way from home," Rigunth replied.

"I didn't mean to intrude on your lands but I'm looking for a human. His name is Peter Pierce and he went missing near the River of Sorrow."

"Pete... Is he alright?" Aisne interjected. She'd assumed that her sister's old boyfriend was safely at home in Jormstad.

"That's what I mean to find out," Aregund replied firmly.

"He's in good health at the moment but your human was caught taking water from the river. As you know, that is forbidden. He will face the Tremerian court tomorrow and could be executed for his crimes."

"Executed?" Aisne's soft expression was suddenly pained. "Rigunth, there must be some way around this... some part of your law that deals with the ignorant..."

Rigunth massaged his chin for a moment before he answered. "Well, there is one alternative but it isn't a guarantee of success."

"Name it," Aregund answered.

"Someone can stand in for him in a test of strength. If his champion is victorious, Peter will be freed."

"I'll do it. I'll stand in for Peter." Aregund spoke quickly waiting for the Prince to accept his offer.

"You don't even know who your opponent will be." Rigunth

moved closer to him with his hands clasped behind him.

"It doesn't matter," Aregund replied. His only thoughts were of the promise he made to Queen Nuestria. There was no way he could return to Merovech without trying everything in his power to complete his task.

"Spoken like a true Garkin soldier," Rigunth teased. "… oh and that reminds me. You must remain in your human form during the contest. No Garkin is allowed on our lands without an invitation. And since you weren't invited…"

"I understand." Aregund nodded his head and took a step back. "I'd like to see Peter."

"Of course. Thoran will show you the way." Rigunth opened the door and Thoran suddenly appeared in the doorway. He motioned for Aregund to follow him out into the breezeway that connected the meeting room and the lower level of the arena. Aregund stole one final glance at Aisne before he was ushered from the room.

Thoran and two other guards led Aregund down the circular staircase to the dungeon. There were four cells in the space but only one of them had an occupant. It was Peter. They put Aregund in the cell next to him and left the room one by one.

Aregund waited until the guards were gone to get Peter's attention. "Don't be frightened… I'm here to save you."

"I'd like to believe you." Peter struggled to get to his feet, sweat pouring from his forehead. "But since you're sitting in a cell just like I am, you'll understand if I'm not optimistic. Who are you anyway?"

"My name is Aregund. I'm a Garkin soldier and I promise that I'll do whatever I can to get you freed."

"I thank you." Peter swallowed hard. "I didn't do what they say I did. They grabbed me before I got within ten feet of that river."

"I believe you Peter but right now I need to rest. If all goes well, we'll be out of here tomorrow." Aregund turned away from Peter and lay down on the concrete floor.

Midi sen was the Faeborn term for the time of day when the sun was highest in the sky. It was also the time of day that Aregund was led up to the arena floor. He was surprised at just how many of the Faeborn had come out to see a match that decided the fate of a mere human. But considering how boring their lives must be, he figured this was the most excitement they'd had in a year.

THE TEMPEST BLOOM: RISE OF THE DARKLING

The arena was twenty rows high with enough seating to accommodate a few thousand spectators. It appeared that every seat was filled. With so many in attendance, Aregund was surprised at how quiet it was.

Prince Rigunth took his place on the dais and waited for Aisne to reach his side. The Faeborn began to clap and cheer when they saw her. She was a vision in a flowing ivory gown with her hair tied in a braid over her left shoulder.

"Let it begin!" Rigunth shouted.

Massive drums sounded from the very top of the arena wall. The three barrel drums played for twelve minutes before silence filled the air again. Peter was brought into the center of the arena just as the cadence ended.

Lorax, the arena master, removed the shackles and pushed Peter to the ground.

"Who stands for this human?" Lorax asked firmly.

"I do," Aregund answered.

"Come forward then. Meet your opponent."

The entire arena grew quiet as they waited for the Faeborn challenger to arrive. Aregund wasn't surprised to see Zephryn, one of Rigunth's most trusted guards, swoop in and land hard in the center of the arena. He was one of the strongest Faeborn alive and Aregund knew that he had no chance of defeating him in his human form. But he'd given his word to fight for Peter and that's exactly what he'd do.

The first few minutes of the match went on without incident. Aregund tried to stay out of the Faeborn soldier's grasp while imagining a way of getting onto his back. If he could get his arms around the Faeborn's throat, perhaps he had enough strength to render him unconscious.

Aregund thought he saw an opportunity when the Faeborn turned to brag to the crowd. But his miscalculation would prove costly. Zephryn turned around just as Aregund drove in and swatted him with his wings. Aregund was hurled twenty feet into the air.

Aisne stood to her feet in a show of concern. "Rigunth, stop this, please!"

"I cannot, sweet princess." He sounded almost bored. "This is the law… who am I to change it?"

"Rigunth, I'll do anything you ask. Just stop this now."

Rigunth moved his hand along her upper arm. "Will you come to my bed chamber tonight?"

"Yes, I will. Now stop this before Aregund is killed!"

Zephryn was standing over Aregund. He was about to deal a death blow when Rigunth raised his arm. The drums sounded again marking the end of the match. There was a disappointed grumble from the crowd but none more than Zephryn himself. He let out a scream that sounded like the roar of a lion.

Aisne stayed in her seat and watched Aregund's unconscious body being dragged from the arena with Peter trailing behind him. She lowered her head as Rigunth stood to his feet.

"I'll expect you at nightfall." He touched his hand to her cheek and left the arena.

Chapter 15

Aisne paced the floor of her chamber as she contemplated Rigunth's words and her own. She promised to give herself to him tonight but she knew she couldn't go through with it. She didn't love him and no amount of time would change that.

She had so many things going through her mind. Seeing Aregund in Tremeria only complicated her feelings. She promised to marry Rigunth but now she doubted that she could even go through with it.

After fighting with herself for as long as she could, she left her bed chamber in search of her promised prince. She'd left him a few hours earlier promising to return for the night. But as she raised her fist to knock on his chamber door, she knew that she'd waited too long. He wasn't there.

She tried to imagine where he'd go at that hour. Only one place came to mind – the arena. Her supposed sacrifice saved Aregund's life, but he and Peter were still Rigunth's prisoners.

As Aisne made her way down the stairs below the arena, she heard strange sounds ahead of her. It reminded her of the soldier's war room back at Merovech. She heard a series of bursts that seemed to be coming through the wall.

She twisted the knob and quietly walked inside. Just as she presumed, Prince Rigunth was standing in the back of the room with his back to the door. He held a silver sphere in his left hand and waved his right hand in the air. Lorax was with him and seemed to be encouraging whatever behavior Rigunth was engaged in.

Aisne was immediately filled with horror as she realized the target of Rigunth's game. Peter was standing shirtless against the wall, with a mass of bruises across his torso. There were a few spheres lodged in the wall behind him but most of them had met their target.

"Prince Rigunth, what in the heavens is going on here?" Aisne moved toward Rigunth.

"Peter is a criminal… therefore he should be punished." Rigunth was playing with a sphere causing it to float back and forth between his left and right hands.

Aisne stared at Peter's battered body again. He was barely able to remain standing. "You're going to kill him!"

"On the contrary, Peter is in no real harm." Rigunth motioned toward a young, Faeborn woman who was crouched in the corner behind Rigunth. "Pilar is one of our youngest and most gifted healers. When we're done, she'll have Peter as good as knew."

Aisne immediately recognized the girl as her former neighbor and schoolmate. Pilar was just like any other girl in Jormstad until the day she bloomed in front of everyone in the town square. There was a lot of speculation about what triggered here transformation but none of it mattered. She was whisked off to Tremeria the next day and no one in Jormstad had seen her since then.

As much as Aisne feared for Peter's safety, she couldn't ignore the way the girl watched her. It was as if she was begging to be rescued as well. But at that moment, Peter seemed to be the closest to harm and she had to act on his behalf.

"This has to stop." Aisne stepped toward Peter and turned to face Rigunth.

"Princess Aisne, please don't interfere. I promise you that Peter is in no real danger."

Aisne stood defiantly in the way. "What you're doing is… torture."

Lorax tensed at Aisne's bravado. He disapproved of the way she spoke to Rigunth but he said nothing.

"I must ask you to leave this room and return to your chamber, princess." Rigunth stared past her at Peter. "This is a time for men to work out their differences."

"Liss-ten to him, Aisne." Peter struggled to compose his words. "I'll be fine."

"Yes, listen to him, princess. *He's trying to be brave.*" Rigunth toyed with Peter in a way that angered Aisne. How could a prince behave in such a way? How could he play with a man's life and enjoy it?

It was then that Aisne realized why the Faeborn were so eager for her to marry Rigunth. They somehow believed she could help him to become a prince who focused on his duty to his family and his people. At the same time, he might learn to deal with his anger toward Garkin and humans alike.

But Aisne had no desire to change him nor did she think it was even possible. Rigunth was cruel and petty and he was hurting her friends. If she married him, how long would it take for him to turn his aggression toward her?

"Rigunth, you must see reason." Aisne stepped closer to him. "If he tells his father that he was punished and without a trial, that information might get back to my aunt."

"And why should I care about the Garkin? They have no authority here…" Rigunth was still playing with the metal sphere.

"But the Garkin are taxed with protecting the humans. You cannot harm them without the Garkin becoming involved."

Rigunth seemed to be considering Aisne's words. Even Lorax relaxed his stance.

"I've grown tired of our guest," Rigunth announced before dropping the sphere to the floor in front of him. He walked toward the door and then turned toward Aisne. "Are you coming, princess?" Rigunth reached for her hand and she gave it to him.

"It has been quite a long day for us all," Aisne replied playfully. She gave Pilar a last cautious look before leaving the room on Rigunth's arm.

It took all the strength Aisne had, to pretend to enjoy Rigunth's company that night. He showed her more of the palace, he explained what their wedding ceremony would be like and he told her of his growing feelings for her.

She tried to return the same sentiment to him but it was very difficult for her. How could she care for a man who was so cruel to so many? She now understood why Soren hated him and why the young Faeborn women feared him.

She lay in her bed that night filled with fear and confusion.

"I thought I was the only person who could make you cry…"

"Aregund!" she whispered as she wiped her face. "How did you get in here?"

"You left the window open." He slowly shifted into his human form. He was smiling but Aisne could tell he wasn't completely himself from what happened in the arena earlier that day. "Peter and I are leaving… I came to say goodbye."

"What do you mean? Has Rigunth released you?"

"We wouldn't be leaving otherwise…"

"Are you able to travel in your condition?' she asked.

"I don't want to stay here a minute longer than I have to."

"I understand." Aisne could feel her heart expanding in her chest. She didn't want to say goodbye to him again but she knew she had to. "Safe travels to you both."

He nodded to her and then shifted back into his Garkin form. It the blink of an eye, he leapt off the balcony.

"It's about time you came back. What kept you?" Peter reacted nervously to Aregund's sudden appearance. "No, don't tell me. I don't want to know."

"Keep your voice down unless you want to go back into that cell." Aregund tried to whisper in his Garkin voice which sounded strange even to his own ears.

With the cover of night to shield them, they made their way toward the forest that surrounded Tremeria. It would be a difficult journey only complicated by the fact that Peter was human. Even though Pilar had healed him, he wouldn't be able to run nearly as fast as he needed to and he refused to let Aregund carry him.

There was another complication in the form of the newly emerged darkling horde. Now that they had resurfaced, it would be impossible to know where they might strike next. But Aregund could only address one problem at a time. And right now, they needed to get a safe distance away from Tremeria.

Aregund led Peter to the sand hills just beyond the River of Sorrow. The sand hills was a desolate place with very little vegetation. Only a few dorkus plants were sturdy enough to grow there. The area was deceptively large and filled with mounds of sand and earth that made it difficult to traverse in a direct path.

Peter had run as far as he could before collapsing onto his knees in the dark. "Aregund, I have to stop." Peter had sweat dripping from his brow.

Aregund kneeled down to get a better look at Peter when he felt someone watching them. "Rest here a moment, I'll be right back." He was trying to whisper again which was just as odd as it was the first time.

Peter lifted his head as he watched Aregund. "What is it?"

"We're not alone," Aregund replied before taking a flying leap toward a cluster of dorkus plants a few feet away. Just when he landed behind the largest bush, a figure flew out of the way and hovered above him.

"Aisne, what are you doing here? I could have harmed you!" Aregund belted out part angry and part surprised to see her.

"You'll need to move faster than that." She slowly lowered herself to the ground and walked over to where Peter was still kneeling.

"You didn't tell me that she could fly," Peter said finally catching his breath.

"She couldn't fly the last time I saw her."

"I've learned a few things since I was away. And one of them is how often the Darkling travel this area. We need to leave."

Aregund moved next to her. "You still haven't explained why you're here."

"I thought it would be obvious by now. I'm going with you. You'll need my help to get Pete safely back to Merovech. He is after all, the governor's son and his favorite as I recall."

Aregund frowned at her. "Your disappearance from Tremeria will cause much more discord between our people than the loss of one human."

"I doubt if Pete's father would agree with you... and what of your mission?" she asked casually.

"What do you know about it?"

"I know that you wouldn't have risked your life and all out war unless you were on a mission from the queen herself."

Aregund turned away from her. "We can manage without you."

"I'm sure you believe that but Merovech is still a half day's journey from here and you'll need someone to shadow you. Pete can barely travel without aid. What will you do if you run into trouble?"

"She makes a strong point, Aregund." Peter struggled to get to his feet.

"Fine." Aregund took a deep breath. "We still have a lot of ground to cover. Aisne will search over head for trouble and we'll make time on the ground."

Peter nodded his head without realizing what he'd agreed to. The only way to speed up the rate at which they travelled was for

Aregund to carry him. With Peter over his shoulder, Aregund moved much more quickly. He ignored the uncomfortable groans Peter made as he held onto his enlarged Garkin shoulders.

After travelling for several miles, Aisne could see the northern edge of the orchards that bordered the town of Jormstad. She landed on the ground just ahead of Aregund. "We should get something to eat. The orchards are just over that next ridge."

"Do you think it's wise to travel so close to town?" Aregund asked.

Aisne closed her eyes and took a deep breath. Then she opened them and smiled. "I don't sense any danger. I think it's safe."

Aregund stared at her for a moment. "So you're a full-fledged fairy now?"

"Something like that…" Aisne turned her attention toward the orchards. "Let's go."

They reached the orchards just as the moon appeared at its highest point in the sky. The clouds were noticeably absent as the succulent fruit fields became bathed in moonlight. All three of them gorged themselves on cassava fruit, cherries and pomegranate the size of melons.

"So you're known as *Aisne* now?" Peter said her name with an extra inflection as he took a huge bite of pomegranate. "I think I finally understand how the naming ceremony works. But the part of the story that escapes me is how you became engaged to someone else."

"This isn't the time to speak about such things." Aisne put a cherry in her mouth before reaching for another.

"Will you change your name now that you're his consort?" Aregund dropped what was left of his third cassava fruit on the ground.

"I am no one's consort!" Aisne glanced at Peter before she turned her attention back to Aregund. "Nothing happened between us," she said softly.

"So he was all set to kill us and then he changed his mind at the last minute?" Aregund was becoming more irritated as the moments passed. "What else could you have used to sway him?"

"I asked him… I begged him to let you live. In the end, I did make certain promises." Aisne couldn't face Aregund now that he knew the truth. But she still wasn't sure if he truly believed her words.

Aregund stared at her for a moment before sitting down on the ground across from her and Peter. "I suppose I should thank you."

"I'd say so. If it wasn't for Aisne, we would have met our end back there." Peter was grateful to her for all that she had done that day. She intervened at his darkest moment. Rigunth might still have been torturing him if she hadn't intervened.

Aregund shook his head slowly. "They were still planning to kill us. I overheard the guards talking when they thought I was asleep."

"My sincerest apologies for disappointing you, Aregund. I was trying to save your life!"

"Shh!! Do you hear that?" Aregund got into a crouched position.

"Hear what?" Aisne replied. "I don't hear anything."

Aregund stared around slowly. "I hear digging…"

When the first darkling broke through the ground behind them, Peter screamed at the top of his voice. Aisne and Aregund both changed into their true forms and assumed defensive positions around him.

"How many are there?" Peter asked.

"Four or five of them now but they'll be more of them soon enough." Aregund lunged forward as three of the darkling were set to attack. He tore at their bodies with a fury that Aisne had never seen.

As the rest of the darkling moved in, Aisne raised her hand sending two of them flying into the air. The fall wouldn't kill them but at least they'd be out of her way for a while. As more darkling appeared, Aisne moved closer to Peter and Aregund.

"There's too many of them," she said. "We have to get out of this orchard."

"Get Peter out of here!" Aregund shouted at her.

"What about you?" she asked. "How will you find us?"

"I'll be right behind you, now go!" His words came out almost as a growl. Aisne hesitated for a moment and then grabbed Peter from behind. She couldn't carry him for long but she could get them far enough away from the darkling for them to lose the scent. She only hoped Aregund would be safe on his own.

Beyond the orchards to the east was a deserted valley. It was home to a small pond and several rock formations that sprung up throughout the area. She decided that this was a good place to wait for Aregund.

"Will you please stop pacing? You're making me nervous, well more nervous." Peter tried to get comfortable balled up on the ground a few feet from where Aisne was standing.

"How can you even think of sleeping, with Aregund out there somewhere? He could be hurt or worse." Aisne had her arms wrapped around her human form. Peter was more comfortable with her that way so she tried to oblige him.

"He's fine." Peter turned in her direction. "I really believe that."

"Thanks Pete. I wish I had your confidence." Aisne sat down on the ground next to him and concentrated. Rigunth taught her valuable lessons during her time in Tremeria. If she relaxed enough, she could tap into someone else's emotional state. It only took a few moments for her to feel Peter's sincerity. If he believed Aregund was unharmed, shouldn't she?

Several hours had passed and daylight was upon them. Aisne was still sitting in the same position watching Peter sleep. She was just about to doze off herself when she saw a large figure lumbering toward her. It was Aregund. She was so relieved that he was alive but she also noticed that he was hurt.

"I'm fine, it's just a scratch." His expression was pained and Aisne could see the blood on his pant leg.

"Will you heal quickly?" she asked.

"Quickly enough," he said as he glanced down at the dry earth that covered most of his body. "I need to wash this off."

Aregund walked the short distance to the pond and pulled off what was left of his shirt. He trudged out into the water and dove under the surface. He allowed himself to become one with the calm waters.

His Garkin form slowly relaxed… his muscles rested, bones constricted. He returned to his human form and emerged from beneath the water. He swam for the shallows and realized that he wasn't alone.

"Who's there?" He was just about to shift when he saw Aisne move from between the trees.

"It's just me." Aisne moved closer to the pond and stood at the water's edge. "Pete's still asleep."

Aregund watched her for a moment and then turned back

toward the trees. "You should be resting too."

"I want to know why you're so angry with me."

"You misunderstood my words. I'm not angry with you."

She moved toward the water and let it tickle her toes. "I can sense your emotions, Aregund. You're obviously bothered about something."

"I'm not angry but I will be if you don't go and get some rest. We can't stay here long." He frowned as he moved toward the trees.

While his back was still turned, Aisne picked up a handful of damp sand and hurled it at him. It landed on his back just above the waist of his pants. He whirled around just in time for another blob of wet sand to land on his face.

"Aisne, stop that this instant!" he belted out.

"What if I don't?" She hurled another blob of sand in his direction but he moved just before it landed on his chest.

Just as Aregund lunged toward her, she bloomed and took to the air. Her strong wings spread out away from her body giving her the thrust she needed. But before she could reach a safe distance, she felt Aregund's hand around her ankle. He'd shifted to his Garkin form and used brute strength to pull her back down to the ground.

Aisne waved her hand in an effort to push Aregund away from her but his grip was too strong. She only managed to land on the ground next to him. She broke into a fit of laughter as she shifted to her human form.

Aregund moved onto his hands and knees as his body began to quiver. His hulking frame became smaller, his features softened. After several moments, he turned toward Aisne. "You are more child than I remembered." An unexpected smile caused the corners of his mouth to turn upward interrupting his serious expression.

"I can't remember the last time I saw that smile."

"There hasn't been much reason to smile of late." Aregund moved into a seated position in the sand next to Aisne.

"I'm sorry, Aregund. I didn't want any of this." Aisne held back tears as she stared out at the pond.

"I know." He touched Aisne's hand as they sat staring out at the still water.

"Maybe we should come back in a few minutes." Peter spoke from behind them.

When Aisne looked over her shoulder, she saw Peter standing there surrounded by half a dozen Garkin soldiers. Aregund slowly stood to his feet and turned around.

"What were you thinking?" Fredegund managed to pull his brother aside before he was to go before the queen. "Are you trying to bring shame on this family?"

"I didn't take her. She insisted on returning with us." Aregund tried to defend himself from the weight of his brother's stare.

"Is that so?" Fredegund answered.

"You're wasting time. I need to speak to the queen." Aregund moved around his brother and headed toward the door to the throne room. Just before he opened the door, he stopped and looked over his shoulder. "What would you have done if you were in my place?"

"I would have taken her a long time ago and been done with it." Fredegund laughed under his breath. "But you're out of time now, brother."

Queen Nuestria was sitting on her throne sharing an intimate conversation with Generals, Guntram and Lok. He couldn't be sure but he thought he heard the queen say something to the effect of, *everything's coming along according to plan.* Of course he had no idea what her plan was.

"Queen Nuestria, please pardon the interruption. I was told you wanted to see me." Aregund dropped to one knee and remained there.

"Aregund, stand to your feet." Queen Nuestria slowly approached him. "You have done well in bringing Aisne and the Pierce boy back safely. I wish I had a hundred more soldiers like you."

"You honor me, my queen."

"And now it is time we honor you, Aregund. Your father has found a new mate for you. Lena, daughter of Lok, will be your wife."

He hesitated as if responding to her caused him pain. "You are most gracious, Queen Nuestria."

Nuestria moved in close to Aregund which was unlike her. She usually reserved such close talking for her generals. "With all of this talk of war, a mating ceremony would do us all well. Don't you think?" She even touched Aregund's shoulder.

He answered her with much less hesitation this time. But his response was brief all the same. "Yes, my queen."

"I'm glad to hear it," she said returning to her throne. "Guntram, Lok, make your preparations."

Chapter 16

Aisne lay quietly in the dark waiting for sleep to find her. She had no idea what her aunt would do with the information she gave her. The Faeborn had threatened a human under Garkin protection. That by itself was enough to destroy the peace between them.

Then there was her discovery of Rigunth's rather egocentric nature. How could she be expected to marry someone with so little regard for anyone apart from himself? Her desire to remain pure until her wedding night meant nothing to Rigunth. She doubted he was even capable of being the kind of husband she desired.

A sudden knock at the door surprised Aisne. She crawled out of bed and approached the locked door with much trepidation. She opened it to find Duran's sleepy eyes staring back at her.

"What are you doing roaming about at this hour?"

Duran yawned and blinked her eyes. But the process of blinking took much longer than normal. "I wasn't roaming about but Aregund was. He wants you to meet him in his training room."

"Right now?"

"Yes," she said letting go of another yawn. "He's waiting for you now." Before Aisne could utter another word, Duran had started off down the hall.

Aisne wasn't sure what Aregund wanted with her but she thought it must be important if it couldn't wait until morning. As she dressed in pantaloons and a short cloak, she thought hard about what she'd say to him. She'd been away from Merovech for a while but the thought of being alone with him still affected her.

"Shouldn't you be resting after your ordeal?" Aisne stood in the doorway of the training room.

"I'm not injured." He dropped the rock he was holding and wiped the sweat from his brow. "Something's happened and I wanted you to hear it from me."

"Let me guess, you're leading an armed expedition into Tremeria." Aisne tried to lighten the mood without success.

Aregund sat down on a large stone and motioned for Aisne to join him. "Sit down, please."

"You're so serious... what's the matter?" Aisne sat down across from him.

"My brother and I will lead a team back to the sand hills."

"How many will go with you?"

"Half a legion... maybe more."

"I pray you'll have success." Aisne wasn't completely sure what to say to him. She stood up and turned toward the doorway.

"There's more," he said.

"Oh?" Aisne turned back around but she didn't sit down.

"While I was out searching for Peter, my father made an arrangement for me." He kicked at a large stone on the ground in front of him. "I have a new mate."

Aisne felt as if the air had been sucked out of the room. She struggled to breath but she forced a smile across her face. Aregund couldn't know how deeply his words pained her. How could she be angry when she'd just spent a month in Tremeria with Rigunth? "You have my congratulations," she said shakily as she backed out of the room.

"Aisne, wait a moment, please..." Aregund called out to her but she'd already started climbing the stairs.

With tears in her eyes, she burst out into the courtyard. As soon as she reached the center of the yard, Aisne bloomed revealing her massive wings. The guards that were patrolling barely had a chance to move out of her way. She almost collided with a few of them as she flew full speed into the air.

"I don't know why I need to be there." Aisne stood up and walked over to the window in Nuestria's chamber. She wore a pink ruffled dressing gown; a gift from the queen no doubt. Her aunt insisted that she dress more delicately even in private.

"It is your duty to be in attendance as my niece and a princess of this kingdom. If it's any consolation to you, he'll attend your wedding as well."

"Who is she?" Aisne asked softly. "His intended, I mean..."

Queen Nuestria moved next to Aisne at the window and stared

at her with a look that appeared almost sympathetic. "Her name is Lena. She is the daughter of one of my generals and a fine soldier in her own right."

Aisne suddenly remembered meeting Lena when she and Aregund were travelling through the Garkin settlement. She didn't quite remember what the girl looked like. The one thing that stuck in her mind was how tall she was.

"Is she pretty?" Aisne wished she could take the question back as soon as she asked it.

"Not as beautiful as you are, my dear." She gently squeezed Aisne's hand surprising them both. It was a well intended gesture and one that gave Aisne cause to believe that her aunt did have a heart after all.

But even the knowledge of her aunt's affections for her couldn't detract from the hurt she felt. Learning of Aregund's betrothal filled Aisne with an anger that she couldn't control or explain. "My apologies, Queen Nuestria. I'm being foolish." Aisne pulled at the pink ruffles around her neck. "If you don't mind, I'd like to go to the courtyard for some training."

"Is that really necessary?" Queen Nuestria's question was more a show of disappointment then an actual quest for knowledge. She wanted her niece to act like a princess and not risk her life surrounded by Garkin soldiers.

"Believe me aunt; it's better for everyone if I'm able to smash something non-living."

A little while later, Aisne got dressed in her most rugged attire and walked out into the courtyard looking for a fight. But she didn't like what she found when she got there. Apparently word had spread through the fortress that Aisne wasn't to be harmed. Not even Brous would accept her challenge.

With her monkey fist in one hand and the other hand attached to her hip, she circled around the courtyard trying without success to get the guards riled up.

"Are the mighty Garkin afraid of one girl?" She stared up at the stone fence where the strongest soldiers now stood.

"I'll take your challenge, whelp!" Aregund walked full stride toward her and shifted as he came. He grabbed Aisne by the throat and hurled her across the courtyard.

She bloomed midair and landed softly on her tiptoes. "That was shifty gargoyle… I like it."

As they walked in a circular pattern at the center of the courtyard, several soldiers moved in to get a closer look. Duran having noticed the event ran to the door of the fortress and yelled inside. "Everybody come quick, Aregund and Aisne are fighting!"

Unlike Brous, Aregund opted to take up a defensive weapon. The shield he carried weighed nearly four hundred pounds. He thought it would offer sufficient protection from anything Aisne might hurl in his direction.

Noticing his weapon of choice, her first order of business was to disarm him. She waved her hand and sent Aregund and the shield barreling toward the stone wall just short of the front gate. He hit the wall hard and landed on the ground.

"My turn," he said moving quickly to his feet and hurling the shield to where Aisne was hovering only a moment ago. She'd taken up a flanking position to his left in what she thought was his blind spot. In actuality, he was aware of her position before she could formulate her next move. He took a flying leap and landed right on top of her.

"What will you do now, whelp?" He wrapped his hand around her throat and slowly tightened his grip. "Do you concede?" he asked.

"Maybe next time, I'll concede." Aisne somehow managed to move her hands down to press against Aregund's torso. She uttered the word, *"fly"* and Aregund when soaring through the air. She was content to let him hit the ground. He wouldn't be seriously injured even at that height.

But halfway to the ground, he shifted back into his human form and started screaming for help. Aisne took to the air catching him right before he hit the ground. She put him down on his feet and landed right next to him. Before she could react, he whirled around behind her and put a dagger to her throat.

"Do you concede, whelp?" Aregund shifted back into his Garkin form. "Don't even think about turning up the heat. I could cut your throat before you gave me a suntan."

Aisne realized she'd been beaten but she still didn't like it. "I concede."

"What was that again? I can't hear you," Aregund teased.

"I concede!" She shouted and then pulled away from him.

There were cheers heard from along the stone fence. Many of the soldiers Aisne had taunted were delighted by her defeat.

As she walked toward the entrance to the fortress, Fyk landed in front of her. "That was a foolish thing you did."

"I know, I lost." She slowed down but she didn't stop walking.

"That's not what I meant." Fyk took hold of her arm more aggressively than normal. "You let every soldier here know that you have a weakness. And if they had to, they'd use it against you."

"So what should I have done?"

"Let him fall." Fyk smiled at her and then leapt back onto the stone fence.

Aisne stood on the wall and watched as Aregund, Fredegund and almost a hundred soldiers marched away from Merovech. She could sense their emotions as if they were one massive being of strength and fortitude. She closed her eyes and tried to focus on their strength to mask her own fear. She was concentrating so completely that she didn't notice Basina beside her.

"Do fairies pray?" Basina asked calmly.

Aisne opened her eyes and turned toward her sister. "I wasn't praying. I was focusing…"

"Focusing on what?" Basina frowned at her. "Only now do I realize how strange you are… how strange you've always been."

"We are not so different, you and I." Aisne turned her attention back to the soldiers who were marching steadily. "Are you concerned for your husband or are such feelings not allowed?"

"What of your own husband? Shouldn't you be in Tremeria helping to secure the peace?"

"I have not taken a husband yet, sister. But I will honor the promise I made in due time."

"I hope that you will, princess. For all our sakes…"

Aisne didn't need to be a Faeborn to know that something was bothering her sister. "What's happened in my absence? Tell me."

Basina kept her attention on the departing soldiers as she spoke. "We haven't suffered many casualties but we are still no closer to ridding ourselves of the darkling. As many as we strike down, there are more to replace them. The queen believes that our only option is to combine with the Faeborn in one final military action."

"So why send soldiers to the valley now?" Aisne replied.

"…because her generals don't share her opinion. They're not so willing to rely on the Faeborn in open battle." Basina finally turned toward Aisne. "You've spent time with them. Can the Faeborn be trusted?"

Aisne suddenly remembered the way Rigunth treated Peter and Aregund when they were in Tremeria. She wanted to tell Basina all they experienced but she decided to leave that disclosure to the queen. "Yes, I believe so."

Just before dawn, the soldiers returned. The queen requested that a small contingent of soldiers meet in her throne room to discuss the results of the raid. She was noticeably irritated by the news that not one darkling was found in the sand hills.

With dozens of Garkin soldiers on the hunt, this was the perfect time to lay waste to the darkling that had attacked Aregund and his companions. No one knew how the darkling could have cleared away without so much as a trace that they'd been in the area.

Aisne watched from across the room as Aregund explained how he led the soldiers back to where he was attacked. She tried to focus on his words but all she could think about was the conversation they'd had in his training room the day before. He wanted to be the one to tell her about the arrangement his father had made but hearing it from him made it all the more painful.

The thought of it burned at something deep inside her. She imagined that Aregund must have felt the same way when she was first promised to Rigunth. He simply handled it better than she did.

Aisne could feel how uneasy Aregund was addressing the queen and her generals. He was much more comfortable in the field. But as a well respected soldier, he was sure to become a general one day.

"Perhaps it is time to put our differences aside and work more closely with the Faeborn. They might be having more success in tracking down the darkling. And since we have something that belongs to the Faeborn Prince, I don't expect that we'll have to seek them out. We should expect a visit from King Tylwyth in the coming days." Aregund glanced at Aisne and so did everyone else.

Chapter 17

Almost a week later, King Tylwyth arrived with a full contingent of guards and his three male children. The Faeborn soldiers lined the left side of the main hall while the Garkin soldiers lined the right. Only the royal families were allowed in the throne room.

When King Tylwyth greeted Queen Nuestria, the mood was much less festive than before. Even his sons, Owain and Dain, moved into the room as if they were on high alert. When Rigunth finally sauntered in, he looked more solemn than anything. It wasn't until his green eyes rested on Aisne that he began to relax.

Standing at her aunt's side and wearing a more conservative gown, Aisne kept her attention on the Garkin crest hanging on the wall opposite her. She was surprised at the concern she felt coming from Rigunth considering how she'd left Tremeria so abruptly. She thought that he would be angry but that emotion was reserved for his father alone.

"Queen Nuestria, we made an agreement that your niece would marry my eldest son. Imagine my dismay when she was taken from our home in the debt of night. How can I take this act by your soldier except in the harshest manner possible?" King Tylwyth had turned a bright shade of green.

"I understand your concerns King Tylwyth but I have a few of my own." Queen Nuestria grasped Aisne's hand in a show of solidarity. "I trusted you with my niece and the guarantee that her virtue would remain intact until a marriage ceremony took place. Imagine my surprise to learn that her delicate nature was in jeopardy at the hands of the one person who was supposed to honor her."

Tylwyth turned to his eldest son and motioned for him to come forward. "Rigunth, what say you to these charges?"

He glanced at Aisne before turning toward his father and the queen. "Father, I cannot tell a lie. Just look at her… she is a vision."

"That's not an answer, Rigunth."

"Okay, I confess. What man, Faeborn or Garkin, wouldn't try everything in his power to sample such a delicious looking creature?"

"That is quite enough, prince!" Queen Nuestria took a step forward in her most dramatic pose yet. "Save your colorful words for the brothels of Sjoborg. They have no place describing a Garkin princess."

"Queen Nuestria, the last time I checked Aisne was Faeborn unless there is something I've missed." A thin smile suddenly appeared on Tylwyth's face as was his normal coloring.

Queen Nuestria quickly swept her statement aside as a simple euphemism. "Aisne is my niece by blood and that makes her a princess of this Kingdom. Unless you now doubt that I am queen…"

Tylwyth realized that he was losing the argument which was the basis for his outrage. His only option now was to fall upon Queen Nuestria's mercy, should she have any to offer him. "I meant no disrespect to you or your family. I still seek a union between our Kingdoms… that is if you'll allow it.

Queen Nuestria, still holding onto Aisne's hand, turned toward her. "The decision is yours, Princess Aisne."

"Whatever you wish, my queen." Aisne bowed to her aunt and stared back toward the crest.

"Very well King Tylwyth, I will allow it. But Aisne will remain here under my protection until the ceremony takes place."

"That is acceptable for us as well." Tylwyth was pleased at this outcome considering the position he was in only moments ago. "As we discussed, I will remain here for the Protectorate Assembly. That will give me time to interact with Governor Pierce as well."

"Queen Nuestria, if you wouldn't mind, I'd like to stay on as well." Rigunth bowed to Queen Nuestria and winked his eye at Aisne.

"That's an excellent idea," Nuestria replied. "We can also discuss the issue that occurred with the human, Peter. I understand that he paid a visit to Tremeria…"

Rigunth's smug expression slipped for a moment. "About that… it seems there was the greatest of misunderstandings…"

As everyone was seated in the throne room, the tension seemed to fade to acceptable levels. With all of the accusations and innuendo out of the way, Tylwyth and Nuestria could get back to what they needed to discuss. They would join forces against the darkling.

Some time later, Rigunth invited Aisne for a stroll in the courtyard. She agreed without realizing she had a Garkin shadow. Nobb was following her at a distance of about ten paces. It seemed that Queen Nuestria stayed true to her word about keeping an eye on her niece.

But choosing Nobb seemed a bit extreme. He hated the Faeborn more than the average Garkin which was probably why he watched Rigunth more closely than was necessary.

"Why is there a Garkin soldier following us?" Rigunth whispered to her.

"He's my bodyguard," Aisne answered. "I'll be a queen someday. My aunt says I should get used to being protected."

"I have a guard. He can protect us both." He motioned in the direction of a large Faeborn soldier standing just out of hearing distance. "You remember Thoran, don't you?"

She waved at Thoran and smiled. He was one of the few Faeborn that she legitimately liked; even if his main duty in life was to keep Rigunth out of harm's way.

"So what happens when you go to bed at night? Do you have a guard for that too?"

Aisne turned toward him with her eyebrows raised. "I seem to remember needing a guard outside of my chambers… or have you forgotten so quickly?"

"You're still angry with me, aren't you?" Rigunth spoke almost in a whisper. "I meant no disrespect…"

"I realize that, Rigunth. You've grown accustomed to getting whatever you want." Aisne forced a smile onto her face. She wasn't bothered by how much he tried getting close to her. She was more concerned with his treatment of her friends.

"Can I walk you to your chambers?" Rigunth asked.

"That's really not necessary. Nobb is more than capable…"

"I know that." Rigunth touched her cheek but quickly pulled his hand away. His father instructed him to behave and he was having trouble already. "I just want to be alone with you for a few moments. I need to apologize for what happened in Tremeria."

"Which part?" she asked calmly.

"All of it… sometimes I feel more of a victim than I like to admit. We have rules in Tremeria that protect everyone and ignorance is no excuse for breaking the law."

Aisne suddenly realized how sincere Rigunth was at that moment. He truly believed that a crime was committed at the river. But the punishment should fit the crime not some bizarre act of torture. She was still angry with him but she would hear his apology. "Give me a moment…" Aisne walked over to where Nobb was standing near the center of the courtyard.

"The Queen made me promise to break his hand if he touched you…"

"She said no such thing! Honestly Nobb, I wonder about you." Aisne shook her head slowly.

Nobb flashed a half smile. "I saw him touch your cheek. If he does it again, I'll have to break at least three of his fingers."

"Very funny… now please wait for me in the corridor. I'll only be a few minutes."

"You're quite domineering. Are you sure you aren't Garkin?"

"Ten minutes, Nobb."

"Ten minutes, princess."

"I'm relieved that you tricked your guard into leaving us." Rigunth followed Aisne up the stairs to the door of her chamber.

"And I'm glad that you're learning how to behave yourself." Aisne spoke in a jovial manner.

"Will you ever forgive me? Aisne, I understand what you expect of me now."

"I'm glad…" Aisne started. But before she could finish her thought, Aregund stepped off the landing and came to stand next to her.

Rigunth recognized him immediately. "What's he doing here?" he asked in a harsh tone.

"I'm here to protect the princess. Nobb was called away." He bowed to Aisne before moving closer to her chamber door.

"This is unacceptable. I will not have your former lover guarding you in your bed chamber."

"He's not my lover, Rigunth." Aisne worked to hide her embarrassment.

"So what is he planning to do, turn down your bed for you?" Rigunth added bitterly.

"I'll do whatever she asks me to do." Aregund smiled.

"Well, if you're staying then so am I." Rigunth crossed his arms over his chest.

Aregund started to reply but Aisne interrupted him. "That won't be necessary Rigunth as Aregund won't be staying either. Grumere will be here within the hour."

"Are you certain you don't want me to stay?" Aregund asked sounding wounded.

"I'm certain. Grumere is quite capable." She wanted to ask Aregund if Lena knew he was outside her bed chamber but she decided against it. What she wanted most was to put space between the two of them.

Neither Aregund nor Rigunth wanted to be the first to leave so they stood there for a moment watching each other. Once Aisne entered her chamber, she waited to hear voices but there was nothing. At some point, they left without incident.

Aisne was relieved when Burl Pierce and the rest of his delegation arrived. Their arrival sparked a new series of closed door meetings between the humans, Faeborn and Garkin. Hopefully, it would result in some effective planning for how to deal with the darkling. But in the short run, the meetings pulled Rigunth away from his constant attempts to endear himself toward Aisne.

One drawback of having the humans at Merovech was Peter. But it wasn't Peter himself that bothered her but his new choice of activity. Aisne had grown weary of watching him watch Basina. He was obviously bothered by the knowledge that she'd married so quickly.

Aisne finally decided that a quick lesson on Garkin marriage would help Peter gain some perspective on his lost love. "Haven't you ever known anybody who left Jormstad and went to live with the Garkin?"

"Of course I have," he replied. "But it's different when the person leaving is the one you were supposed to marry."

Aisne couldn't hide her surprise at this revelation. "When did you and my sister ever speak of marriage?"

"We'd spoken of marriage many times. But I hadn't asked her until the last day we were together... you know, when she changed."

"What did she say?" Aisne asked almost in a whisper.

"She never had a chance to answer." Peter took another

sorrowful look in Basina's direction.

"Come on. Let's go outside." Aisne stood up and motioned for him to follow her. When they reached the courtyard, Aisne transformed and grabbed Peter by the arm. She set him down on the stone wall of the fortress and shifted back to her human form.

"I'll never get used to you doing that," Peter said as he steadied himself. "Is it safe up here?" he asked moving around a soldier to catch up to Aisne.

"It's as safe as anywhere, I suppose." She walked along the wall until she reached the corner high booth where two guards stood on look out.

Peter stood next to her and stared out at the valley below. "So what will happen with you and Aregund?" He obviously wanted to think about something other than Basina but Aisne wasn't sure she was comfortable moving the focus to herself.

"Why do you ask?"

"Well, I've heard you talking about the law that means to keep the Faeborn and Garkin apart. But when we were at the pond, you and Aregund seemed quite close."

Aisne swallowed hard. "You know the story… we were supposed to be married and now we're promised to other people."

"I suppose things would be easier if you were born Garkin. If you could change what you are, would you?"

"I'd rather be born into a world where it didn't matter…"

He nodded his head slowly. "So would I." Aisne knew that he understood perfectly what she meant. He watched the woman he loved stare at another man the way he wanted her to look at him. Aisne could sense his pain quite easily.

Minutes passed without either of them speaking a word. Peter shuffled in place as if the silence added to his discomfort. "So you'll marry Prince Rigunth?" he asked calmly.

Aisne laughed to herself. "Why are you asking so many questions?"

"I'm concerned for you. Rigunth is obviously a psychopath."

"I can understand why you feel that way…"

"But you don't think he'd ever try to harm you?"

"I wouldn't let him," she added firmly.

Peter stared at her for a moment. "You have changed so much from when we were children."

"Yes, it's called growing up. Everyone changes in time…"

"That's not what I'm talking about. Your abilities are quite impressive. You probably could take Rigunth on and any other Faeborn that came your way. You're a strong fighter, you can fly, what else can you do princess?"

"It's not really as exciting as it sounds. I'm still working out how I fit into this world. Will a marriage to Rigunth really strengthen the bond between Faeborn and Garkin? I don't' know."

"Well, if you want my opinion, I think you should marry Aregund. He's a strong fighter and brave… don't forget brave."

"You don't really know him," Aisne said trying to discourage Peter from waving Aregund's hero banner too high.

"I know that he risked his life for me. He believes in his duty above all else."

"I must agree with you there. Duty is the most important thing in the world to him." Aisne knew that better than anyone. As long as Garkin law forbids a Faeborn and Garkin from marrying, Aisne had no hope of being with Aregund. It was a painful reality to be sure.

Peter gave her a sideways glance. "I know that he cares for you too."

Just when Aisne was formulating what to say to Peter, she noticed Aregund climb on top of the wall and move toward them.

He nodded to Aisne before focusing on Peter. "Your father needs to speak with you. It's important."

Chapter 18

"Were there any survivors?" Peter asked struggling to hold his composure. He stared around at the drab walls of the queen's main sitting room feeling as if they were closing in on him.

"A few people fled to the mountains beyond Elbrus peak but most have come to Jormstad seeking shelter." Burl Pierce sat motionless as he struggled with his own sadness.

"William always told me he was prepared for a darkling attack. I wish I knew what went wrong."

"He was one of the first casualties, I'm afraid. He may have even been targeted by the darkling."

Peter stood up and turned away from his father. "But that doesn't make sense. I thought the darkling were mindless, creatures that killed recklessly…"

"It doesn't make sense to me either but we must accept the reality of what has happened. Sjoborg is lost. Most everyone there was killed, captured or fled to the wild lands."

"So we do nothing to avenge my brother's death?" Peter turned toward his father with tears in his eyes. "Thousands of people without a home and we just sit here and lick our wounds…"

"What would you suggest, boy? That we run into the ground chasing an unknown enemy? We might as well dig our own graves."

There was a sudden knock at the door. "Governor, you're needed in the throne room at once!"

"We'll finish this discussion later…" He gave Peter a weak smile and then hurried from the room. Burl Pierce wasn't as brave or gallant as his ancestor, Lad Pierce but he would do what he thought was right. He would work closely with the Faeborn and Garkin for the preservation of all three species.

Peter slumped back down into his chair and tried to imagine how his life could get any worse. His only brother was dead, the woman he loved was now married to someone else and the life he imagined for himself was a distant memory.

There was only one thought that brought him any comfort – revenge. He hurried out into the hall and raced out to the courtyard. Aisne was still where he'd left her on the wall. "Aisne, I need to speak with you!"

She bloomed in an instant and drifted down to the ground next to him. "What is it, Pete?" She could tell by the look on his face that something was wrong.

"William is dead…" Peter didn't try to wipe the tears from his face.

"I'm so sorry." Aisne felt a rush of despair coming from him. His emotions were so strong that she didn't know how to shut them out. "I wish there was some way that I could ease your pain."

"There is something you can do… you can teach me how to fight. I want to avenge my brother."

"Pete, I don't know if that's a good idea… you're not a Garkin. Training is difficult and you won't heal overnight."

"Please, Aisne. I need to feel like my life means something again. I have to do this or I'll lose my mind."

Aisne stood watching Peter for a moment. She remembered how much he idolized his brother. When William moved to Sjoborg to take over as governor, Peter couldn't have been more proud.

William was truly a free spirit. He was also fiercely independent. He refused any aid from the Garkin or Faeborn choosing instead to live completely separate. He even kept the interaction with neighboring Jormstad to a minimum. His honest and benevolent nature was lost to the world but it didn't need to be in vain.

"Meet me right here at first light. We'll get started." Aisne nodded her head at Peter.

He nodded to her. "You won't regret it."

The next morning, Aisne walked out into the courtyard and found Peter standing exactly where they were the night before. He had a brown cloth wrapped around his head and his clothes looked like they were three sizes too big.

"What are you wearing?" she asked.

"I wanted to wear something sturdy while I trained." He pulled at the shirt. "Of course I had to borrow the clothes. If you haven't noticed there aren't any Garkin who share my shirt size."

"...maybe a Garkin child." Aisne laughed under her breath.

"I'll accept your mockery for now... but only because you're training me." Peter smiled widely.

Aisne motioned for Peter to follow her. "Let's go."

"Where are we going?" he asked.

"You my friend are a whelp. Actually, you might be less than a whelp so we need to start with the basics."

When they reached the lower training room, Aisne leaned against the back wall and stared at Peter. "Pick up that rock over there."

He did what he was told and then turned toward Aisne. "Now what?"

"Now you're going to hold it out in front of you for as long as you can." To her surprise, Peter dropped the rock carelessly onto the stone floor. "Why did you do that?" she asked.

"I know what you're doing and if you didn't want to train me you should have just said so." He started walking toward the stairs when Aisne grabbed his arm.

"Why are you leaving?"

"Aregund told me how he had you lifting stones to try and distract you from fighting and now you're doing the same thing to me."

Aisne stared at him for moment. "How about a contest then? When you can hold the stone longer than I can, you will start your training."

"That doesn't help. You're stronger than I am right now."

"Then I will hold a bigger stone." Aisne reached out her hand to him.

"Agreed." Peter shook her hand more firmly than was necessary firmly and walked back over to the stone.

He was more determined than Aisne had ever seen him. But after holding the stone for just over an hour, Peter dropped it on the ground mere inches from his left foot. Aisne could sense the aching in his upper body and what remained of his determination slipping away.

"Let's go again," he said breathlessly.

Aisne dropped her stone and walked over to him. "That's enough with the stones. We're going to accelerate your training."

She could see the relief flash across his face. "So now what?"

"Now we will see how fast you are, how strong you are and how far we can push you." Aisne walked over to the doorway of the training room. "Follow me."

Aisne led him up to the training room she used with Fyk. When they walked inside, Grumere was putting a large battle axe back on the shelf by the window. He watched them as they came in but he didn't say anything. He nodded to Aisne and then left the room.

"Pick something," she said staring around the room full of weapons.

"What do you mean?"

"Look around and see if any of these weapons appeals to you."

"I like the axe that soldier was just holding..."

"...pick something smaller," she added quickly.

Peter turned toward the wall again and glanced around at all of the shelves. After a few minutes of searching, his eyes rested on a wooden sledgehammer. It was a formidable weapon, but the material it was made from was lightweight and easy to carry.

"Good choice but you'll need power to use that and the right stance."

"Let's start with my form and then we'll work on the power." Peter smiled at her and lifted the sledgehammer up over his head.

"Easy there warrior prince, you don't want to injure yourself." Aisne took the hammer from his hand. "You hold it like this." She changed her stance so that she could pivot onto her back foot. Then she held the hammer across her midsection as if she were about to defend herself.

Peter was soon able to mimic the way Aisne stood and the way she held her arms at her side. He didn't have a hammer in his hand, but he could stand like he did. "I've got it," he said proudly.

"Yes, you do." She put the hammer back on the shelf. "Now we can work on your strength."

After spending the next week in the courtyard running, jumping and turning stones, Peter was ready for a change of pace. He could see that Aisne was trying to condition his body but he wanted to focus on fighting.

As Peter finished another lap around the courtyard at full speed, he came to stop in front of her. "I can't do this anymore. Can't I learn some fighting styles while I work on my speed?"

"Pete, as a human, your speed is a big part of your defense. You're not as strong as a Garkin or as agile as a Faeborn but your speed could save your life."

"The only thing I want to do is kill the darkling." Peter rested his hands above his knees in an attempt to steady his breathing. He wasn't in condition to kill anything at that moment.

"The only person that will be killed is you unless you increase your stamina."

Brous was watching from across the courtyard but for some reason he didn't find his view suitable enough. He moved closer to the center of the space and stared over at Aisne. She noticed him watching her but she decided to ignore him – she did at first anyway.

"Aisne, why don't you let someone train him who actually knows what they're doing? Teaching him to be a fairy is just going to get him killed."

"Who should train him then, you?" She turned toward Brous and put her hands on her hips. She could see the large Garkin sizing her up as if he were about to strike. She changed her stance to prepare for the assault when Peter suddenly stepped in front of her, sledgehammer in hand.

Brous let go of a throaty laugh but Aisne could tell he was impressed by the human's courage. "What are you planning to do with that hammer whelp?"

"If you step any closer you're going to find out," Peter replied. Aisne could see Peter's arms trembling a little but he still held his stance.

Aisne slowly bloomed and placed her hand on Peter's shoulder. She wanted to reassure him that he wasn't alone. The commotion they caused started to attract other soldiers in the courtyard. They didn't know what to make of the scene.

Brous and Aisne had taken several runs at each other in the past. But they had no idea why a mere human was standing in front of Aisne. She didn't need anyone's help to defend herself.

"You have one chance, Brous, to walk away now while you still have your dignity intact." Aisne gave the impression of trying to be reasonable but in truth she was taunting the Garkin. He would never back down from a human and a Faeborn.

Just as Aisne moved into a slight hover above the ground, Brous darted forward. Peter made an impressive attempt at a swing of the axe but his timing was off, way off. Brous moved to the right avoiding the blow. He would do what he typically did which was to take his opponent by the throat.

"Peter, drop to your knees!" Aisne screamed. He responded slowly so Aisne helped moved him away from Brous's grasp. The Garkin let out a frustrated groan as he came up empty handed.

Peter scrambled away from Brous and reestablished his stance behind him. With axe raised, he took another swing. He landed a blow but it wasn't enough to do any harm.

"That tickles," Brous teased. "May I have another?"

"You know what they say, ask and you shall receive." Peter took another swing with the sledgehammer but this time, Aisne was helping add power to the swing. When the sledgehammer struck Brous' face, it sent him flying against the east wall of the courtyard.

"Yes!" Peter yelled.

Out of the corner of her eye, Aisne saw Fyk approaching her. She thought for sure he would scold her for sending Brous to the infirmary again. "Aisne, I'd like to have a word with you."

"Yes, Fyk." Aisne returned to her human form in hopes of appearing less threatening not that she could threaten Fyk in any way.

"Go and get Aregund and Prince Rigunth," he yelled to Bale who was standing closest to the entrance of the fortress. He watched Aisne and Peter for a few moments. "Why did you stay back out of the fight?"

"I knew that Pete couldn't beat Brous alone. Brous is bigger, stronger and he could carry out maneuvers that Pete wouldn't anticipate."

"Precisely," he said. "You'd taken away Brous' advantages without him even knowing. That is what we must do with the darkling."

When Aregund and Rigunth arrived, they weren't alone. Queen Nuestria, Burl Pierce and even Tylwyth Teg crowded into the center of the courtyard. The entire war counsel had abandoned the queen's throne room to join them.

Fyk wasted no time getting into the discussion of why he'd disturbed their meeting. He held everyone's attention while he talked of strategy and a lost advantage.

"We fight the same enemy but we do so foolishly. Even as we stand here together, we are stronger than the darkling. So why is it that when we meet them in battle, we are separate?" Fyk walked around in a small circle which represented all of the space the crowd allowed him. "We need to train differently; we need to train together, to fight together. I fear that is the only way we can defeat this evil."

"How do you suggest we do this, Fyk?" Queen Nuestria moved forward and stared at him. "The strengths that we have and the strengths of the Faeborn are very different."

"But that is exactly how we can flourish together." Fyk turned toward Aisne with pride in his eyes. Even though no one knew that he'd been the one to train her, he felt immense pride at all that she'd accomplished. Now the game she played with her human friend might save them all. "Aisne, show everyone what you and Peter just performed here."

Aisne felt as if her skin was tingling all over. She loved to fight and practice in the courtyard but having everyone watching her – Aregund and Rigunth included – left her largely uncomfortable. Even with her feelings of unease, she knew that her action was required.

"Pete was standing over here and I was behind him. Brous came up for a challenge so I bloomed and elevated myself. From that angle, I could surmise every move he was going to make before he made it; even more than usual."

Grumere suddenly stepped forward. "This can be a very useful strategy. The darkling attack from all angles. We never know where to expect them. If the Garkin are on the ground and the Faeborn above, they can pick off the ones who would sneak up on our brothers from behind."

"But the Faeborn will still have their share of the fight I presume…" Rigunth added boldly.

"Of course, Prince Rigunth," Fyk added. "We will need to work together once we've discovered the location of their nest."

Rigunth walked up to Fyk and smiled. Then he glanced in Aregund's direction. "We are pleased to assist the Garkin as long as you admit the truth… without us, you wouldn't survive."

Aregund could barely contain his anger. He clinched his fists and stepped forward. "If we don't work together, none of us will survive this threat."

King Tylwyth quickly spoke up. "We need to work together indeed. I believe Prince Rigunth understands this."

There were grumblings from some of the Garkin standing

around the courtyard. Rigunth's sudden pronouncement didn't resonate well.

"Why am I the only one not afraid to speak the truth?" Rigunth added.

"…because your truth is nothing more than fiction." Aregund took another step forward.

"Then why don't we find out once and for all Garkin." Rigunth moved directly in front of Aregund. "Let's see who is stronger."

Aregund was surprised by Rigunth's challenge but he recovered quickly. "What will a fight between us accomplish?"

"Maybe it would prove that you aren't a coward!" Rigunth was trying to goad Aregund and it was working. Rigunth bloomed and started hovering above the ground. His wings swayed back and forth as he welcomed the surge of energy from his Faeborn form.

Aregund quickly shifted and assumed a defensive position. His enlarged body resonated with sheer power. Everyone started moving back from the center of the courtyard as Aregund and Rigunth locked eyes on each other.

No one tried to stop the skirmish from happening. A fight between Rigunth and Aregund had been anticipated by many of the soldiers since the day the Faeborn prince arrived. Rigunth wanted everyone to believe he was fighting Aregund to prove that he was stronger but in truth, he was really fighting for Aisne.

At the same time, Aregund knew that if he injured Rigunth, the alliance between the Garkin and Faeborn would be threatened. As badly as he wanted to teach Rigunth a lesson, he wouldn't risk the alliance. There much more at stake than his Garkin pride.

Aregund did little to defend himself as Rigunth charged him. He knocked Aregund to the ground and then circled around to make another pass. Before Aregund could get to his feet, Rigunth flicked his wrist pulling a rack of battle axes on top of him.

Aisne wanted to pull Aregund away from the mountain of metal that was about to fall on him but she caught Fyk's gaze. Even in his Garkin form, she noticed the slight gesture he made. He shook his head telling her not to intervene.

Instead she turned away and hurried from the courtyard. If she couldn't help Aregund, she certainly wouldn't watch him be harmed. She was well into the fortress before the distance prevented her from hearing the grunts of pain as Aregund engaged in a fruitless battle.

Chapter 19

Aisne was leaning against the wall of the basement training room when she heard someone coming down the stairs. A few moments later, she saw Aregund's battered body limp into the room and drop against a large stone in the far corner. He pulled off the top of his uniform and winced when the fabric moved over his right shoulder.

She kneeled down in front of him and noticed how much of a beating Rigunth had given him. There were a number of bruises on his chest and arms. But the worst of his injuries was to his right shoulder where he'd taken a spear.

Aisne's vision blurred as tears filled her eyes. "What can I do?" she asked.

Aregund didn't speak. He just shook his head and leaned his back against the cool stone wall. He'd never felt such pain in his life. His wounds weren't life threatening but he'd need several days to heal even in his Garkin form.

Instinctively, Aisne reached for his shoulder. Her body began to glow and she reflexively bloomed. She didn't know how to help him but she felt an overwhelming desire to ease his pain.

Aregund flinched at the heat that was emanating from the palm of her hand. But the heat was soon replaced with a soothing vibration. The bruises on his body began to fade and the punctured flesh on his shoulder began to mend.

"How are you doing that?" Aregund finally spoke.
"Shh!" she said closing her eyes. Aisne imagined his skin smooth and unmarked. She didn't want to think about the suffering he'd endured because of her.

"Aisne, open your eyes." Aregund was smiling at her but it only lasted a moment. His expression soon changed to one of concern. He stood to his feet pulling Aisne up with him.

"That's incredible." Aisne touched the place where his flesh was broken before. Then she touched his chest where only moments ago, he'd had a host of large, purple bruises. She was about to touch his stomach when she heard someone on the stairs coming toward them. Aregund took a step back from her and turned toward the wall.

Peter stepped into the room realizing that he'd interrupted something. "Fredegund sent me to check on you."

"What does he want?" Aregund asked still facing the wall.

"He wanted to make sure you reached the infirmary. But of course he couldn't bring his Garkiness down here and check on you himself."

"I didn't expect him to…" Aregund finally turned toward Peter.

"By all the lights in the heavens," Peter stared at Aregund with wide eyes. "Your injuries… how have you healed so quickly?"

Aregund stood with his arms folded over his chest. It was obvious he wasn't in the mood to share.

"I healed him," Aisne blurted. "I don't know how exactly."

"You mean you literally healed him?" Peter moved closer so he could get a better look.

Aregund didn't appreciate the attention so he pulled his uniform shirt back over his head. "I've heard of fairies with healing ability but it's not that common."

"You need to tell someone; you need to tell everyone!" Peter was more animated than normal.

Aisne stared at Aregund and he nodded his head slowly. As they made their way up to the queen's throne room, Aregund noticed several of the guard staring at him with surprised expressions. They must have witnessed the beating he'd taken at the hands of Prince Rigunth.

As expected, Queen Nuestria was standing at her high table staring at maps with miniature representations of Garkin and Faeborn soldiers. She was surrounded by King Tylwyth, Prince Rigunth and two of her most trusted generals. They must have combined their war talk over a meal because there were platters of meat and fruit at the opposite end of the table.

Aisne's entrance into the room was met with several furrowed brows; that was until Aregund and Peter walked in behind her. "Queen Nuestria, we need to speak with you," Aregund said bowing to her.

"You're looking quite well from your skirmish in the courtyard." Nuestria stared around him and looked at Aisne. "What has happened?"

"I was in the training room when Aregund came in," Aisne started. "When I saw him, I had the sudden urge to help him."

Rigunth stepped around the table and stood in front of Aregund. "What trickery is this? No Garkin could heal himself so quickly."

"That's what I'm trying to tell you," Aisne replied steadily. "I healed him. I touched him and he was healed."

Rigunth knew that Aisne cared for the Garkin soldier but he refused to show those feelings now. Instead of showing his discomfort with their closeness, he decided on a different approach. "Could you heal me if I were injured?"

"Why don't we find out?" Without hesitating, Aisne grabbed a knife from one of the serving trays and wiped the tip of the blade across Rigunth's left forearm. She only hoped it was the arm he used to pierce Aregund's shoulder with the spear.

Rigunth winced and took a step back from her. "You could have warned me," he said staring at the cut that was now bleeding.

"My apologies, Prince Rigunth." Aisne put the knife down and held her hand out to him. "I didn't realize you were so delicate. Should I attempt to heal you now?"

'That would be ideal," he said stepping toward her.

Everyone in the room, including the Queen, moved closer to Rigunth to get a closer look at his arm. Aisne hoped that she could heal him or she might have to answer for why she cut the prince with a knife.

Even with everyone's eyes watching her, Aisne let herself relax and focus on Rigunth's left arm which was now bleeding pretty well. She held her hand a couple of inches above his arm and closed her eyes.

"Aisne, you're glowing!" Peter announced. Queen Nuestria quickly hushed him into silence.

"It feels warm," Rigunth added but he didn't sound as if it pained him.

A few moments later, Aisne's glow faded into nothing and Rigunth's arm was as smooth as before it was cut.

"It worked," Rigunth said holding his arm up and waving it around. "How do you feel, princess?"

"I feel fine," Aisne answered.

King Tylwyth moved forward and touched Rigunth's arm. "All

the same, princess… we need to be sure your gift is what we think it is."

"Can you heal humans as well?" Guntram asked as everyone turned toward Peter.

"No," Peter replied nervously. "This human doesn't need to be healed." He considered bolting from the room but he could be too easily caught to bother.

Nuestria took Aisne's hand and led her towards the door to the throne room. "Aisne, there is a very important matter that could use your… attention."

"What is it?" Aisne glanced at Aregund before she was ushered from the room.

Nuestria led Aisne up the stairs to a section of the fortress she'd never seen before – the infirmary. Aisne wasn't privy to all of the details of the fight against the darkling. But as soon as she walked into the room, she became fully aware of just how dangerous their land had become. There were a dozen soldiers at various stages of healing lying in cots along both sides of the room.

Some of the minor injuries included skin abrasions and puncture wounds. One of the soldiers had even lost a limb. Aisne wanted to look away from a couple of the soldiers but she was afraid to appear weak in front of her aunt.

"You want me to heal them?" Aisne asked.

"Not all of them." Nuestria wore a solemn expression as she stared around the room. "Just one." Nuestria led Aisne pass the soldiers and through another door at the other end of the room.

Once through the door, Aisne noticed a single soldier lying on a cot against the wall of the small room. Aisne knew right away that the soldier was gravely ill. The opening in the wall was proof enough that soldiers who entered here, rarely walked back out.

"What's wrong with him?" Aisne asked in a small voice.

"A fellow soldier mistook him for the enemy. He took a lance in the center of his chest… there isn't much time left." Nuestria stiffened as the realization of her own words washed over her. It had to be difficult for her to watch her soldiers die with no promise of impending victory over their enemy.

Aisne approached him and stopped cold when he opened his eyes. As a Garkin soldier, he'd never show how much he suffered, but Aisne could feel his pain.

"I'm going to help you," she said to him.

He gave Aisne a confused look and then stared up at Queen Nuestria.

"Do not be troubled, Heziel." Queen Nuestria smiled at the soldier. "She's here to help you."

He stared warily at her but he didn't try to move. As she held her hands out toward him, they began to glow. Aisne let out a deep breath making the only sound in the room.

At first, nothing happened. Aisne started to think that the severity of his wound was beyond her power. She kept her hands over his chest and concentrated harder. Eventually, the broken flesh and bone fused together. The only true remnant of his injuries was the blood soaked clothes covering his chest.

Heziel's eyes grew brighter almost immediately. He started moving his torso to make sure that the wound was truly healed. "How did you do that?" he asked in a voice that was deeper than Aisne expected.

"It's an ability that I've only just discovered." Aisne smiled at him as her vision began to blur. She tried to ignore the sensation as she watched the soldier try to sit up.

"I wouldn't recommend that you get up just yet." Aisne touched him arm gently.

"I am in your debt," he said.

"Rest now, soldier." Queen Nuestria moved closer to his cot. "They'll be plenty of time to show your loyalty to the princess."

Aisne followed Nuestria into the main room of the infirmary. As they neared the entry door, Prince Rigunth walked inside. Nuestria gave him a strange look before turning toward Aisne. "I'll see you downstairs." Nuestria smiled at her and left the room.

"Have you healed another Garkin soldier?" he asked playfully. "I hope that means that I'm next." Rigunth raised his right index finger. "Can you heal this for me?"

Aisne glanced at his finger and then gave him a stern look. "There's nothing wrong with your finger."

"You're not looking at what's broken." He pointed the finger at his heart. "You haven't forgiven me yet."

"Rigunth, is there something you need?"

"Can we speak in the hallway?" Rigunth spoke in a softer voice than normal. "It's rather a delicate matter."

Aisne followed him into the hall where they could be alone. After slipping his hand into his coat, Rigunth pulled something from his pocket. "You left this behind." He held out the silver bracelet he'd given her back in Tremeria. "I wanted you to have this."

"Thank you, Rigunth. I didn't know if I should keep it or not."

"I'd prefer that you kept it on at all times." Rigunth hesitated for a moment. "There's something else."

"What is it?" Aisne asked cautiously.

"I'm concerned about the future, princess."

"Go on." Aisne gave him her full attention.

"You're angry with me over what happened with Peter… but did you ever ask him what he was doing at the river?"

"I should ask you the same thing, Rigunth. Did you offer Peter Pierce a tribunal before you set Aregund against one of your best soldiers? When you realized that Aregund wouldn't harm you in a fight, did you have to mutilate his body?"

"Is that where your real concern lies… with Aregund?"

"Pete and Aregund are both my friends and I will defend them if I have to."

"What about your promise to me? We're supposed to be fortifying an alliance between our people."

"I haven't forgotten the promise I made." Aisne closed her eyes tightly. She was starting to feel the weight of the day. "I need to rest."

"Will I see you tomorrow?" he asked softly.

"I don't see why not."

Aisne intended to go up to her chambers but ended up going to the training room instead. Aregund was lifting a large stone when she walked in.

"Shouldn't you be… anywhere but here?" he asked.

"I wanted to make sure you were still healed." Aisne leaned against the wall near the entrance.

"I'm doing well." He placed the stone on the floor and turned toward her. "I didn't thank you properly before."

"Seeing you well is thanks enough." Aisne felt as if the room was closing in on her but she couldn't bring herself to leave. A part of her felt comforted when she was around him even with the knowledge that he was promised to someone else.

"So I was curious about your intended. Why does she not attend the queen's functions? She has that right as your future wife."

"In truth, I don't believe she's comfortable around the Faeborn."

"…any Faeborn in particular?" Aisne asked casually.

Aregund shifted his stance slightly. "There are Garkin among us who have never seen a Faeborn. It's normal to feel some anxiety when confronted with a different species than your own."

"Have you known many Faeborn?"

"Besides the royal family and their guard… no, I haven't."

"You didn't seem uncomfortable when you saw me changed at the cabin."

His expression turned solemn as some memory of their past returned to him. "That was different. You were already familiar to me."

"So I was…" Aisne pretended to be focusing on the small weapons display against the wall. Only now did she realize that her being Faeborn wasn't an issue for Aregund. If only she could convince everyone else of that. "Will you attend the Protectorate Assembly? It begins tomorrow."

He shook his head. "My presence is not required and for that I'm grateful. Fredegund will represent the 2nd legion."

"I wish I could say the same. I'll need to be at the queen's side tomorrow."

"You don't enjoy being a princess?" Aregund had an almost teasing tone.

"Not really. I just wish everything could be the way that it was before I bloomed." Aisne realized that she'd admitted too much.

"I've learned that we don't always get what we want." He turned his back to her and picked up an even larger stone than before.

"Goodnight, Aregund." Aisne turned to leave.

"Goodnight, princess."

Chapter 20

Aisne woke slowly to find Laila's green eyes watching her. Sitting on the bed dressed all in white, she looked like an angel. "Laila, is it really you?"

"It is I." Laila touched her hand to Aisne's cheek. "I'm so relieved that you're awake."

"What do you mean? How long have I been asleep?" Aisne slowly sat up on the bed.

"You've been asleep for two days."

"Two days?" Aisne pressed the palm of her hand to her forehead. She was struggling to remember what happened right before she went to bed. She had a vision of Aregund's eyes looking at her but that was all.

"You healed someone... and while your intentions were pure, you actions were unwise."

"I don't understand." Aisne tried to quiet the panic she was feeling.

"You healed the soldier but in order to do so, you tapped into your own life force... depleting it."

"Are you here to heal me?"

"You could say that... I'm also relieved to see you after the way you left Tremeria."

Aisne shook her head. "I'm sorry that I left that way. I needed to make sure my friends wouldn't be harmed."

"I understand." Laila squeezed Aisne's hand.

"Is sleeping beauty finally awake?" Soren tucked his head into the doorway of Aisne's chambers.

"Soren, what are you doing here?" Aisne smiled widely at him.

He moved into the room and stood at the foot of the bed. "I wasn't going to let my mother come here without me. I don't trust the gargoyles as much as you do."

"So who's training your new candidates?"

Soren glanced at Laila before he spoke. "There won't be any more training. Tremeria is preparing for battle."

"That reminds me," Laila interjected. "Do you feel strong enough to attend the Assembly?"

Aisne had almost forgotten about the Protectorate Assembly. She'd missed the entire opening day. She only hoped the Garkin and Faeborn were on their way to an uneventful transition.

When Aisne reached the door to the throne room, Brous and Grumere were standing guard. Brous tried to hide his surprise at seeing her up and about. Grumere on the other hand was stoic as always. Aisne could have grown a third arm and he still wouldn't have flinched.

There were only a handful of dignitaries standing at the back of the room including Nuestria's generals and Lieutenant Governor, Nathan Kenbridge. Peter stood behind his father who was seated at the head of the table. Queen Nuestria and King Tylwyth were standing on either side of him embroiled in a heated debate.

Queen Nuestria wore a uniform similar to that of her soldiers, a metallic vest over her jacket and a gold crown that was lined with five inch blades. She hadn't noticed Aisne standing just inside the doorway. "King Tylwyth, there is no need to rush the transfer of support. If Governor Pierce needs time to consider the arrangement, we should give it to him."

"I am unmoved by your sentiment, Queen Nuestria. We have conducted the Protectorate Assembly in the same way for centuries. I see no reason to make a change now." King Tylwyth's pale complexion had turned a bright shade of green, further evidence of his annoyance.

"King Tylwyth, I believe we have arrived at an impasse. Before you direct your anger toward the Garkin, you must consider the responsibility that your son carries in this. His treatment of Peter Pierce calls into question his suitability as your heir."

King Tylwyth was left speechless but that didn't stop Prince Rigunth from coming to his father's defense and his own. And that led to a rather colorful response from Peter as well.

"Queen Nuestria, may I have a word?" Aisne's voice trembled as she tried to speak over the men. Her efforts were hardly needed though. As soon as everyone realized Aisne was standing there, the room grew quiet.

Aisne stared around at the shocked expressions and swallowed a large lump in her throat. Of all of the faces in the room, Rigunth's pulled at her attention most. He started toward her with his arms outstretched. "Princess, I'm so happy to see you!"

"Thank you, Rigunth." Aisne smiled at him and immediately started to relax. She glanced over his shoulder to see Queen Nuestria moving toward her.

"Aisne, my darling." Queen Nuestria put her hands on either side of Aisne's face. "You gave us quite a scare. How are you feeling?"

"I feel rested, aunt." Aisne attempted to add levity to the room. "I've discovered that I'm not a healer… that mystery is solved."

"You are most brave, Aisne." Queen Nuestria added kindly. "I couldn't be more proud of you."

King Tylwyth cleared his throat pulling at Queen Nuestria's attention. She glanced over her shoulder at him but quickly turned back to Aisne. "Prince Rigunth, would you be a dear and escort the princess to the banquet hall?"

"But of course, Queen Nuestria. It would be my pleasure." Prince Rigunth raised his arm so that Aisne could wrap her arm around his. But instead of leading her toward the ballroom, Aisne insisted he take her out to the courtyard. With so many dignitaries in Merovech, there were extra guards everywhere. They still managed to find a quiet area to talk.

"I wanted to thank you for allowing Laila to come to Merovech." Aisne wanted to impede the quiet that was gathering around them.

"I have to admit my decision was selfish in part. I know that you're very fond of her and she feels the same way about you. I'd hoped she could influence you to return to Tremeria."

Aisne still had her doubts about Rigunth but she certainly wasn't going to discuss that now. She was enjoying the feel of the air on her face. If not for the gown she wore, she might have taken to the sky above the fortress. "Do you think we can defeat the darkling?"

"Yes, I do." Rigunth turned to look at her. "We will defeat them… together."

"I hope you're right." Aisne smiled at him.

"Would you like to go to the banquet hall? I'm sure your friends are there and they'd enjoy the chance to see that you are well."

"That's an excellent idea."

Aisne walked into the banquet hall on Rigunth's arm. He preferred to enter the room first even though he wasn't in his own kingdom. It was just as well, she thought.

She didn't want the attention that came with being a princess. Everything she said or did was closely watched. But there were worse things that Aisne could think of. Her chest started to tighten as she watched Aregund and Lena moving toward her.

Rigunth noticed her changed emotional state and grasped her hand. His touch helped her to relax reminding her of the comfort her mother's touch provided. "Better now?"

"Yes, thank you," Aisne replied. There were definite advantages to being engaged to an empath.

"Princess Aisne, you've recovered, I see." Aregund bowed slightly before turning toward Rigunth. "Prince Rigunth..."

Rigunth smiled and clutched Aisne's hand. "Well, if it isn't my favorite Garkin soldier. How are you?"

"I'm well." Aregund turned toward Lena. "I'd like to introduce my intended. Lena is daughter of General Lok and half legionnaire to the 3rd."

Lena slowly bowed showing a beautiful gold headband. It complimented her knee length lavender dress. It was much showier than Aisne expected for a Garkin soldier but Lena was obviously trying to make an impression.

She was tall for a woman even by Garkin standards. In her satin shoes, she was eye level with Aregund. If it hadn't been for the tension on her face, she'd have been beautiful. "Prince Rigunth." Lena bowed slightly and then turned toward Aisne. "It's an honor to meet Princess Aisne, the Faeborn with a touch like the sun."

Aisne felt her face warming as the memory of her attack on Brous came to mind. If not for Aregund's interference, she might have burned Brous alive. "Hello Lena, what a lovely dress."

"Thank you, princess." Lena smiled weakly. "What a peculiar looking charm. Wherever did you get it?"

Aisne touched the silver bracelet on her wrist. "It was a gift from Prince Rigunth. The stone is nephrite."

"A rare jewel for a rare beauty." Rigunth moved his arm around Aisne's waist.

Aregund stiffened slightly before turning toward Lena. "We should let you get your dinner."

"Yes, I haven't eaten in days," Aisne said smiling. She turned toward Rigunth and he was smiling back at her.

As Aregund and Lena headed for the door, Aisne held her breath. "I hope they aren't leaving because of us."

"Of course they are," Rigunth said laughing. "Lena doesn't care very much for you which is understandable. But what I don't understand is why she thinks even less of me. We've only just met."

"I am confounded as well. How difficult it must be for you to meet women who don't throw themselves at your feet." Aisne raised her eyebrows at Rigunth but he failed to find her comments amusing.

"Spin yarns if you will, princess. But it is my duty to enthrall my people. They must find me captivating in every way possible."

"Why is that?" Aisne could hardly believe Rigunth's rationale. "Your people must respect and admire you, sir. They don't need to find you physically appealing."

Rigunth leaned closer to her. "I suppose you're right. Why should the people love me when my own princess does not?"

"Do you really want to have this discussion now?"

"Of course not." Rigunth smiled but it barely reached his eyes. In truth, he was disheartened that Aisne didn't desire him at least in the same way she seemed to desire Aregund. His one consolation was the promise he and Aisne made to one another. Once they returned to Tremeria, there would be no one to compete with for her affections.

Aisne closed her eyes as the first spoonful of stew reached her taste buds. She felt as if she hadn't eaten in a full week. Having Rigunth watch her with wide eyes did little to slow the pace at which she emptied her porcelain bowl.

She was tempted to dip her spoon into Rigunth's bowl but she thought better of it. Even the threat of wasted food wouldn't affect the breach of etiquette she was imagining. Drinking the last of her ale, Aisne noticed the small group making their way toward her table.

Duran was the first to greet them. She bowed to Rigunth more times than Aisne could count so of course he liked her immediately.

It was promising to see that he could carry on a nice conversation with at least one Garkin.

Unfortunately, the pleasantries wouldn't last long. Once Brous started spouting off about sparring and the courtyard, Rigunth's mood quickly changed. He would never allow Aisne to go back to the fight. It wasn't proper for a princess and the future queen of Tremeria to be rolling around on the ground with Garkin soldiers.

A few minutes later, the soldier Heziel approached the table. Before Aisne could address him, Heziel bowed and said, "Greetings princess. We are pleased to see you well this night."

"Thank you, Heziel. I'm pleased to see that you are fully recovered as well." Aisne smiled at him hoping that Rigunth wouldn't be offended by the gesture.

"I have you to thank for that." Heziel bowed to her again before returning to his table in the far corner of the room.

"Well, princess. You are becoming even more popular among the soldiers here. I didn't think that was possible." Rigunth leaned toward her in hopes that no one else could hear his words.

"It's not what you think," Aisne replied softly. "He was the dying soldier I healed. He might feel some guilt because of what happened to me."

"I suppose you're right," Rigunth said turning his attention toward the room of soldiers. He watched them eat large pieces of meat with their bare hands and speak in voices that were much louder than he thought acceptable in the presence of royalty. There were so many ways that the Garkin were different than the Faeborn. He would be glad when he was able to return home.

"Are you finished your dinner, Prince Rigunth?"

"Yes, I've had my fill."

"Can you escort me to my chambers?" Aisne wanted to leave the room before any more Garkin well wishers approached them.

"Of course, it would be my pleasure." Rigunth rose from his chair and reached for Aisne's hand.

He led her up the stone stairs to her chamber with Nobb a few paces behind them. They finally decided to pretend that he wasn't watching her every move. Queen Nuestria was insistent about Aisne being guarded. Perhaps now, she was finally accepting it.

"Would you like me to join you inside?" Rigunth was being his most charming self.

"I don't think that Nobb would allow that." Aisne glanced over at the large Garkin who'd just stepped onto the landing. "Will I see you in the morning?"

"If you let me come in, you don't have to wait." Rigunth moved closer to Aisne and stared down at her.

Aisne shook her head and smiled. "If you entered my chambers tonight, I'm quite sure that Queen Nuestria would kill us both."

"I'm sure you're right." Rigunth smiled back at her. "I will be so relieved when we are back in Tremeria. We are not nearly familiar enough with one another."

"Once we are married, we'll have a lifetime to become acquainted." Aisne laughed to herself. She still wasn't comfortable speaking with Rigunth this way.

As she lay in bed that night, Aisne stared out her window at the stars. She knew there wouldn't be many more nights spent sleeping in that room. Soon she would be married to Rigunth and living in Tremeria as his Queen.

A part of her was still frightened by the idea of leaving Merovech for good. She didn't want to think of how much she would miss it. But at the same time, she'd be starting a new life in Tremeria. That life would include solidifying peace between the species and continuing a Faeborn bloodline that had lasted thousands of years.

For the first time since she'd met him, Rigunth's face was the last image she had in her mind before falling asleep.

Chapter 21

Aisne sat at the breakfast table with Queen Nuestria watching her every move. "I'm fine aunt. You don't have to be concerned."

"Let me be the judge of that..." Queen Nuestria seemed quite emotional for the early hour. "I thought I might lose you."

"I simply needed to rest. Laila explained it to me."

"Well, why don't we leave the healing to Laila and the rest of the fairies?"

"In case you haven't noticed aunt, I am a fairy!"

"You are also a princess and my heir." Queen Nuestria finally ate the dorkus root she had been holding between her thumb and index finger. "I asked Laila to stay behind with you and she has agreed."

"What do you mean, stay behind?"

"King Tylwyth and the rest of the Faeborn delegation left at first light this morning. We agreed to postpone the Protectorate Assembly for another month."

"What of Prince Rigunth?" Aisne asked trying to keep her voice even. She still wasn't sure how she felt about the Faeborn prince.

"He asked to remain here with you." Nuestria leaned back in her chair and crossed her long legs. "The two of you will depart with your entourage once the naming ceremonies have concluded."

Aisne knew it wouldn't serve her well to complain about her role in the Garkin ceremonies. In two days time, she would have to watch Aregund marry Lena. She didn't know how she would hold her composure.

She would also witness Tog and his younger sister Kebi take part in their own naming ceremony. With the darkling threat looming, these might be the last ceremonies for some time. Aisne tried to think less about her own feelings and more about the positive influence the ceremonies would have on the soldiers' morale.

"Queen Nuestria, there's something I've been meaning to ask… why have you not considered Basina as your heir? She is after all, the older sister." Aisne toyed with a strange looking fruit on her plate.

"She has taken a soldier's oath. She has no taste for the ceremonies, the politics of what we must do…" Nuestria seemed to be choosing her words carefully.

"What are you trying to say aunt?" Aisne could feel herself becoming uneasy.

"When I learned that Basina was Garkin, I became quite concerned." Nuestria moved forward in her chair. "But when you bloomed, my dear… I knew that we were saved. Your union with Rigunth is most important to us all."

"Rigunth wants to have the ceremony soon after we arrive in Tremeria. What do you think?" Aisne asked cautiously.

"That is an excellent decision. Your marriage will most certainly soften the tension between the humans and the Faeborn. Of course I will make every effort to attend."

"Will I be able to return to Merovech?" Aisne asked.

"Perhaps one day…" Aisne could sense that her aunt wasn't being truthful. "Don't let yourself be worried about such things."

With Nuestria's words fresh in her mind, Aisne found herself roaming the streets of Merovech city. She hadn't spent much time there but she would miss it. As beautiful as Tremeria was, it didn't feel completely real to her. It certainly didn't feel like her home.

"Are you lost, Princess Aisne?" A familiar voice spoke from behind her.

"Hello Lena, I was hoping to run into my sister this morning. Is she on patrol?" Aisne wasn't completely telling the truth but she thought it sounded genuine enough.

"Basina is still in her chambers. Is there something that I can assist you with?"

"No but thank you." Aisne started off toward the main road.

"Are you recovered, princess?" Lena yelled from across the road.

"I'm quite well," Aisne replied pasting a smile on her face.

"I heard a couple of the soldiers speaking of your ordeal."

"Yes, I need to learn what my limitations are." Aisne softened a bit. "I'm all better now."

"Well, that's good to hear." Lena seemed genuinely pleased by the news. "I'd better be off then."

"Good day to you." Aisne smiled at her before heading back

toward the fortress. Aisne couldn't deny the fact that Lena and Aregund seemed like a good match. At least she wouldn't have to worry about him being alone once she left for Tremeria.

"So what happens now?" Duran asked as she spun a monkey fist haphazardly above her head.

"You should put that thing down." Peter dropped the stone he was holding to watch Duran more closely.

Aisne was watching them both from the other side of the training room. "Duran, I think Pete is right."

"Forget about the weapon." She hung the monkey fist on the wall and moved closer to Aisne. "What's it like to have a hand maiden waiting on you? Did she make the gown you wore last night?"

Aisne glanced over at Peter and then turned back toward Duran. "Can we talk about this some other time? I promised Pete that we would focus on his training today."

"Don't worry about me. I'm just the human weakling trying not to get myself killed." Peter was holding a stone shakily over his head.

"Pete, that's fine. You can put the rock down now."

"Excellent." Peter placed the stone on top of a pile in the corner just when he was about to drop it. "Now what?"

"Now I want you to challenge me..."

"This should be amusing," Duran added as she moved into the corner of the room closest to the doorway.

Peter put his hands on both knees as he worked to steady his breath. "Are you serious?" He looked at Duran sternly.

"Duran, I think I should work alone with Pete." Aisne knew that Duran's presence would only be a distraction for both of them.

"Are you certain?" Duran asked sadly.

"Yes!" Aisne and Peter both answered at the same time.

Once Duran was gone, Aisne took two steps toward Peter. She started shifting her weight from one foot to the other. "I need to ask you something… It's important."

"What is it?" Peter stood straight up dropping his hands to his side.

"What were you doing near the River of Sorrow?"

Peter suddenly looked wounded. "Why do you ask? Did Rigunth ask you to question me?"

"Of course not... I just want to know."

"I was looking for my friends. We were out for the day and decided to go for a hike."

"You do know that the area around the river is forbidden..."

"You're starting to sound like him... that ridiculous Faeborn prince of yours..."

"That's not fair," Aisne shot back.

"Life isn't fair, princess. If it was my brother would still be alive, Sjoborg would still be intact and I would be married to your sister." Peter stepped back from her. "The Faeborn cannot be trusted. Soon everyone will know the truth of it."

"I have no idea what you're talking about." Aisne started feeling defensive but she refused to fight with Peter. She knew how hard he was struggling to deal with everything he'd lost. "Why don't we go back to training?"

Peter stared down at the floor. "Perhaps I should have Aregund to train me."

"You can ask him but I doubt if he has the time. He's getting married the day after tomorrow."

"I don't think it will be a problem. He's the one who approached me about training."

"That's very kind of him," Aisne said feeling somewhat uncomfortable. Did Peter lack the confidence in her for his training? "I'm sure he can help you."

"I think so too."

Aisne felt an immediate sense of urgency to escape the training room. "I should probably go..."

"I thought you had some free time," Peter said calmly.

"Yes but Rigunth asked me to meet him when I was done. He's making sure I don't change my mind about returning to Tremeria."

"Are you having second thoughts?" Peter asked almost under his breath.

"No, not really. I know what has to be done. I made a promise and I intend to keep it."

"You won't forget about me when you're queen of the fairies, will you?"

"Pete, I couldn't forget you if I tried."

"Have you done something to your hair? It's quite nice."

THE TEMPEST BLOOM: RISE OF THE DARKLING

Rigunth twirled a lock of Aisne's hair between his thumb and forefinger.

"Rigunth please," Aisne said moving a map closer to him. "We are supposed to be discussing strategies." They were sitting near the head of the table in the queen's throne room. Instead of spending the evening strolling the courtyard and holding hands, Aisne convinced Rigunth to review the map with her.

"The darkling launched attacks in these three areas." Aisne pointed to the map as she spoke. "We should also intensify our efforts in those areas. The entrance to their nest must be near one of them."

"Aisne, why do you concern yourself with such things? Let the soldiers handle it." Rigunth stood up and walked over to the queen's throne. He moved behind it and motioned for Aisne to join him. "Why don't you leave the war map and come take a seat? You know you want to."

Aisne laughed to herself. "No, I think you're the one who's waiting to sit in a thrown. I just want to wake up one day and not have to worry about the darkling."

There was a sudden knock at the door. Thoran walked into the room and said, "Prince Rigunth, you're needed in the courtyard. Another darkling has been captured."

They both followed Thoran into the main hall and out to the courtyard. There were a number of soldiers gathered around the center of the space. Aisne fought her way past a half dozen soldiers to see what they were watching. She could hardly believe her eyes.

Aregund was tying what appeared to be a darkling to a huge spike. The creature's body was beaten but it didn't appear to be dying. When Aregund had the darkling secured, he turned to find Aisne watching him.

"I didn't harm it," Aregund said to her. He took a step back realizing that Rigunth was watching him closely.

"Well, perhaps you should have. Why would you bring that creature into this fortress?" Rigunth spoke with such distain. "Does anyone have a spear?"

"No!" Aisne bloomed and moved toward the creature. "No one will hurt it unless they want to deal with me first."

"Aisne, what is going on?" The Garkin soldiers stepped aside as Queen Nuestria moved toward the center of the courtyard. "Where has this creature come from?"

"I found the creature hiding in the woods not far from here. It was carrying these." Aregund pulled four stones from his pocket and held them out for the queen to see.

"What are they?" she asked.

"They appear to be made of nephrite," Aisne replied. She glanced at Rigunth but he looked as confused as she was.

"I still don't understand why you brought it here. What do you plan to do with it?" Rigunth's mood hadn't improved since he first saw the creature.

"We can study it…" Aregund replied flatly.

"Or maybe we can communicate with it…" Aisne stepped closer to the creature but Aregund grabbed hold of her arm.

"That's close enough, princess. It's not safe." He realized everyone was watching him so he let go of Aisne's arm.

"It doesn't want to hurt me." Aisne took another step closer to the creature. It smelled of pure sulfur but she tried to ignore it. "He's frightened."

"Can you detect anything else?" Queen Nuestria moved closer to Aisne.

"No, that's all. He's just so frightened." Aisne closed her eyes and opened them quickly. "Perhaps if I touched it…"

"That is out of the question!" Rigunth stepped in between Aisne and Aregund.

"Then why don't you do it?" Aregund shot back. "We need answers this creature can provide."

"I have no intention of touching that creature. We should kill it and be done with it."

"Queen Nuestria, what is your decision in regards to this creature?" Aregund ignored Rigunth's outburst and gave the queen his full attention.

"For now, I want the creature moved to the dungeon. Aregund, Heziel, make sure the creature gets there intact. I'll decide what to do with it later." Queen Nuestria started walking toward the entrance to the fortress. "Everyone else get back to your duties."

Aisne reached the door of her chamber with Rigunth close behind her. This was usually the time he spent trying to convince Aisne to let him join her. His efforts always failed.

"I already know what you're going to say so I won't even ask."

Rigunth leaned against the wall closest to the chamber door.

"Would you stay with me until I fall asleep?" Aisne asked softly. Seeing the darkling in the courtyard bothered her more than she wanted to admit.

Rigunth smiled widely. "Of course I will, princess."

Chapter 22

"Aisne, wake up!" Duran gently tugged at her shoulder.

"What is it?" Aisne sat up on the bed blinking her eyes slowly. The room was still covered in darkness giving proof that morning had not yet arrived.

"Queen Nuestria's called an emergency meeting."

Aisne pulled a heavy dressing robe on over her nightgown and followed Duran down the stairs. She noticed a handful of soldiers filing into the throne room as she reached the main corridor. One thing was for certain, something was very wrong.

Queen Nuestria was sitting on her throne wearing the gravest of expressions. Seated to her left a few paces back was Prince Rigunth. His usually glowing complexion was ashen. His shoulders were slumped and he seemed to be staring out at nothing in particular.

Laila was standing directly behind him with her hand on his shoulder. But what Aisne found most bizarre was the way Thoran and Soren stood on the platform. They appeared to be protecting Rigunth - but from whom?

Aisne followed Duran over to an empty row of chairs near the back of the room. She hoped to draw little attention to herself but Queen Nuestria noticed her immediately. It was obvious that Nuestria was disappointed that Aisne didn't join her on the platform.

She pushed her disappointment aside and finished addressing the room. "The council members sent Soren back to Merovech to bring us the news about the King." Queen Nuestria chose her words carefully. "At first light, a search party will track down the whereabouts of King Tylwyth and his sons, Dain and Owain."

"Queen Nuestria, I would like to lead the search party to find my father," Rigunth's voice was crackled and pained.

Queen Nuestria took a deep breath before turning toward Rigunth. "I understand your desire to search for your father but that's just not possible. You could be the only surviving male of your father's bloodline. You must act as king until his return."

Queen Nuestria's words were difficult for Rigunth to hear. But in his heart and mind, he knew the truth of it. His place was in Tremeria with his people.

The queen turned her attention toward the small group of soldiers she'd gathered. "We need two teams. The first team will deliver Prince Rigunth safely to Tremeria and the second team will search for King Tylwyth."

Fyk stood to his feet and approached Queen Nuestria. He bowed slowly. "As legionnaire for the 1ˢᵗ, I feel some responsibility for what's happened to King Tylwyth. If you'll allow me, I'd like to lead the team to track him."

Queen Nuestria's strained expression softened a bit. "Fyk, you are the truest soul I know. I accept your offer." Queen Nuestria glanced slowly around the room at the others she would send with Fyk. She knew full well what a dangerous task this would be, but it was essential.

As the meeting carried on, Nuestria made additional selections for the two teams. The room was filled with soldiers who offered to go on the hunt. With all of the discord between the Garkin and Faeborn, it was surprising just how willing the Garkin soldiers were to risk their lives.

Aisne felt a similar desire. She didn't know how her aunt would react to her offer but she needed to try. She couldn't sit there and do nothing.

Aisne calmly stood to her feet and waited for Queen Nuestria to recognize her. But when her aunt finally turned in her direction, she didn't give Aisne the response she was looking for. Nuestria shook her head and then turned her attention toward Fredegund who was standing closer to her throne.

Once Queen Nuestria had gathered a search party for King Tylwyth and a protection detail for Prince Rigunth, she ended the meeting. Everyone else was ordered back to their duty stations.

"Aunt, may I have a word?' Aisne caught up to Queen Nuestria as she too attempted to leave the room.

"I already know what you want and the answer is no." Queen Nuestria started up the winding stairs to the floor of her chamber with Grumere and three other guards following at a safe distance.

"Won't you at least hear me out?" Aisne added.

"I won't change my mind, Aisne. You are needed here and that is final." Nuestria walked into the room and motioned for Aisne to follow her inside.

"But I can help. Why won't you let me?"

Queen Nuestria removed her heavy, plush robe and sat on the chaise next to the largest window in the room. She leaned back and crossed her legs watching Aisne carefully. "Are you certain your desire to help has nothing to do with Aregund? After all, he is joining Fyk in the hunt."

"How can he leave now? He is set to wed Lena tomorrow."

"This is no time for weddings or other trifling about… the king must be found."

"I understand completely and that is why I wish to help. If you won't let me search for the king then let me accompany Rigunth home."

"I can't allow you to do that either." Queen Nuestria raised her shoulders slightly.

"Do you expect me to wait here and do nothing?"

"I expect you to follow the orders given to you by your queen!" Queen Nuestria stood up and took a step toward Aisne.

Aisne quickly bowed her head. "As you wish."

Queen Nuestria took another step forward placing her hand on Aisne's shoulder. "Why don't you return to your chambers? You look like you could use some more rest."

"You're right as always." Aisne smiled and walked into the hall. It was obvious that Queen Nuestria wasn't going to change her mind. But there was one more person in Merovech who might sway the Queen.

"Why must you question everything you're told?" Basina asked flatly. She turned away from Aisne and stared out at the darkened sky above Merovech city. She placed her left foot on a stone slab that represented the narrowest part of the stone fence.

Basina was surprised that her sister had returned to see her but the surprise she felt quickly turned to annoyance. "I will not speak to the queen on this matter."

"If King Tylwyth is to be my father-in-law, shouldn't I be doing everything in my power to locate him and bring him home safely?"

"That is not a task that you've been given." Basina shook her head slowly before turning back toward Aisne. She had a way of looking at her younger sister that bestowed so much disappointment.

"I want to help, Basina. Don't you understand that? I know the queen would listen if you supported me."

"Aisne, you would be at great risk of harm if you left Merovech. And there is no guarantee that the king will be found alive."

"We still need to try… I need to try." After several moments of silence, Aisne turned away from Basina and leapt off the stone wall.

Fyk led his team quickly over the plains. This wasn't difficult to accomplish with the Garkin having cleared the land near the fortress centuries ago. They didn't want to give any foe the ability to sneak up on their city.

But once they reached the valley above Jormstad, their safety was no longer a guarantee. Even in daylight, this area was treacherous. There had been many darkling sightings in recent times, so everyone was on edge. They'd reached the first cluster of rock formations below the water's edge when Fyk announced that they would be taking a break.

Dax and Roden secured the perimeter of the temporary camp site while Peter practiced swinging the small axe he'd brought as a defensive weapon. Aregund couldn't help being amused by his efforts. Peter would never be as strong as a Garkin or nimble as a Faeborn but he was whole in enthusiasm.

Before long, the group moved in around Soren as he began to recount the events that led to the king's disappearance. The more he spoke, the more obvious it was that he still felt anguish at the loss of King Tylwyth. His admiration for the king was a stark difference from the disdain he felt for Prince Rigunth.

"The scout had just given us the all clear. The path ahead for a few hundred feet should have been without incident. But just as we left the edge of the valley, they moved in around us." Soren's face was marked with pain as he spoke. "They seemed to come out of nowhere and from every direction."

"Why didn't you go to the king?" Fyk asked. He used a less harsh tone than normal. It was obvious he didn't want to accuse Soren of any wrong doing.

"I tried but by the time I reached where the king had been only moments ago, they had already taken him. I fought off a half dozen of the beasts but not before they took a piece of me." Soren pulled aside the neckline of his jacket to reveal several fresh claw marks.

"Why didn't you let someone heal you? Your own mother has the gift, does she not?" Aregund asked.

"I keep these scars as a reminder of my failure. Why should I be healed when my king is out there somewhere?" Soren nodded his head in the direction they would be travelling.

Although he would claim otherwise, Soren had the heart of a Garkin. That fact had never been more obvious than at that moment. His words were an echo of what every Garkin felt in their hearts and minds. If something catastrophic would happen to Queen Nuestria, they would react just as Soren had.

If not for Soren's light brown hair and eyes, he could have easily blended into the Garkin legions. But that would never be a reality for him. He'd never known his Garkin father so he felt no allegiance to them. Soren's only knowledge of his biological father came in small doses. His mother didn't like to talk about him and Soren didn't press her on it.

THE TEMPEST BLOOM: RISE OF THE DARKLING

Chapter 23

It was never Aisne's intention to deceive her aunt but she desperately wanted to help Fyk. If any sense of normalcy was to return to the land, the Faeborn king would need to be found alive. Aisne hoped that helping to make that idea a reality would be enough to diffuse the queen's anger at her leaving Merovech that day.

Aisne's plan was to follow Fyk's team far enough into their journey, that they would be unable to send her home. The only issue with her plan was in the execution of it. After making her way across the plains, she realized she'd drifted too close to them. They were downwind of her position and only sixty or so feet away. Any of the Garkin could have picked up her scent by now.

They hadn't marched far from their camp site when Aregund suddenly stopped. He lifted his nose into the air and took a deep breath. "We have company," he said in a gruff voice.

"I know," Fyk said without turning around. He was leading a single file line through the valley. Travelling this way was useful by Garkin soldiers because it helped to conceal their numbers.

"And you saw no need to mention it? She should return to Merovech at once." Aregund tried to leave some hint of respect in his voice for his superior.

"We can use her help. King Tylwyth will be her family soon. She'll want to find him more than any of us." Fyk added. He knew the truth of his words and so did everyone else.

Aisne had gifts that would be useful to them. Unlike Soren, she had all of her Faeborn instincts. Moving objects with her mind and flying were very useful skills. Soren could do neither of those things. He was probably the most eager to have Aisne join them.

Aregund soon ended his protest against Aisne joining them. No one knew why he protested at all. Not long ago, they seemed quite fond of each other. Surely his feeling hadn't soured so completely.

"The fact that none of you turned to acknowledge my approach tells me what I already guessed. I ventured too close too soon."

"What can I say?" Soren mused. "You smell of fairy dust and jasmine. We knew you were coming the moment you left Merovech."

Aisne cared little for Soren's words. It was obvious he was trying to endear himself toward the Garkin soldiers. Until that moment, Aisne felt pity for him being part of two species and fitting in with neither of them. But now, she felt a hint of irritation.

"That's odd Soren… I thought the smell of fairy dust was coming from you." Peter surprised everyone as he openly mocked Soren.

"I understand now," Soren replied completely ignoring Peter. "You've come to collect your human."

"He's not *my human*. He's my friend. A concept you know nothing about." Aisne fell in line behind Aregund as they continued their march toward the area where the king and his sons went missing.

Peter, who was walking just ahead of Aregund, glanced back at Aisne and gave her a reassuring nod. It was the first time in a long time that she felt like smiling. Peter was the only human among them and by far the weakest member of the group. Yet he felt inclined to try and make Aisne feel welcome on the hunt.

With the sun shining at full strength, the air around them was almost fully saturated with moisture. But they pressed on further with a single goal in mind – to find the king.

With such a heavy task ahead of them, it was no wonder the group was light on conversation. That time spent walking in silence left Aisne's mind to wonder to less important matters. She couldn't shake the discomfort she felt about Aregund's reaction to her. At that very moment, she marched behind him and he didn't so much as glance over his shoulder to greet her.

Aisne hated how the memories of their time together still haunted her. She hated the way his very presence excited her. Just the smell of the sweat from his body made her stomach tie into knots. Even if he had forgotten how close they once were, she could not.

The fact that Aregund was a Garkin was of great consolation then. He couldn't read her thoughts so he had no idea of how she longed to be with him. The promise of becoming a Faeborn Queen couldn't erase the memory of how she felt in his arms or the way her heart ached when he watched her with piercing brown eyes.

Aisne was pulled from her thoughts when the men ahead of her stopped marching. She watched Soren take a few long strides away from the trail. When he turned toward them, he wore a look of utter confusion. "The king's broken carriage was right here. I don't know where it is now and I don't feel his presence anywhere."

Soren's senses were slightly better than a human's so they were somewhat useful. Fyk and the other Garkin weren't any more successful in detecting which way to go. The king's scent had faded too much.

Aisne suddenly bloomed and shot up fifty feet into the air. She glanced around in every direction. Moments later, she noticed a mound of earth that was freshly disturbed. "That way," she said pointing on the opposite side of the trail from where they were standing.

She landed delicately on the ground just ahead of the mound of earth and raised her right hand with her palm facing down. The loose dirt began to shift as a wooden spoke became visible before them. Aisne lowered her hand and started walking pass the mound of dirt. "This way," she said firmly.

Dax and Roden were the first to follow Aisne into the orchard but Peter wasn't far behind them. He felt more comfortable around Aisne no matter how strangely her actions seemed.

Soren watched as Fyk and Aregund followed behind Peter. He could only assume that Aisne was using her Faeborn senses to pick up a trail of the king, a gift that he lacked. If there was any time in his life he wished to be more Faeborn, this was one of them. But as it were, they would have to rely on Aisne.

She led them deeper into Jormstad which wasn't expected. Soren assumed the darkling would take King Tylwyth north of the sand hills. That way it would be harder to track them. But figuring out what the darkling might do was impossible. If they had taken the king, no one knew why. And no one wanted to ponder the larger question… was he still alive?

As Aisne led the team through the western region of Jormstad, Soren suddenly grew impatient. He stepped from his position at the rear of the team and caught up to Aisne. "Why would the darkling bring him this way? This doesn't make sense," he barked.

"I don't think they're bringing him to Jormstad either," Aisne replied. "I think they are moving him someplace else. Some place where no one would think to go."

"And where would that be, princess?" Soren asked flatly.

"They're taking him to Sjoborg," Fyk interjected.

Aregund nodded his head slowly. "Yes, of course. They're taking him somewhere that's hard to reach and easy to defend."

"Why do you think that?" Peter asked.

"Because that's what we'd do." Aregund swung his axe over his shoulder and started walking in the direction they'd been travelling.

The rest of the team started marching again. They continued south passing many of the places Aisne frequented before her change. There were homes and a few small shops that lined the road they traveled on. A few of the locals came out to watch as they moved through the area, but no one spoke to them.

It was a feeling that Peter had never felt before. The humans felt less safe and less concerned with who supported them. It was obvious that the threat of the darkling outweighed the might of the Garkin and the Faeborn. No one was safe and no place was safe for them to hide.

Did the humans know that King Tylwyth was missing? Perhaps they did. It was just further evidence of the discontent that grew across the land. Peter knew that the quest they were on was more important than anything he'd done up to that moment.

He thought of questioning Mr. Farley, one of the only people who had the wherewithal to give Peter a nod of acknowledgement. But he knew it would be fruitless. If any human saw the darkling move through town, they would probably have been killed or taken by the darkling themselves. Fyk and his team would have to rely on themselves alone for this quest.

After travelling in silence for some time, Peter turned to Aisne who'd decided that walking in pairs was more efficient. "After what happened to the people in Sjoborg, the darkling are surely wagering that no human would come there again."

"So you will prove them wrong." Aisne smiled at him. "If that is what you wish."

"I can think of no other course." Peter was speaking more to himself than anyone. Although he was afraid, he knew this was something he had to do. If he didn't face his fears, he would always be haunted by them. He finally accepted that the fate of all of the species was tied together somehow.

The border between Jormstad and Sjoborg was a natural dissection of the land where a large cluster of Cebus trees sprung up in a bizarre pattern. Peter was the last of the group to cross the border into Sjoborg, for obvious reasons. His brother, William had died not far from where they stood.

The governor's home in Sjoborg was called the First Residence. It was a beacon of sorts for visitors or those wishing to leave the somewhat rigid life in Jormstad. Although it wasn't the closest structure to the border, the second floor was easily visible from almost anywhere in Sjoborg.

The protectorate quarters where the Garkin soldiers lived stood directly adjacent to the border. It was meant to serve as a secure facility for anyone in Sjoborg who decided they wanted help from the other species. The single story wooden structure was broken and bent towards the ground. On the day the darkling took William, they killed a number of other humans and all five Garkin soldiers.

Now emptiness and quiet filled the air giving Sjoborg an eerie atmosphere that affected practically everyone in the group. Aisne felt herself being led toward the First Residence but when she reached the gardens at the front of the building, she felt the urge to hold her position.

Fyk noticed her trepidation and moved next to her. "We'll make camp here tonight. Dax and Roden will take the first shift."

"I have another suggestion…" Soren said as he moved toward Fyk. "We can all rest at once. I'll set up a circle of protection for us using this." Soren pulled a large green stone from his pocket and held it out toward Fyk.

"What is that, you say?" Fyk asked.

Aisne couldn't help noticing how closely his stone resembled the one Prince Rigunth had given her. Reflexively, she reached down and touched the stone as it hung around her wrist.

"This stone has a specific ability. It can protect the ground and air inside our circle from anyone of another species entering it." Soren held the stone toward Aisne. "It is the same stone that hangs from your wrist. A gift from Rigunth, I'd wager?"

"Yes it is," she answered wearily. "But tell us more of this magic you speak of."

"It is quite simple, princess." He held the stone out to her again. "I need you, Fyk and Peter to touch the memory stone. Then I will set it about its work."

Everyone did as he asked but no one seemed particularly convinced of his claim. His next act seemed even more ridiculous. He started dragging the stone on the ground. He kept the pattern around the entire house including the gardens until he approached the point at which he'd started. As soon as he dragged the memory stone over his starting point in the dirt, the entire trail glowed bright green.

Aisne instantly felt the truth of his words. "So that explains it. That explains why no one in Tremeria lives in fear. You have this same protection in the whole of Tremeria, do you not?"

"Yes, it is true," Soren admitted.

"Why have you kept such a secret from us?" Aisne seemed almost distraught. "How many human and Garkin have died while the Faeborn protected their entire settlement from harm?"

"There are other measures against the darkling." Soren tried defending himself but it was obvious that his efforts were mostly in vain. "They cannot crawl through granite. King Tylwyth shared this knowledge with your queen. That is why your fortress is built upon it."

"What about the humans?" Peter interjected. "We don't have granite or pieces of that green stone. We are at the mercy of whatever whim the darkling have seen fit to burden us with."

Fyk stepped forward putting himself between Soren and the others. "Let us rest now. Once we have found the king and returned him home, then we can discuss these so-called memory stones."

Fyk stood next to Soren and waited for the others to move into the house. As soon as Peter walked inside, he set about lighting candles all along the lower level. Most of the house was intact except for the floor in the back corner of the governor's office. The darkling knew exactly where to find William. He never stood a chance at survival. But how did a human offer a threat to the darkling? Their tactics made no sense.

Aisne expected to smell the remains of an animal or worst yet that of a human but there was only the smell of dust in the air. She was relieved until she noticed Peter drifting down the main hall.

Peter stood in the doorway of William's office staring at the hole in the floor. There was a battered tarp covering the hole but Peter still watched the corner of the room as if the darkling would crawl through at any moment. Realizing that Aisne stood next to him, he tried to adjust his bent posture. "He must have been so frightened."

"Perhaps or maybe it happened quickly."

"There was a time when I wanted to be him. I wanted his life. He had the perfect family and a wonderful position here."

"Well now it can be yours… if you want it." Aisne stared around the room at the broken furniture.

"Yes, of course. I'll be the governor of dirt and misery. It pains me to admit this but Sjoborg is lost…just as Luftohk was lost centuries ago."

Fyk's heavy footfalls on the wooden floor caused Aisne and Peter to turn in his direction. "The house is secure. Get some rest, both of you." Fyk hesitated for a moment before walking back toward the entrance to the house.

Fyk had ordered the others to set up lanterns in the rooms upstairs while he went over the perimeter again. Fyk was the ultimate soldier but he'd never take risks with their lives. With the sky now dark and cloudless, he'd stay up most of the night making sure they didn't fall under attack.

After consuming some fruit and a bit of spice juice, Aisne headed upstairs for the night. She'd made it halfway up the stairs when she heard someone coming behind her. She turned to see Aregund's tense expression.

"I was surprised you didn't stop to see your parents." Aregund moved around her and leaned against the wall where she stood.

"That would be the human thing to do but I'm on a quest," she replied flatly.

"Are you?" he asked raising an eyebrow at her.

"Does it bother you so much that I can be of help? Maybe even more help than you…"

"It bothers me that you're here at all. The queen gave you a direct order."

"How do you know what the queen instructed me to do?"

"Because I spoke to her…" He seemed to be choosing his words carefully. "I told her how uncomfortable I would be if you joined us."

"Since when do Garkin soldiers worry about comfort?"

"That's not what I meant." Aregund clinched his fists together. "I cannot focus on this quest while I'm worried about keeping you safe."

Aisne was surprised by his admission. Now she was the one unsure of what to say. "I'm stronger than you realize," she replied backing up the steps away from him.

"I know that. It's not as if you haven't saved my life before." Aregund remembered the time he and Aisne spent on Elbrus peak surrounded by darkling. "We would have perished on that mountain if not for you..."

"I suppose I was properly motivated," she replied lightly.

"You were indeed." Aregund's crooked smile reappeared pulling at Aisne's resolve to keep her distance from him.

Before she could make an excuse to run away, she caught the sound of Peter whistling. He was climbing the stairs two at a time.

"Sorry to interrupt..." Peter stopped just below where they were standing on the stairs. "Fyk needs Aregund."

"Of course." Aregund nodded at Peter and then followed him back downstairs.

Chapter 24

"You don't have to watch me, Pete. I'm fine." Aisne was sitting on the bed in the room at the top of the stairs.

"What kind of friend would I be if I left you alone?" Peter was sitting on the floor next to the door. He could barely keep his eyes open. "Just think of me as another Garkin soldier." He let go of a large yawn.

"Why don't you at least sit in the arm chair? Even soldiers have to rest some time."

"Well, if you insist." Peter collapsed into the chair and immediately started smiling. The chair was much more comfortable than he thought it would be.

Within minutes, Peter was fast asleep. He'd removed one of his boots and his head was leaning back in an odd position. Aisne took a blanket from the foot of the bed and laid it over him.

Other than Aisne and Peter, everyone else found a place downstairs to sleep. She couldn't help wondering if that arrangement was part of Fyk's orders. As she glanced over at Peter asleep in the chair, she realized that she too was starting to feel the weight of their journey.

She closed her eyes and tried to remember what life was like before she'd changed. When she lived with her parents, her greatest concern was having her father lecture her about being more productive. What she wouldn't give to be back behind the counter of her father's carpentry shop listening to his gentle instructions.

Aisne was still half asleep when she felt someone calling her name. It wasn't an audible sensation but it was real all the same. She glanced over at Peter who was fast asleep in the chair. But it wasn't his voice she heard. It was coming from outside the window.

She grabbed her boots and headed toward the door. When she reached the top of the stairwell, she thought about how she would explain her late night wandering to Fyk. That was a conversation she didn't want to have.

Backing away from the stairs, she returned to the small bedroom. She quietly opened the window and crawled out onto the ledge. Focusing on the air around her, Aisne bloomed and glided quietly away from the house. She allowed her body to glow just enough to see her way in the dark.

She couldn't tell if the voice was male or female. It registered as nothing more than a whisper. But she could hear her name quite clearly.

Aisne landed on the soft grass just beyond the Cebus trees that bordered Sjoborg. Her entire body tingled with a sensation that meant one thing – danger. She was being watched. She turned around and came face to face with a creature like nothing she'd ever seen before.

Its skin was pale gray with eyes that were blacker than the darkest night sky. Its wings were larger than necessary for the size of its body. The creature's mangled hair did little to conceal the large pointed ears on the sides of its head.

As Aisne stood watching the creature, she noticed the beginnings of a smile on its face. The smile did little to lessen the fear Aisne felt at that moment. She finally managed to find her voice. "Can you speak?" she asked.

"If I choose," the creature replied gruffly. Its voice sounded like the blending of two voices in one.

"Who are you?" Aisne asked.

"Who are you?" the creature mimicked Aisne's words but in its own binary tone.

"I am Aisne, Princess of Merovech."

The creature leaned its head to the side. "You are Faeborn. How can you be a Garkin princess?"

"So you know of my people… how is that possible when we know nothing of you?" Aisne tried to sense something from the creature but she felt as if she was being blocked somehow. It's as if the creature's essence was purposefully hidden from her.

The creature started flapping its wings raising itself up off the ground. "Where is Ungotha?"

"I don't know who you mean," Aisne replied cautiously.

"You wear the memory stone... you must know where she is." The creature pointed at the bracelet on Aisne's wrist.

"It was a gift." Aisne touched her hand to her wrist.

"Where is Ungotha?" The creature moved closer to Aisne. "I won't ask again."

"I don't know." Aisne realized that the conversation was ending. Whatever patience the creature had with their exchange was gone.

Before Aisne could react, Aregund moved from within the trees and took a defensive position in front of her. He was in his Garkin form and carrying his battle axe.

"What are you?" Aisne asked. She floated a few feet off the ground so that she could see the creature from behind Aregund's large frame.

"Move away, princess." Aregund raised his right arm out to the side as if that one gesture would keep Aisne safe from the creature. "I will not allow you to be harmed."

The creature focused its dark eyes on Aregund. It seemed confused by his sudden appearance but it didn't appear threatened by him. In the blink of an eye, the creature spread its large wings and flew off through the trees into Sjoborg. Aisne flew up into the air and followed after it.

"Aisne, no!" Aregund shouted to her before running back through the Cebus trees. He didn't have much confidence in finding them. In flight, they could be almost anywhere by then.

Much to his surprise, Aisne was leaning against the only standing wall of the protectorate house. Aregund moved toward her and sheathed his axe over his shoulder.

He reached a supporting hand out to her but she shook her head and leaned away. "I'm fine," she said struggling to stand up straight.

"If you insist," Aregund replied calmly. He wanted to throw her over his shoulder but he knew she would protest. He reluctantly started off toward the First Residence. "We must speak with Fyk."

Aisne and Aregund recounted the story of what transpired in the woods, as Fyk paced back and forth across the living room floor. He allowed them both to speak only making the occasional sound with his throat or cracking whatever bones in his hands or arms that needed cracking.

He was an intimidating man even in his human form. But when Fyk finally spoke, his tone was softer than Aisne expected. "At least now we have some idea of what we're dealing with. Get some rest.

We leave at day break."

Fyk was in William's old office sitting with his back against the wall when Aisne walked in. He opened his eyes to meet her nervous expression.

"Fyk, can I speak with you for a moment?"

"Aisne, I have heard your report. You need to rest now."

"…but I wanted to explain."

"There is no explanation for your actions. Leaving the house alone to pursue an unknown enemy was reckless, at best." Fyk stared at her with a look that she'd never seen from him. It was disappointment. "You are a vital part of this quest. But if you go rogue again, I will return you to Merovech."

"I understand." Aisne backed out of the room and hurried up the stairs. With only her shame to accompany her, she fell onto the bed and turned onto her side facing the wall. She didn't know what made her act so impulsively. But Fyk made it clear that her bravado wouldn't be tolerated. All she could think of now, was why the creature called to her and what it wanted.

She heard the door open and close but she didn't bother turning around. "You're welcome to the chair again, Pete."

"That's very generous of you." Aregund stood by the door and stared around the room.

Aisne sat up quickly. "I thought you were Pete," she said softly.

"That much is obvious." He smiled but it only lasted a moment. "Are you alright?"

"I'm fine," she replied quickly. "The creature didn't harm me."

"That wasn't what I meant…"

Aisne nodded her head and smiled. "Fyk was right with what he said. I should have taken someone with me before I left the house."

Aregund took a step closer to her. "Fyk should have been the one to decide if you went at all. He is leading this hunt."

Aisne felt her face becoming warm. The last thing she wanted was a tongue lashing from Aregund as well. "I understand completely. Is there anything else?" Aisne stood up and turned her back to him.

"I want to know more about what happened before I arrived." He moved closer to her.

"I already told you everything." She stared out the window. Part of her was tempted to jump out but she remembered the reprimand Fyk had just given her. "I think that creature is…"

"What? Tell me." Aregund moved next to her.

"I believe that creature is the Tempest Bloom."

"So why didn't you tell that to Fyk?"

"Why? So he could laugh in my face. Garkin tell the story of the Tempest Bloom to their children to scare them."

"That doesn't mean it isn't true."

"So you think that creature is part gargoyle and part fairy?" Aisne asked firmly.

"Not exactly…" Aregund massaged his chin for a moment. "But it could be part fairy."

"It looked like a darkling with wings… but not. There was something so strange about it."

"But darkling have no vocal ability." Aregund took a deep breath. "I wish we knew more about it. That creature is obviously linked to King Tylwyth's disappearance."

Aisne sat down on the bed. "Perhaps Fyk will have a strategy for us by morning."

"He might indeed." He glanced out at the sky before turning back toward her. "It appears that Soren's charm worked. The creature needed to call you out instead of coming in."

"That's something to be glad about at least." Aisne tried to appear relaxed but she couldn't shake the memory of the creature's voice in her ear. Knowing that they were safe inside the memory stone's boundary line was comforting. "We should get some rest; Fyk's orders."

"You're right." He walked over to the open door but instead of leaving the room, he closed the door and pulled his axe from over his shoulder. He started removing his uniform jacket when Aisne approached him from behind.

"What are you doing?" she asked but not unkindly.

"I need to rest. Don't you?"

"Yes, of course." Aisne tried to keep her voice from shaking. "I just wasn't expecting you to sleep in this room."

"Is that a problem?" he asked turning toward her.

"I don't suppose that it is." She wasn't sure how to respond to him. "Does Fyk know that you're in here?"

"He's the one who sent me."

"You're here to keep an eye on me… I should have known." Aisne walked over to the window and stared out at the sky as if that simple act would offer her some escape from Aregund's presence.

"We are in this together, you know. We need to keep you safe."

"I can keep myself safe." Aisne turned around not realizing that Aregund had covered the distance between them. He was standing so close to her that she could see the overgrowth of hair on his usually clean shaven face.

"That's where you're wrong." He kept his eyes locked on her. "We don't know what that creature is capable of. We don't know what it wants or if others of its kind are out there."

"I know exactly who it wants… Ungotha."

"That name means nothing to me," he replied.

"I don't know it either," she answered calmly.

"We need to follow in the direction the creature was travelling and hope that the king is still alive somehow."

"You don't really believe he's alive, do you?"

"Whoever took the king was strong enough to overpower him. If they are that capable, they certainly wouldn't need to keep him alive. I fear that the king has met the same fate as Queen Harmonia."

Aisne assumed that Aregund would have some words of encouragement but none came. Hearing the doubts he had about the king resonated more deeply with her than she would admit. She felt panic and anger all at once. She started toward the door but Aregund caught her by the arm.

"Where are you going?" he asked.

Aisne decided that being angry at Aregund was better than worrying about the king. If the king was dead, Rigunth and all of the other Faeborn would be devastated. Who knew what his death would do to relations between the Faeborn and Garkin? "Why would you even come on the hunt if you truly believed it was fruitless?" she asked him.

"I have a duty…"

"A duty to whom? Queen Nuestria? Lena? What will any of that matter if the king is dead?" Her eyes filled with tears as she found herself leaning against Aregund.

He held her gently with one arm as she waited for him to speak to her. He didn't. Instead he just held her in his arms as she wept.

After several quiet moments, she felt the pull of emotion slip away. She slowly wiped her face with her hand. She knew that her emotional display would be distasteful for most Garkin but Aregund was different. He'd always been accepting of who Aisne was. But when she looked into his eyes, it was obvious that his tolerance had turned into something else – love.

In just that instant, Aisne had allowed herself to read his emotions. She was usually so careful to block out what he was feeling or to stay far enough away from him that his emotions would get lost in the sea of emotions swimming around a crowded room.

But there was no hiding from his feelings now. He was in love with her as sure as the sun would rise in the morning. And she knew that she loved him just as well.

Before she could stop herself, she moved onto the tips of her toes allowing only a fraction of distance between her mouth and his. Her heart beat so rapidly it almost lost its rhythm. In the time it took for her to blink her eyes, he'd pressed his lips to hers.

It was a tender kiss, soft and inviting. It reminded Aisne of the first time Aregund had kissed her. These moments she cherished above all others.

But as beautiful as the moment was, it had no place on this quest. She kissed him once more before burying her face in his chest. "I'm sorry, Aregund," she whispered. "This is wrong…"

"I know." He spoke softly into her hair.

Aisne backed away from him but she still couldn't look into his eyes. She felt embarrassed but the only emotions she could detect from him were desire and a bit of amusement. When she moved onto the bed, she thought that he might leave the room.

Instead he followed her onto the bed and pulled her against him. It was a benign act but it let Aisne know that he still wanted to be close to her. She wanted the same thing, needed it in fact. Tomorrow might bring her worst fears into reality but at least she would be comforted tonight.

Chapter 25

The town square was a shell of its former self. The once bustling shops were silent and gloomy. The windows that stood open showed tattered curtains hanging loosely or bare openings where the curtains had completely fallen away.

Aisne remembered how excited she was as a child to visit Sjoborg's square with her father. In one of her fondest memories, her father allowed her to pick the fish they bought at market. She was even allowed to wrap them in sack cloth. Her fingertips smelled of quale for two whole days.

The memory brought a smile to her face but it was soon followed by sadness. Aisne hadn't seen her parents in months. She only hoped they were well. With the sudden disappearance of the Faeborn king, everyone would be on edge.

Fyk led the team through the southern edge of town in search of the mysterious winged creature. They marched along the only cobblestone road that led to Sjoborg's sandy beaches. The tall stalks of sea grass could make an excellent hiding place for any creature seeking to approach them unnoticed.

Aisne tried to keep her mind on the hunt but she couldn't stop thinking about Aregund. Last night, she'd been closer to him than she'd been in quite some time but he didn't seem effected by it. He marched behind Fyk and kept his eyes searching around them. Not once did he turn in her direction.

After hours of marching cautiously through Sjoborg, Fyk knew that they needed to move more quickly. The sun would only last a short while longer and then the darkling would be able to travel above ground. Their search for the king would become much more perilous.

Aisne stared up into the sky and noticed a shadow moving quickly above her. The winged creature swooped down and landed on the ground about a hundred feet ahead of them. The creature gazed at them for a moment before turning and running full speed toward the beach.

Aisne barely noticed the others reacting around her as she reflexively bloomed. She moved to launch herself from the cobblestone, when she felt a firm grip on her forearm. "Aisne!" Fyk bellowed. "Stand down."

"But I can catch it!" Aisne felt the tension growing within her.

"Aisne, the creature is obviously toying with us. It wants to be followed." Fyk released Aisne's forearm and turned away from her. "Aregund!"

Aregund nodded quickly and started off after the creature. He shifted into his Garkin form propelling himself forward at inhuman speed. Both he and the creature disappeared from sight.

"Soren!" Fyk called out. "We need to secure another camp site. Use your stones. We'll wait for Aregund here."

There were a handful of cottages built along the beach just off the cobblestone road. There was only one that was still habitable. The main wall of the cottage faced the ocean. It was made entirely of glass and still intact. Soren made quick work in setting up a safe zone around it.

The glass wall exposed a small kitchen and a fairly large sitting room. The furnishings of pale coral and taupe were made to mirror life in the ocean itself. If it weren't for the intense feelings of death and loss, Aisne might have found the cottage beautiful.

Peter started searching for any supplies they could use but it was obvious that the former owner had taken everything with them that they could carry. Fyk stood look out for Aregund while Dax and Roden searched the nearby cottages for supplies as well.

While the men busied themselves, Aisne inspected the rest of the cottage. There was a washroom connected to the bedroom on one side. On the other side there was a mudroom that the former occupant used to store fishing equipment. The cottage was more than sufficient for Aisne and the others to take up refuge for the night.

Aisne tried to keep her spirits up but they had been searching for the king for two days without success. What they did find, was a strange winged creature they hadn't known existed. Fyk strongly believed that it was involved with King Tylwyth's disappearance but they didn't know how.

A quick succession of heavy footprints sounded against the roof of the cottage. Fyk was moving quickly but for what purpose? A few moments later, Peter burst into the bedroom where Aisne was sitting on the bed.

"Come quickly!" he shouted. "It's Aregund."

When Aisne reached the sitting room, she saw Fyk holding Aregund's body up. In his Garkin form and barely conscious, Aisne could tell that Aregund was hurt.

"What happened to him?" she asked softly.

"Darkling." Roden looked down at Aregund's pant legs which were shredded and bloodied.

"Can you heal him?" Fyk asked firmly.

"Yes but I'll need to see the wounds. Take him into the mud room and lay him on the floor." Aisne rushed into the washroom to get water and towels. She filled a bucket about halfway before pulling it out of the sink. She felt her hands begin to shake so she closed her eyes and focused on steadying them.

She knew full well that healing Aregund was risky. She hadn't the gifts of a true healer and she didn't know how healing him would affect her. But there was no question in her mind that she'd do it.

After shrugging off her nervousness, she entered the mudroom and knelt down next to Aregund. She lifted the damp rag over his body and noticed that he was only wearing a loincloth. She'd never seen so much of his skin before. "Why is he in his human form? These injuries could kill him."

Roden knelt down by her side wearing a confused expression. "He thought you could heal him more easily if he were human."

"I'll be the judge of that," Aisne added under her breath. She started rinsing his wounds that had become caked with blood. She discovered two large wounds that would have been fatal for a human; a set of puncture wounds on his left leg that started just above his knee and a much deeper gash on his right upper thigh.

When the darkling encountered Garkin kind, they used one main tactic to weaken them. If they could destroy a Garkin's ability to jump, they could overpower him with their numbers. Judging by the position of his wounds, they had attempted this tactic with Aregund.

Aisne first healed the area above his knee and at his ankles. Then she focused her attention on the worst of his wounds. She placed her hand on his upper thigh where fresh blood oozed from his torn flesh. His body shuddered as the palm of her hand glowed hot against his skin. Once the wound was closed, Aregund opened his eyes and looked at her.

"That should do it." Aisne stood up and carried the blood soaked towels into the washroom. She'd just started rinsing them out when Fyk came in after her.

With Fyk standing in the washroom, it felt smaller than it actually was. "You did well."

"I should've been with him." She spoke without looking at him.

"That is not your decision to make nor would it be a wise one. You could have both been lost. At nightfall, we are at a disadvantage." Fyk was trying to be delicate with her as much as he knew how. It wasn't a position he found himself in often. When he gave orders to his soldiers, they complied without question.

"I'm aware of that." Aisne couldn't think of what else to say so she focused on cleaning the towels.

"When you're finished here, join us up front. Aregund should be well enough to tell us what happened."

Aisne nodded her head and kept cleaning. Once Fyk was out of the room, she realized she'd been holding her breath. It was one of her methods of keeping out the emotions of others. She didn't want to experience the disappointment Fyk must have felt at her constant disobedience.

When she entered the sitting room, Aregund was already speaking to the men. He noticed her walk in but continued with his story.

"I followed the creature into the rough just beyond the western border of Sjoborg. It moved up into the air just out of my reach and waited as if it thought others would follow." Aregund scratched at his neck and then turned toward Fyk. "When no one came, the creature darted off in a northern direction. I tried to follow it but it was flying so fast... by my third jump, I realized I'd lost it."

"What do you think the creature is after?" Soren asked.

Aregund turned to Aisne again. "I think it wants her which means that none of us will leave Sjoborg until it gets what it wants. I moved north to try to pick up the creature's scent and that's when the darkling moved in. I couldn't get passed them."

"Me?" Aisne asked. "I thought the creature was looking for

Ungotha."

Fyk moved closer to Aisne. "Whatever the creature is after, we must stand fast. At first light, we'll return to where the creature led Aregund."

"We're sure to find answers there," Aregund replied.

Fyk nodded his head and folded his arms over his broad chest. "Agreed," he said.

A knock at the bedroom door woke Aisne from a light sleep. She knew immediately who it was. Aregund walked into the room and knelt down next to the bed.

"Aisne," he whispered. "Come outside… I need to speak with you." Without waiting for an answer, Aregund walked back out of the room.

Aisne sat up on the bed and stared after him. She hadn't a chance to read his thoughts so she had no idea why he wanted to speak with her. She slowly crawled out of bed and pulled on her clothes. Fyk and the others were asleep at the front of the house so Aisne slipped quietly through the mudroom door.

The sky was quiet and full of stars. The clouds that dared show themselves were few and far between. It seemed as if they were banned from Sjoborg completely. Even the crickets that normally filled the night were absent, further evidence of the memory stone's power.

"It was dangerous for you to heal me." Aregund spoke in a harder tone than normal.

"You didn't need to bring me out here to tell me that." Aisne answered him just as sternly.

"That's true. But I also wanted you to know that I'm grateful to you." Aregund stared up at the sky as if he expected someone to suddenly appear. "I didn't tell Fyk everything."

"What did you leave out?" Aisne swallowed hard. Part of her wished she was back in the cottage.

"The darkling had me cornered but they let me escape."

"Why?"

"I think they wanted me to lead them to you." Aregund turned back toward her. "You need to return to Merovech at first light".

"Aregund, if what you say is true that means I'm more valuable to the hunt than we thought. I can't leave."

"We can find the king without you. Won't you listen to reason?" Aregund was almost pleading with her. It certainly wasn't what she expected from him.

"What happens if one of you is injured? I could never forgive myself if you fell because I abandoned you."

"Aisne, it's obvious you have an important role to play in all of this. You must not be harmed."

"So my life is more important than the king's?" Aisne stepped closer to him.

"It is to me," he said intently.

Aisne felt warmed by his sentiment. But she had no intention of leaving Aregund and the others to face the winged creature and whatever other horrors might present themselves. "I won't leave."

Aregund was angered by her stubbornness but he realized that she wouldn't change her mind. He took a deep breath and folded his arms over his chest. "Let's get you back inside. You'll need your rest." He nodded his head in the direction of the back door.

Aisne leaned back on the bed and stared up at the ceiling. She was waiting for the mass of emotions she felt to subside enough for her to get some much needed rest. Between the threat of the darkling, the mysterious winged creature and Aregund's intended dismissal of her, she hardly found herself able to sleep.

Most unexpectedly, Aregund walked back into the room and sat down on the floor against the wall. Resting his arms across his knees, he closed his eyes.

"Are you planning to sleep there?" she asked realizing that her watcher had returned. Perhaps he and Fyk thought she might escape out of another bedroom window.

"Not exactly... I was performing a meditation of sorts. I hoped to encourage you to take my advice and return to Merovech." He opened his eyes and showed a half smile. "But you're too stubborn to listen to a mere soldier."

Aisne was caught off guard by his words. Aregund frequently exercised his ability to take her from one set of emotions to another. "What exactly does that mean?"

"You're promised to the son of king. How could I possibly influence you to do anything?" His eyes remained close as he spoke.

"I will do what I know in my heart is right, Aregund. That means helping to find the king with or without your blessing." To further illustrate that her decision was final, she turned her back to him and pulled the blanket up over her shoulder.

Aisne wanted to convince Aregund of her good intentions without her fairy emotions getting in the way but that was a gift she might never attain. As quiet filled the room, Aisne realized that she had won this battle with him at least for now.

"As you wish, princess." With that, Aregund walked out of the room. He hadn't gone far though. She could sense him clearly. He wasn't angry but he wasn't completely relaxed either.

She wished that he'd understand her position. But even if he didn't, it wouldn't change her mind. No matter what the result, she was determined to find the king and help to bring an end to the tension and distrust between Faeborn and Garkin kind.

Chapter 26

There was no real border between Sjoborg and the wild of the jungle expanse that went on for unknown distances to the east and west. As soon as Aisne left the grey sands of Sjoborg beach, everything around her changed.

It appeared as if nature was at war with itself as much of the more delicate vegetation had died long ago. Only the strongest trees survived and grew wild with vines spreading across the ground connecting to other nearby trees. Some of the trees appeared to be dying now with branches that pointed toward the ground.

"Is it much further?" Aisne yelled to Aregund.

"No," was all he said in response as he led the others through the thicket in what seemed like a winding pattern only occasionally stopping to pull a branch out of his way.

"I think he's confused," Peter whispered to her. "But he'd never admit it." Peter found himself at the end of the line directly behind Aisne. His marching order was another reminder of his human frailty.

"He'll get us there, don't worry." Aisne tried to reassure Peter. "We'll find the king and everything will be well."

"So what will you do then?" Peter whispered to her hoping the others couldn't hear his words.

"...after we find the king?" Aisne glanced back at him. "Rigunth and I will marry... I don't know after that."

Peter gave her a strange look. "You're still going to marry him?"

"Of course I am," she replied. "Why does that seem strange to you?"

"I only assumed that you would change course. Rigunth will be a tyrant, the worst kind of ruler. He believes that Faeborn are better than all other species and he would like nothing more than to see the rest of us grovel at his satin boots!"

Aisne stopped walking and turned toward Peter. "But that is why I must be at his side. I can help him to become the king we all need him to be."

"I've known you all of my life, Aisne. I have seen you do incredible things. But helping Rigunth change so completely is a task that even you cannot manage."

Aisne started walking again but more slowly than before. "Pete, I need to ask you something and I need a straight answer. Why were you near the river of sorrow that day?"

"To be completely honest, I was looking for proof… evidence against the Faeborn to confirm what I'd already known. They can't be trusted." Peter lowered his voice even more than before. "Look at how they concealed the power of those stones from us. What else could they be hiding?"

Aisne glanced back at Peter with surprise in her eyes. "You sound like one of the Garkin. We cannot let skepticism rule our lives."

"And we can't ignore the truth when it's right before us." Peter raised his voice more than he wanted to.

"We can discuss this later," Aisne replied. "Let's catch up with Fyk."

"As you wish, princess." Peter spoke firmly and with indignation. He wouldn't let the conversation end there.

When Peter and Aisne caught up to the team, they were approaching a clearing where the earth was scorched almost black. The nearby trees were wilted and dead. It appeared as if the sun had focused its intense heat on this area and nothing else. Just as Aregund reached the edge of the clearing, he turned left and kept walking.

"Wait, are you sure this is the right way?" Soren asked.

"I believe so," Aregund replied but it was obvious he wasn't sure.

"Are you sure we shouldn't be moving north?" Soren added. He hadn't moved from the edge of the clearing. "What made you decide to head west?"

Aregund stopped walking and turned to face Soren. "I don't know. I just felt that moving north was the wrong way. But I must admit, I don't remember moving west from this point last night."

"That's because you didn't," Soren advised. "There's a memory stone at work here."

"How do you know?" Roden asked stepping around Fyk.

"…because I can't move any further north. I've tried but I can't do it," Soren added calmly. "Peter, may I have a word?"

Peter joined Soren near the edge of the clearing. "At your service," he said cautiously. The thought of being useful to the team both frightened and intrigued him.

"I want you to walk over to that stump." Soren pointed at a large tree stump at the center of the scorched clearing.

Peter did as Soren asked. He walked over to the tree and then turned to see the surprised expressions on the faces of his companions. "Now what?"

"There's a memory stone over there somewhere," Soren replied flatly. "Check around where you're standing."

Peter nodded his head and started looking around on the ground. He saw only the stump itself and the rest of the tree that appeared to have been ripped out of place.

After searching a short while, Peter noticed a small section of the ground that had recently been disturbed. The dirt appeared loose and somewhat damp. He moved closer to the area to get a better look and realized that his feet were sinking deeper into the dirt.

By the time he reached the bottom of the fallen tree, the dirt was almost up to his knees. "Soren, I need your help!"

"Peter, I can't approach until you find the stone and bring it to me." Soren's patience was wearing thin.

"Are you finding anything, Peter? Take your time." Fyk's voice was firm but calm. He was accustomed to leading soldiers through difficult situations and Peter was no different.

"There's some loose dirt over here but I don't see the stone yet."

"Check around in the dirt. It has to be there," Soren added.

Peter reluctantly got down on his hands and knees and searched around in the loose dirt. He felt ridiculous in this position with four Garkin, one Faeborn and Soren watching him. The only thought that gave him any consolation was the fact that they needed him to find the stone. Without him, they would never be able to walk across the clearing.

He moved as close to the tree as he could without scraping his arm on the jagged edge. Just when he felt he couldn't reach any further under the tree, he felt not one but two stones that fit into the palm of his hand. He dragged them along the ground toward him and raised the stones above his head. "I found them!"

"Great! Now bring them over here…" Soren sounded almost

sarcastic not that Peter minded.

"As you requested," Peter said sounding slightly winded as he handed the stones to Soren. "There are two stones, Soren. What does that mean?"

"Let's find out, shall we?" Soren took the stones from Peter and held them out so that everyone in the group could touch them. Soren explained that this was the only way to break the memory that had been set in the stones. Now all of them could cross the clearing.

"This is an odd place for a tree to fall." Aisne stared at the tree.

"This tree didn't fall," Fyk said as he shifted into his Garkin form. He lifted the tree as if it were a twig and sent it sailing away from the clearing. "It was meant to hide something."

"But what?" Aisne added.

Dax shifted as well. "We'll soon find out." He moved to where Peter had been kneeling and started pulling at the loose dirt. Roden shifted and clumsily joined Dax in the digging. Waves of brown dirt went flying in several directions. It was hard to tell if they were actually looking for something or if they were playing like children in a sand pile.

"Enough!" Fyk bellowed. In his Garkin form, his voice could shake the ground around him. He jumped into the air and landed between Dax and Roden. The brothers moved out of the way as Fyk began rubbing his hands around the large whole.

In a matter of moments, he found what appeared to be a trap door. He pulled at the edge of the wood plank revealing a large hole beneath it. The opening was just large enough for him to fit inside so he stepped forward and disappeared into the ground.

Aregund glanced over at Dax and Roden. "Stay here," he said before dropping into the hole himself.

"I'll wait here too," Peter announced as he stepped back from the hole.

"Ladies first!" Soren stepped toward the hole and motioned for Aisne to join him.

She bloomed and allowed herself to drift slowly through the trap door. When her feet reached the ground below, she immediately felt warmth coming from the space. She started searching the room for the source willing her own internal light to burn brightly.

Soren suddenly appeared next to her wearing a concerned expression. "There is something strange about this place."

"I feel it too," Aisne replied. "There's someone here." She started moving forward but was soon met with the weight of a large hand around her wrist.

"Wait!" Aregund said. He glanced at Fyk who had moved just ahead of them.

"Its fine," she said pulling her wrist from his firm grasp. She started moving forward toward the larger section of the room. There was a dip in the floor making the room seem as if it was falling deeper into the earth.

As Aisne moved forward, she noticed a figure slumped against the wall in the far corner. With Soren and Aregund closing in behind her, she moved deeper into the room realizing that the warmth she felt was coming from the figure.

"Someone's alive down here," Aisne whispered over her shoulder. She felt a measure of delight that they might have finally found the king. And finding him alive meant that they could go home.

But after moving a few steps closer, Aisne realized that the person crouched down on the floor was not King Tylwyth. The small frame and long tangled hair were further evidence of that fact. It was definitely a female. She was wearing a long color-faded dress and no shoes.

The woman appeared to be sleeping. But once Aisne kneeled down next to her, she jerked away from the wall and turned around. She let her green-eyed gaze rest on Aisne. They were eyes that had looked at her so many times before – they were Rigunth's eyes.

"It cannot be!" Soren fell to his knees behind Aisne. He seemed too afraid to move closer to the woman.

Aisne smiled and bowed her head. "It's a pleasure to meet you, Queen Harmonia. We've been looking for you for a very long time."

Aregund bowed to her as well before kneeling down next to Aisne. "How did you get here?" he asked.

"We thought that there was one of them but there were two…" Her voice was low and gravely. Her body seemed weak but her spirit was strong. She was certainly relieved to see them there.

"Are you speaking of the winged creature, my queen?" Soren finally found his voice.

"You've seen it?" Queen Harmonia looked almost afraid. She glanced from Soren to Aisne and then stared down at her battered hands. "That means she let you find me and King Tylwyth will soon be dead."

"You've seen the king?" Aisne asked.

"The creature brought him here two days ago to prove that I was still alive."

Fyk finally walked over to them. "Can you travel, Queen Harmonia? We should leave this place."

"But I have so many more questions…" Aisne stood up and turned toward Fyk.

"…and you can ask them on the road. The creature could return and we would be defenseless down here." Fyk turned and walked toward the opening in the ground.

When they all reached the surface, Fyk ordered Dax and Roden to check the perimeter. He watched the space around them but it was obvious he was avoiding Queen Harmonia. Aisne was surprised at how uneasy he was around the Faeborn queen.

Or perhaps it was his memories of the day Harmonia went missing. King Tylwyth accused the Garkin of taking her which was not the case. Many soldiers lost their lives on both sides because of Queen Harmonia's disappearance.

"It's our fault that the creature is so angry." Harmonia hobbled along as they made their way back to Sjoborg. The muscles in her legs struggled to support her weight. She wasn't strong enough to fly having sustained herself on so little over the centuries. She could convince some edible vegetation to grow beneath the scorched ground but little else.

"You killed Ungotha… didn't you? That's why the creature is so angry." Aisne didn't look at Harmonia but she felt the fairy watching her.

"We tried but she was too powerful. So I imprisoned her in an underground tomb not unlike the one you found me in."

"But why?"

"Why else? Fear," she replied moving several strands of matted hair from her face. "The power the creature possessed far exceeded anything that Tylwyth or I had ever seen. Sometimes when we fear a thing, that thing becomes an enemy."

"Where did Ungotha come from?"

"I don't know. Communicating with her was… difficult. But we assumed that her immense power was born of nature itself."

"How did you end up in that hole?"

"Her symbiot put me there. A creature part darkling, part something else. After centuries in the ground, I managed to make contact with some humans who'd ventured nearby. I could feel their presence but so could the darkling. Once the symbiot realized the humans might find me, she destroyed them. At least it felt that way when I reached out for their energy."

Aisne watched Peter's reaction to Harmonia's words. At least now he knew why his brother and the other humans were targeted.

"We've encountered her symbiot as well," Aisne added. "That creature is far more dangerous than any darkling I've ever seen." Aisne wanted to explain how much damage the darkling had done over the last few centuries and how much more dangerous she imagined this other creature would be, but she knew that information wouldn't make Harmonia feel any better about the state of things.

"It will kill him you know, once it finds out that I cannot free Ungotha."

"King Tylwyth?" Aisne was trying to digest the queen's words.

Harmonia nodded her head slowly. "He's being forced to reveal Ungotha's location. Once that monster realizes my powers are depleted, it will kill Tylwyth. I trapped Ungotha under a shell of memory stones. No other fairy alive can destroy that barrier."

Aisne glanced at Aregund as he stared cautiously at her. "I can," Aisne replied firmly.

Queen Harmonia could only smile. "Is that so? Then we'd better hurry." Harmonia's unsteady hobble was just a bit faster than before.

"Where are we hurrying to?" Aisne asked.

"The river," Harmonia replied. "We need to get to the river."

When they reached Sjoborg beach, Fyk ordered the team to rest before they would march northward again. The Garkin would never ask their commander for rest or food but Fyk knew they all needed it. The dangers they would face at the River of Sorrow might be more than they had ever faced before.

Harmonia protested the delay but she was quickly overruled. Everyone in the group knew of the deaths and injuries that resulted from what Tylwyth and Harmonia had done. Even though none of them would admit it, they weren't particularly interested in rushing to their deaths to protect Tylwyth anymore.

All of the Garkin had lost family in the war between the Garkin and Faeborn. Dax and Roden had lost their parents, Aregund's mother was taken by darkling, and Fyk had lost all of his siblings except for one. It was difficult to learn that they had all died for a lie.

Then there was Peter. Still dealing with the loss of his brother, he burned with the knowledge that his death was in vain. He could only wonder what his father would do with the knowledge as well.

Peter kept his distance from Queen Harmonia and refused to bow to her. He could barely stomach looking at her. His desire to remain on the hunt had been dashed away into nothing.

In that moment, he made a silent promise to William. He would find a way to avenge him and take back his home. No other human would have to bow before a member of another species again.

Chapter 27

They reached the edge of the River of Sorrow just before nightfall. Fyk was given everyone instructions on how they would proceed when Harmonia stepped forward. "Something is wrong," she said shakily.

"What is it?" Aisne asked. She immediately felt the change in the queen's emotional state.

Harmonia stared up into the largest of the hibiscus trees that lined the back side of the river. She held her hand to her mouth and shouted, "Get them… someone get them, please!" Harmonia was too weak to fly. All she could do was point into the trees at the large cocoons.

When Aisne realized where Harmonia was pointing, she immediately took to the sky. She reached the two masses, and laid her hand on the one closest to her. She breathed a sigh of relief when she realized, the body was still warm.

Dain and Owain had been wrapped tight in a dark cloth and hung from the highest branch of the hibiscus tree. She could only imagine how they got there but what mattered now was getting them down safely.

She held onto Dain and using her free hand, flicked her wrist to undo the mess of knotted vines that were attached to his feet. She lowered him to the ground and then went back for his brother. Harmonia and Soren quickly tended to Dain, pulling at the sticky cloth he was wrapped in.

"I suppose we should be relieved that it let them go," Fyk announced. "Now we just need to get them to safety."

"This is so strange. Why take them in the first place?" Aisne returned to her human form.

"They were used as bait… to let us know that we're in the right place." Fyk's brow seemed more furrowed than normal. "Peter, you will lead Dain and Owain to your father's home. Dax and Roden will accompany you." Fyk motioned to Soren who then handed Peter one of the memory stones.

"But how will you defeat that creature with so few?" Peter asked. He stared at Aisne, his face full of fear.

"If my suspicions are correct, two more soldiers won't make a difference for us…" Fyk nodded toward Dax and Roden and they moved into action.

"Be well, Pete." Aisne smiled weakly at him.

Dain and Owain had barely recovered from the shock of seeing their mother alive when they were asked to explain what happened to them. Owain described how they were overpowered in an exchange with some sort of darkling but they had no idea where their father was taken.

They both showed courage as the realization washed over them that they might never see their father again. It couldn't have been easy for Queen Harmonia either. She had just been reunited with her two youngest sons and now she was about to face a terrible evil to rescue their father. There was no guarantee that she would survive the ordeal.

As Harmonia watched her sons be taken off by Garkin soldiers, the fear she felt became more obvious to Aisne. It was pitiful to see her this way. At one time she was thought to be the most powerful being in the world. Now she was reduced to a frail, broken queen without her king.

There were no Faeborn guards around the river which was strange in and of itself. Aisne watched the Garkin change to their stronger forms giving credence to her own concerns about their circumstance. She knew that the next few minutes or hours would decide the future of the Faeborn and Garkin people and their reality. With Harmonia at her side, Aisne bloomed and took to the air.

After assuring that no other creatures were hovering about, Aisne lowered herself to the ground. "How do we reach Ungotha?" she asked Queen Harmonia as calmly as she could.

"Come this way." Harmonia led Aisne and the others toward a large, round stone that was hidden by ficus bushes. "Beneath this stone is a tunnel that leads to Ungotha."

Without hesitating, Fyk walked in front of Harmonia. He moved toward the boulder with clear intentions of moving it.

"We should move quietly, my lord." Harmonia was trying to be tactful in her words.

"Why so? They are already expecting us. This entire journey has been a ruse designed by the winged creature. It wanted us to follow it here and to bring the one person who could free Ungotha – Princess Aisne." Fyk spoke the words out loud that everyone else was thinking. "From here, we have a clear mission: retrieve the king's body, destroy the creature and put an end to this darkling threat by any means necessary. I cannot promise that we will all survive, but we will give our all to meet these tasks before us."

"You don't believe the king still lives?" Aisne asked solemnly. Fyk snorted and shook his head. "There would be no reason to keep him alive. But let your heart not be heavy. We have much to do." With that, Fyk turned toward the boulder and ripped it from its place. He flung it over his shoulder and took a step toward the dark entrance.

The tunnel itself was difficult to traverse. The air became thinner as soon as they were all inside. The sunlight that spilled into the tunnel's entrance was all but depleted about halfway through the downward, sloping passageway.

Aisne slowly intensified her inner glow. She was now capable of changing her physical state without much effort. An ability that had not gone unnoticed by the others around her.

They were all relieved to finally reach the end of the tunnel that opened into a large oval-shaped room. The walls were smooth and damp with drops of water occasionally falling from the ceiling, further evidence that they were below the edge of the river. There was also the smell of damp earth and sludge emanating from just ahead of them.

"Brace yourselves," Harmonia announced. "Ungotha is unlike anything you have ever experienced. "Come this way."

Queen Harmonia led them all forward. Even though this next room was larger than the previous one, Aisne felt as if she'd been pulled into a smaller space.

"I thought you'd never get here," said a voice from the other end of the room. Aisne immediately recognized it as the voice of the creature she'd encountered in Sjoborg. "Now we can begin."

Aisne knew immediately that the creature was speaking directly to her. Fyk was right. This entire journey was designed by the creature to find Ungotha and to have Aisne set her free. If only she knew what step to take next.

"Move closer, Aisne. You'll want to get a closer look." The creature slowly flapped its wings pushing away the magical mist that covered the rear of the room.

Aisne waved her arm in front of her face hoping to clear her line of sight. When she focused in the direction of the creature's voice, she noticed that it was sitting on a throne near the right hand corner of the room. It was covered in a drape of grey cloth that seemed to serve no purpose in particular.

But what caught Aisne's attention next forced a gasp from her lips that she couldn't contain. Directly ahead of her, near the back of the room, was a large mound of earth covered in a hardened, green veil. It was Ungotha, the creature she was meant to free.

She also noticed a clump of a man in shackles surrounded by a mess of brown leaves and loose dirt that appeared as unstable as any in the room. Aisne could just make out a few arches in the king's crown and flecks of his pale blond hair.

"What have you done to him?" Aisne finally found her voice. "He lives for now. That should be your only concern."

"What do you want?" Aregund asked showing his growing impatience. "Because if you think you're walking out of here alive, you're mistaken!" He walked slowly forward with his canine teeth exposed. He appeared ready to pounce on the creature at any moment.

"How can you speak to me that way, Aregund?" The creature rose from its chair and released a small howl from its mouth. Its body began to shrink and its skin began to change in color and texture. The wings disappeared as its round face came into view. The winged creature's human form was that of Lena, daughter of Lok.

"This cannot be," Fyk bellowed. "I watched you born with my own eyes."

Aregund stood still, too shocked to move. He realized how fully the creature had been toying with them all. He was just as much a pawn as Aisne had been.

Aisne struggled to merge her reality with what she was witnessing. How had Lena fooled everyone so completely? Aisne thought back to every time she had been in Lena's company and there had never been a clue to her true identity.

In an instant, Aisne remembered the first time she'd seen Lena. She and Aregund were travelling through Merovech city headed for the mountains. That night was also the first time she'd seen a darkling and now she knew how they'd found her.

"Why did you send the darkling after me and Aregund?" Aisne ignored everyone else in the room and focused on Lena.

"I was planning to get rid of you… just as I had so many others." Lena toyed with the garment around her thin body. "Imagine my surprise to find that you possessed Harmonia's most powerful gift. I realized that I could make use of you."

Fyk took another step forward. "What happened to you? I've never seen such a change in a Garkin."

Lena took her seat on the throne contemplating how she would respond. "My father struck a bargain with Ungotha… she wanted to use me as a tool for communicating with the Faeborn and Garkin. My father had other plans."

"General Lok is involved in all this?" Fyk asked firmly.

"After my Faeborn mother was murdered, he swore to avenge her. Giving me to Ungotha was his way to do that. She changed me, made me stronger."

"Would Ungotha be pleased by your actions now?" Queen Harmonia hobbled forward moving closer to Lena than was probably safe.

"How dare you speak her name… you tried to destroy her for nothing more than existing!" Lena quickly stood to her feet. "When I am done here, I will give my father the power to kill Queen Nuestria. Only then will his revenge and mine be complete!"

"You're mad, Lena! You haven't the power to avenge your mother or you'd have done it by now!" Aregund stood between Harmonia and Aisne but it was obvious who he meant to protect.

"That's where you're wrong. Everything has happened the way I planned." Lena moved along the wall closer to where the king lay unconscious on the ground. "I have the king secured atop a pool of quick sand. Once I remove the memory stone protecting him, he will sink to his death."

Harmonia wore a pained expression. "You mustn't harm him! Take me instead…"

"That's not going to happen, my queen." Soren stepped in front of Harmonia and shifted into his hybrid form; a mixture of both

Faeborn and Garkin attributes. He had no wings but his body glowed brightly. His facial features hardened slightly and his body mass almost doubled. With claws exposed, he moved to Harmonia's side.

"Well, what have we here?" Lena turned her attention toward Soren. "So which of your parents do you honor, the Faeborn or the Garkin?"

"I honor my Faeborn mother and my queen." He glanced over his shoulder toward Harmonia. "You have power that is true. But none of us will let you harm Queen Harmonia or Tylwyth."

Lena threw her head back and laughed. "So which of you will stop me?"

"You might be surprised," Aisne replied.

"Oh you don't scare me little fairy." Lena focused her eyes on Aisne as if she had just noticed her in the room. "Your burning touch is impressive but I have gifts of my own."

"So what's to keep me from taking the king and walking out of here?" Aisne spoke with a new confidence.

"I can think of a few things…" Lena's skin began to quiver as her hidden nature fought through her olive skin. Her eyes darkened and turned black. She raised her arms over her head as large wings unfolded behind her. She started to chant something that was unrecognizable and that's when they appeared.

The walls started moving as darkling clawed their way into the room. Several of them came out of the floor and joined the darkling that had already gathered alongside Lena. Even more of them moved into the room through the open doorway. The smell of sulfur filled the air replacing the scent of moist soil.

The majority of the darkling surrounded Fyk and Aregund. Lena obviously wanted to keep them occupied so that she could convince Aisne to do her bidding. Fyk turned his back to Aregund and they assumed defensive positions. Likewise, Soren turned to put himself between Harmonia and the darkling that would soon be upon them.

In all of the commotion, Aisne felt she had an opportunity to take action. She shot up into the air and flew toward the king. Before she could reach him, Lena caught up to her mid air destroying her momentum. Using her superior strength, she grabbed Aisne by the throat and lowered her to the ground.

"All of you will stay where you are," Lena announced in her dual toned voice. She moved behind Aisne restraining her body with her left arm and holding Aisne's throat with her right. "If any of you makes a move toward the king or any of my brethren, I will rip out her throat."

"Don't listen to her!" Aisne shouted as she struggled in vain to pull herself from Lena's grip.

"I don't think you want to return Nuestria's favorite niece to her in pieces but that is exactly what will happen… I promise you."

Aregund was the first to stand at ease even shifting to his human form. "Do not harm her," he said softly.

Lena's face eased into a wide grin of grey teeth and gums. "I knew I could count on you to behave with your fairy in danger."

Fyk relaxed his own stance but he didn't change to his human form nor did Soren. He maintained a protective stance in front of Queen Harmonia.

"Now we will have an end to this." Lena released Aisne's throat and pushed her onto the ground. "Release my mother now!"

"Will you release the king and my companions?" Aisne asked as she moved shakily to her feet.

"You are in no position to make demands of me. If you don't release Ungotha, all of you will die!"

Aisne glanced at Fyk before moving toward Ungotha's tiny prison. As soon as she was close enough to touch the shell, Ungotha placed a three fingered claw against it. Aisne couldn't hide her distress at the sight of Ungotha.

Ungotha had no mouth. Her eyes were large, round and black as night. Instead of a nose, she had two large slits at the center of her face.

To say that Ungotha was hard to look at was an understatement and communicating with her didn't seem possible. Swallowing hard, Aisne placed one hand against the shell and the other at her side. She had to make an impossible decision and no outcome seemed to lead toward her escape with her companions.

Aisne hesitated for a moment taking a look over her shoulder at King Tylwyth. He'd started stirring against the ground. She had a quick thought to move quickly in his direction. But when Aisne turned back toward Ungotha, she noticed the creature shaking her head. Could she have read Aisne's thoughts and decided to warn her against trying to reach the king? Aisne couldn't be sure.

"What's taking so long?" Lena shouted. "Do you require

motivation?" Lena pointed her finger toward the king and he began to sink into the quicksand. The darkling also began moving toward the rest of Aisne's companions approaching from every angle.

Fyk and Aregund fought off the few that had started attacking. Even Soren grabbed one that had moved too close to Queen Harmonia. But the darkling had the numbers and it would only be a matter of time before Fyk and the others were overpowered.

"I'll do it!" Aisne shouted. "Don't harm the king." Aisne's hands began to glow white hot. She pressed them both against the hard shell of fused memory stones.

Almost immediately, the shell began to weaken where Aisne's hands met with its surface. She didn't know how much energy she would need to break the shell but she wouldn't be able to maintain the power surge for too much longer. The immense power she was calling to the palms of her hands was draining her energy at a rapid rate.

"It's working," Lena proclaimed. Realizing that her mother would soon be free, she waved her hand bringing the darkling to a standstill. They retreated from the Garkin but they still surrounded them.

Fyk and Aregund continued their circling motion back to back in a defensive pattern. Even though the darkling had retreated from them, they didn't know when Lena would change her mind and attack. For the moment, Aisne's companions were safe but the same couldn't be said for the king.

Lena waved her hand in his direction, moving the stone that secured his position. He began to sink deeper into the quick sand.

"No!" Harmonia screamed. Soren, you must save him!"

Lena suddenly turned her attention toward the queen's protector. Before he could cross half the distance to the king, she ordered her darkling brethren to focus their attack on him. Fyk and Aregund soon found themselves divided in their efforts to continue protection of the queen and helping Soren stay alive.

Realizing that he couldn't help Tylwyth, Soren was forced to return to the queen's side. As much as she protested, Soren had to focus on her safety. The greatest tragedy would result from both the Faeborn queen and king being lost to the darkling.

Just as Aisne watched Ungotha rise to her feet, she felt her own legs give way beneath her. Aisne lacked the strength in her body to remain upright. With her energy spent, she could only watch the events unfold in front of her.

Lena flew over to the king and stepped on the top of his head. His body became completely submerged under the quick sand. The queen could only scream in agony as she watched her husband being murdered.

Aisne prayed for her strength to return to her but none came. Her worse fear was realized. King Tylwyth was dying and soon her companions would be lost as well. They fought off the darkling that were closest to them narrowly avoiding claws that sought to strike at the weakest points in their bodies. But for every darkling they destroyed, another waited to take its place in the battle.

Without making a sound, Ungotha covered the small distance between her and Lena. The hem of her dust-colored robe dragged the ground collecting traces of wet soil but her feet never seemed to touch the ground.

Watching Ungotha embrace her adoptive daughter reminded Aisne of how much had been lost to make their reunion a reality. But in her heart and mind, she couldn't regret her decision to free Ungotha. No creature should be restrained against their will and for someone else's purposes. What Tylwyth and Harmonia had done was a cruel injustice and King Tylwyth paid for it with his life.

Queen Harmonia's crime would be repaid through her suffering. She stood with her eyes fixed on the area where her husband disappeared beneath the dirt. She wrapped her arms around herself and sobbed like a small child.

Aisne wanted to console the queen but she still didn't have the strength to stand. She could only experience the emotions of those in the room. But even those sensations were overrun by the immense heat in the space. The energy Ungotha released was unlike anything Aisne had experienced before.

Ungotha suddenly glanced at Harmonia and then Aisne. It was a moment that Aisne would never forget. Ungotha seemed to be making a decision but no one could have imagined what it was.

She wrapped her arms around Lena and then released her causing a loud spark to explode between them. Lena's body landed on the ground with a thud. Her skin turned darker; as dark as the damp ground beneath her. In the few moments that followed, Lena's body blended into the ground and disappeared from sight.

Darkling and Garkin alike turned in Ungotha's direction. She stood for a moment watching the place where Lena's body lay only a moment ago. There was sadness in her or longing; Aisne couldn't fully distinguish between the two emotions. What she found odd was that she could feel anything from Ungotha at all. Perhaps the enclosure she was held in masked more than just her power.

Aregund slowly moved between the darkling and went to help Aisne up off of the ground. She let the soldier hold her close to him before she turned back toward Ungotha. The fighting was over still no one knew what her intentions were. That was surely about to change.

Ungotha took a few steps forward and then motioned toward Harmonia. The Faeborn queen moved shakily ahead of Soren and bowed. It was an awkward gesture but it seemed appropriate. Ungotha had destroyed Lena, ended the fighting and most probably saved their lives. A thankful queen was the least Ungotha could expect.

In a surprise gesture, Ungotha motioned toward where King Tylwyth's body was buried in the sand. Soren didn't know what the gesture meant but he assumed she was giving her permission for them to collect the king's body. He moved quickly to pull King Tylwyth from under the quick sand laying him gently on the ground at Harmonia's feet.

Ungotha stood watching as Fyk and the others moved closer to Tylwyth's body as well. They surrounded him on the ground and bowed their heads. Aisne could feel the weight of the sorrow in the room and it made her chest feel as if it might fold in on itself.

After a silent exchange with Ungotha, Harmonia kneeled down next to Tylwyth's body and touched her hand to his cheek. She seemed to be waiting for his eyes to open but they didn't. It had become clear that his body suffered distress before they arrived.

Lena never intended to free the king. She intended for his life to be the sacrifice for his treatment of Ungotha. It was a heavy price to pay but no more than what countless others had given in the name of fear.

Harmonia turned her attention toward Ungotha once more. She nodded her head and then smiled weakly. No amount of sympathy could heal Harmonia's heart but this creature found something to lift her spirits; it was the promise of peace.

Ungotha floated out of the room and the darkling followed after her. It was one of the strangest things Aisne had ever seen. What made the moment even more bizarre was how much lighter the room felt after Ungotha was gone.

Still struggling to catch his breath, Fyk was the first to break the silence. "What just happened?" he asked in a gruff voice.

"She's gone," Harmonia replied. "The darkling are gone and they're not coming back."

Chapter 28

After waiting in the main hall for almost an hour, Aisne and the others were ushered into the throne room at Tremeria. Prince Rigunth was sitting on the throne dressed in a uniform Aisne had never seen before. His normal attire was covered in a golden chest plate. He wore a blank expression but his inner emotions were much more telling. Anguish and regret filled his aura so completely that Aisne needed to take a step back from him.

The room was filled with Faeborn of the highest order. Members of the Tremerian council were seated on rows of cushioned benches that were positioned along both sides of the red carpet. A carpet that stretched from one end of the room to the other. The heads of the finest Faeborn families were in balcony seating behind the council members.

"I would think that you Garkin would have respect enough to take a knee in my throne room," Rigunth spouted as he stood to his feet. "Or have you no respect at all?"

"Apologies, Prince Rigunth." Aisne knelt down with Fyk and Aregund beside her.

"We mean you no disrespect, Prince Rigunth." Fyk got down on one large knee and remained there with his head lowered.

"Then why have you returned my father's body to me? Why is he not riding in at your side?" Rigunth walked slowly down the stairs of the royal platform and moved toward the large Garkin.

"The good king fell in a battle below the river." Fyk hesitated for a moment. "We made every effort to free him alive."

Rigunth moved in front of Fyk and stared coldly at him. "Look at me when I'm speaking to you!" He struck Fyk across the face and waited for the Garkin to make a move. Fyk did nothing. He was in a room full of Faeborn soldiers. Any aggression on his part would've led to his immediate death.

"What are you doing?" Aisne stood to her feet. "This man risked his life to find your father and you punish him? This makes no sense." Aisne had never been good at masking her emotions and this interaction with Rigunth was more evidence of that fact.

Rigunth could not hide his surprise at her outburst. As the prince and subsequent heir to the throne of Tremeria, his word and deeds became law. No one in their right mind would dare defy him.

"Princess Aisne, you are on dangerous ground!" Rigunth shot back at her. "I suggest that you take your place behind me or you can take your place with them."

Without a moment's hesitation, Aisne knelt down next to Fyk and lowered her head. An immediate burst of whispered conversations filled the room. Aisne's choice to kneel at Fyk's side wasn't sitting well with the Faeborn, least of all Rigunth.

He didn't attempt to hide the flash of hurt and surprise that crossed his face. "Princess Aisne has taken up with her brethren against me and you have all witnessed it." With his anger at a fevered pitch, Rigunth moved his attention back to Fyk. "You led the team to rescue my father and now his body lies cold. What do you have to say for yourself?" Rigunth raised his hand again giving the impression he would strike Fyk once more. But before he could make contact with the Garkin, Aisne stepped between them.

She quickly bloomed and grabbed hold of Rigunth's arm. With a flick of her wrist, she flung Rigunth back on the floor. Everyone in the room watched as Rigunth rolled over landing hard on his back.

Thoran and a dozen other Faeborn surrounded Aisne and Fyk. They waited for orders from Prince Rigunth and everyone knew what would be the result.

"Take them!" Rigunth yelled. He'd bloomed and started hovering above the floor. He ordered the Faeborn soldiers to remove Aregund and Fyk which wasn't an issue. They'd remained in their human forms. Fyk motioned toward Aisne and she returned to her human form as well.

"Isn't this a fine mess?" Aisne said as she leaned against the back wall of her cell next to Fyk's. The dungeon was dimly lit by two fire sconces hanging on either side of the entry way. It contained four iron cells of which only three of them were occupied.

"Yes, of course it is and we have you to thank, princess." Aregund was in the cell across the room from hers. She could feel the disappointment he felt toward her and it gave her the desire to break free of her cell and fly far away.

"I couldn't stand there any longer and watch him assault Fyk." Aisne noticed the way Aregund was looking at her and made the decision to try and ignore him. "I don't expect you to understand."

"Understand what? That you're going to get us all killed? I understand that very well."

"Rigunth can't kill us. He just wants to punish us…" she answered wearily. "He got what he deserved." Aisne looked over at Fyk who'd suddenly turned in her direction.

"Aisne, you shouldn't have engaged with Prince Rigunth that way. He didn't harm me. He's merely a man in grief looking for an outlet for his pain." Fyk finally spoke to calm the conversation.

"I can get us out of here." Aisne tried to appease Fyk. She hated the idea of disappointing him so fully. "We could be in the forest before they knew we were gone."

"If we run, that would only make matters worse," Fyk added. "Queen Nuestria will come for us in due time."

Aisne turned her body toward the wall of her cell so that no one could see her somber expression. The knowledge that her companions thought she acted poorly did nothing to brighten her mood.

She pondered Fyk's words but something inside her wouldn't accept Rigunth's reaction. Blaming him for King Tylwyth's death was wrong. At the same time, Rigunth showed no joy for his mother being found alive. That should have given him some measure of comfort.

After almost three days in the dungeon, Aisne felt a new sense of anxiety. She couldn't understand why they were still being held in these cages. Why hadn't Queen Nuestria come for them?

In a very short time, she'd transitioned from sleeping in the Prince's chambers to sleeping in his dungeons. The whole experience showed her just how Rigunth treated those in his custody. She suddenly remembered Peter's words to her. Everything that he'd warned her about Rigunth was coming true.

Somewhere around midnight on the third day, Aisne was awakened by an unexpected visitor. She squinted her eyes as the light from their lantern moved shakily toward her cell.

"Who's there?" she asked. After what seemed like an eternity,

Soren knelt down and put the lantern on the floor at his feet.

"Quiet down, you'll wake the whole of Tremeria," Soren answered almost in a whisper.

"What are you doing here?" she whispered back.

"This is my fault," Soren answered refusing to look directly at Aisne. "I told Rigunth what happened in the cave but he twisted my words."

"Soren, you needn't worry. Once my aunt arrives, we'll settle all of this." Aisne couldn't believe she was trying to make Soren feel better when she was the prisoner.

He shook his head slowly. "Your aunt isn't coming. Her messenger informed Rigunth that she intended to do her own assessment. She's requesting that you all be released but he refused."

"So what are we supposed to do now?" Aisne felt herself becoming angry. Her whisper was gone and so was her assumption of a peaceful resolution. "We can't stay locked up down here."

"That's exactly why I'm here." Soren opened Aisne's cell door and motioned for her to come out. "I'm getting you all out of Tremeria tonight."

"What about the guards?" Aisne replied cautiously. By then Fyk and Aregund were listening. She knew that Fyk would never agree to leave if it meant hurting any of the Faeborn.

"Let's just say that I created a diversion to get them away from the arena."

"So how are you here now? Won't they know that you returned to the dungeon?" she asked.

"No, they won't make that assumption." Soren unlocked the other two cells and moved back toward the entry door. "I had help. Not everyone believes in Rigunth's philosophies."

"Wait!" Aisne started to follow after him but returned to her cell. "I need to do something first." Aisne concentrated on her right hand which started to glow. After partially melting the lock that was on her cell, she did the same with the cells that had held Fyk and Aregund. She wanted the Faeborn to believe that she freed the Garkin. It was enough that Soren had helped them. She didn't want him to suffer Prince Rigunth's wrath too.

Within minutes, they were all standing on the edge of the arena. Soren had given them instructions on how to travel through the forest and to get safely out of Tremeria. With the Faeborn soldiers chasing decoys in the opposite direction, security near the forest would be minimal. But no chances could be taken.

"We are in your debt, Soren." Fyk grabbed Soren's forearm and nodded toward him.

"Safe travels to you." Soren replied.

"Aisne, are you coming?" Fyk asked realizing that Aisne was standing apart from him and Aregund.

"I'll be right behind you," Aisne said calmly.

Aregund gave her a strange look but he didn't protest her announcement. Perhaps the last three days of captivity had bothered him too much to give her a heartfelt goodbye. "Be safe, Aisne," he said before starting down the stairs that led away from the arena.

With the Garkin on their way home, Aisne realized that there was one more matter she needed to address. "Soren, where is Queen Harmonia now?"

Aisne stopped walking just outside the royal mausoleum at the edge of the garden. Surprisingly, she could still see the arena from where she was standing. After covering her face and hair as Soren suggested, she moved through the arched entryway and into the viewing room. Harmonia was standing quietly watching her husband's still body. He was in a glass case at the center of the room covered in a golden shroud.

His body would remain in its current state for many moons. Unlike humans, whose bodies began to decay immediately after death, the Faeborn and Garkin would appear to be merely asleep for weeks after they'd taken their last breath. Faeborn customs required that the king be encased in stone just as his ancestors before him. However, no Tremerian alive would disturb the queen's grieving process. King Tylwyth would remain on display until the queen wished otherwise.

"I never offered you my condolences for your loss." Aisne spoke softly as she approached Harmonia.

"I have a feeling that's not the reason you're here." Harmonia spoke through the sheer, white veil that covered her face and hair.

"You're being kind, my queen." Aisne smiled shyly.

Harmonia turned toward Aisne with tears in her eyes. "I won't ruin Rigunth's impression of his father especially now."

"He should know the truth. Everyone needs to know. Our people have been fighting the Garkin for centuries. It needs to end."

"Destroying my family won't change history. The answer is no."

"Is this really about history or the future… your future? How do you think your children would feel knowing the part you played in all this?"

"It's true. My relationship with my eldest son was never a good one. He didn't agree with the influence I carried with the king. When he saw me returned, he barely took notice."

"You and Rigunth have time to mend your relationship. What of the rest of us?"

"He won't marry you now… you disgraced him in front of everyone who matters here."

"I wasn't referring to myself." Aisne was suddenly reminded of her actions in the throne room. She remembered the look on Rigunth's face when she struck him; a mixture of shock and embarrassment. "I'm speaking of the thousands of innocent people who will die from continued conflicts between the species."

"Think clearly of what you're asking, Aisne. There's more at stake than just my family. This knowledge could plunge us into civil war and no one would survive this time." Harmonia turned back toward the king's body and leaned closer to the glass enclosure. "Please leave me so that I can properly grieve the loss of my king."

Aisne knew that there was some truth to Harmonia's words. She wasn't in any better condition to confront Rigunth than Harmonia was. So much had happened in the span of a few days.

The only thought that gave her comfort now was leaving Tremeria. Her decision to stay behind and speak with the queen was a risky one but Aisne knew it was worth the risk. "Queen Harmonia, I think it best for me to leave now but I'll need your help."

Aisne felt a hint of panic as she waited just inside the doorway of the great room. She could see the shadows of the two guards standing in the main hall. After King Tylwyth was taken, Rigunth decided to step up security in the palace. Of course this didn't bold well for Aisne's plan of escape. Harmonia promised to help her but she had no idea what the queen had in mind.

Suddenly the sound of Queen Harmonia's high pitched scream filled the air. The guards in the foyer reacted immediately as did the guards from the main entrance to the palace. Aisne watched as a flurry of wings and ice colored uniforms whip passed her. She waited a few moments more before she hurried down the main hall and out the palace doors.

Much to her surprise, there was a horse waiting for her at the bottom of the massive circular stairs.

"Mra!" Aisne half whispered when she realized it was Rigunth's favorite steed. The horse made the most excited blur as Aisne moved toward him.

He lowered his head giving Aisne some help mounting him. She gave his mane a quick tug signaling that she was ready. That was all of the push he needed to take off across the plains. Mra seemed to already know where they were headed as he moved into a full gallop. Aisne did her best to hold on tight.

As Aisne raced away from Tremeria, she thought about everything she was leaving behind; the idea of a lasting peace, a broken engagement, and a queen in mourning. She also thought of Fyk and Aregund. Hopefully, they'd made it far enough that the Faeborn wouldn't be able to retrieve them.

Ice cold tears fell on her cheeks and were quickly swept into the wind. She had never ridden a horse this hard but Mra seemed to be sympathetic to her desire to get as far away from Tremeria as possible. As much as Mra was cooperating, Aisne knew that he couldn't ride like this forever. Worse yet, he didn't belong to her. Rigunth's favorite horse would certainly attract unwanted attention when her goal now was to blend in.

After stopping at a small, forgotten creek well beyond Tremeria's borders, Aisne rested and Mra drank. He seemed to enjoy the dull glow that Aisne released. He seemed comforted by it. Aisne struggled to find some comfort for herself. Her future was as uncertain as was the peace between the Garkin and Faeborn. King Tylwyth's deception might be the undoing of them all.

Aisne mounted Mra and coaxed him into a slow gallop. They travelled that way for several hours until the sun threatened to pierce the dark sky. Reaching the orchards just beyond Jormstad gave Aisne only one thought and that was of home.

She hadn't seen her parents in such a long time. What would she even say to them? *'Hello Majka, I'm on the run from the Faeborn prince...*

can I come in for a cup of ale?' The conversation sounded comical in her mind but she was out of options and in need of a good rest.

After circling around behind the orchards, Aisne waited until she saw Ms. Miller take her morning stroll up to the pear trees. The sight of the old woman in the orchards made Aisne smile. At least one of her memories hadn't been tarnished by pain or death.

Chapter 29

By the time Aisne led Mra through the few remaining streets to her parent's home, the sun was high overhead. She knew that her father would have already left for his shop which was somewhat of a blessing. Mra would have been quite unsettled around her Garkin father.

Aisne tied Mra's reins to a small tree on the side of the house and made her way toward the back door. She tried turning the knob and was relieved to find that the door wasn't locked. She walked into the kitchen to find her mother's wide eyes staring back at her.

"Aisne, is it really you?" Emma's green eyes twinkled brightly.

"Yes, it's me Majka." Aisne hugged her mother tightly. She remembered how safe she felt as a child in her mother's arm. But nothing could remove the cloud she felt hanging over her.

"What has happened, daughter? We heard things… terrible things. Did you find the king?"

Aisne pulled away from her mother and sat down at the kitchen table. "I failed in the hunt. The king is dead."

Emma sat down across from Aisne and reached for her hand. "I know you did everything you could. You mustn't feel personally responsible for this loss," Emma said calmly. She wasn't as upset as Aisne expected but she wasn't completely allowing her feelings to be known either. "His children must be completely distraught."

"Yes they are… but there's more."

Aisne exchanged two pieces of bread and a cup of tea for conversation. She recounted everything that happened over the last few days including the discovery of Lena's true identity and her father's plan to assassinate Nuestria. But nothing surprised Emma more than the knowledge that Queen Harmonia was still alive.

There was something therapeutic about confessing the whole story to her mother. How quickly her reality had changed since she started on this latest quest, how differently her life would be now that there was no purpose. Aisne no longer felt connected to the Garkin nor did she identify with the Faeborn. She had no idea who she was anymore. Everything that she'd been fighting for was a lie.

Sometime later, Aisne found herself in her old bedroom. Having succumbed to the utter fatigue that she felt in her mind and body, she collapsed on the bed. How strange it was that her parent's home remained so much the same when the whole of reality had changed so completely?

Aisne had no idea how long she'd been asleep but she immediately noticed the large figure seated at the foot of her bed.

"Hello, Aisne." Ansoald's voice was low and gravelly. He leaned closer so that she could see his face more clearly. "How was your rest?"

"It was good," Aisne replied pulling herself up to a seated position. The room was darker than it should have been or at least that's what she thought. "How long have I been asleep?"

"…half a day at least."

Aisne moved quickly off the bed. "I have to go. They'll be looking for me."

"You don't have to leave now." Ansoald sat up taller and groaned under his breath. "Let us help you."

"I don't want your help!" Aisne shot back at her father without thinking. She started digging in her closet for sturdier shoes. "I have to leave now. It's not safe for you that I'm here." She searched the floor of the closet for high ankle boots and then slid them on one by one. "I don't know what I was thinking coming here…"

"This is where you belong. It's your home."

"It was my home but not anymore." Her voice was softer then.

Ansoald started to show the frustration he felt on his face. "Well at least let me get you somewhere safe…"

Aisne turned to see the look in her father's eyes. It was a look he'd given her so many times before. As a little girl, she depended on his strength and kindness in equal portions. She would've loved nothing more than to run into his arms and bury her face in his chest. But that wouldn't fix her problems now.

"There's a settlement just beyond the mountains. Right before your sister was born, a good friend of mine left with his family. That's where they were headed," he added kindly.

"Tell me more." Aisne sat down on the bed next to him. "How sure are you that they're still there?"

"I've received a few messages from him over the years. Others have gone but they rarely return to Jormstad. Life there is difficult but at least they have avoided the conflict between Garkin and Faeborn."

"Why have you never told me about these people before?"

"There was no reason to mention Mikael and the others. Our life was always here."

Aisne stared at her father for a moment before standing to her feet. "Thank you father. I'm sure I can find my way. Can you promise me that you will try not to worry?"

"I can do anything but that," he said as he hugged her tightly.

Before Aisne left her parent's house, she asked her mother to take Mra to the orchards and set him free. He would find his way back to Tremeria quite easily. As much as she loved the horse, she couldn't take him into the mountains with her. And even he she could, Mra would be too afraid around the Garkin to have any kind of life.

Of course Mra was none the wiser as Aisne stroked his mane for the last time. He probably thought he was getting special attention for carrying her such a great distance without complaint. "You are a good boy, aren't you Mra?" Aisne could feel her throat tightening as she realized she would never see him again.

Aisne started on the road that would lead her toward the mountains with her knapsack full of Emma's fruit loaf. She could hear the horse neighing as if he was calling to her. She didn't turn around, she couldn't. Instead she focused on the road ahead.

It didn't help that her mother was standing just inside the front door making neighing sounds of her own. Aisne didn't bother asking her mother not to cry or to stop worrying about her. Asking a Faeborn to control their emotions at a time like this would've been a wasted effort. Emma watched her daughter walk up the road until she disappeared out of sight and into the darkness.

The main road that Aisne was on could lead her directly to Merovech but she had no intention of going there. Instead, she turned onto the partially paved road that would lead her north toward the mountains.

Her mood became instantly lighter as she moved further away from Jormstad and into the unmanned valley. Even at this distance, Aisne could see the three highest peaks of the mountain range; the tallest of which was called Cebus. It was named for the leafy green trees that covered its mount.

Several hours later, Aisne reached the spiny miscus trees that bordered the deep forest. She was about to take her first rest when she heard voices from behind her. Fearing capture, she ducked into a nearby bush landing square into a freshly made bushwag nest. Her presence was problematic for the four legged beast but neither of them seemed poised to change locations with Garkin soldiers nearby. The Garkin were known to eat bushwag when they were on the hunt.

Once the voices faded into silence, Aisne crawled from under the bush. She waited another few moments before getting shakily to her feet and lumbering forward. Were the Garkin tracking her so quickly? She couldn't be sure.

A part of her now regretted stopping at her parent's house. That brief respite allowed the Garkin to get out ahead of her and now she was cut off from the north. Her options were limited. In a panic, she changed direction and headed toward the one place she knew to be safe.

The little cabin Aregund had taken her to was far from Merovech. Few soldiers knew of the old Garkin settlement and even fewer had any cause to return there. Even when they hunted oxen, they preferred to travel south through the sand hills where the animals were plentiful.

Aisne couldn't see the cabin from where she stood but she knew it was there all the same. It would make the perfect hiding place for a fairy on the run. She just hoped she could reach it before one of the Garkin soldiers reached her.

Her heart continued to race as she darted through the low land forest region. It seemed the closer she moved toward the cabin, the more frightened she was that she wouldn't make it. After stumbling around in the dark for another hour, she finally arrived at the front door of the cabin.

She walked inside and braced a wood plank against the back of the door and into the two large hooks on either side of it. It would be little protection if a Garkin soldier tried to break down the door but it offered some mental comfort. She stared around the cabin checking for any traces that someone had been there.

From what she could see of the darkened space, nothing seemed out of place. She was standing on the mole hair carpet trying to remember where all of the furniture was. Using a light source was unwise since she hoped to avoid detection.

Aisne carried her knapsack into the bedroom and sat down on the bed. She wanted to rest but the smell of bushwag nest was entrenched into her clothing and her skin. Her fear of detection was somehow superseded by her desire to clean herself. She filled the metal tub in the washroom and set about getting the stench of the last few days off her body.

Aisne suddenly found herself shaken by the fear of what lay ahead of her. She was alone and unsure of her future. King Tylwyth was dead and Queen Nuestria had left her to suffer at the hands of a cruel prince. Now she was left to flee her home and everything she'd known.

She felt some consolation in knowing that she wasn't the first to leave. Mikael and the other families fled Jormstad in search of a better way of life. Perhaps joining them would offer her the life that she desired away from the kingdoms of the Garkin and Faeborn. It was certainly worth a trip through the mountains to find out.

A little while later, Aisne crawled into the bed. The wind howled against the small window creating a sort of lullaby. The only sound that was more comforting to Aisne was the sound of crickets chirping in the distance. But their sound had suddenly faded from the night.

A large thump suddenly sounded on the roof of the cabin. Aisne reflexively shifted into her Faeborn form as every inch of her body moved into high alert. Her heart raced with the realization that she'd been found.

At least one Garkin was outside but she had no idea how many more were out there. In her heightened emotional state, she couldn't rely on her fairy instincts to help her now. The adrenaline coursing through her body was her primary defense.

She waited for what felt like an eternity for the Garkin to show themselves. She didn't know what they planned to do with her. Would she be taken back to Tremeria or held in Merovech? Neither idea was agreeable to her.

Her patience nearly depleted, Aisne moved toward the front

THE TEMPEST BLOOM: RISE OF THE DARKLING

door of the cabin. She flicked her wrist and plucked the wood plank away from the door. Then she opened the door and floated out into the night.

To her surprise, there was no one there. She drifted up into the air but there was no one on the roof. She started to wonder if she had imagined the whole thing.

Just to be sure, she flew around to the back of the cabin. There was no one out there but her. Not wanting to attract unwanted attention, she hurried back into the cabin. Using the cover of darkness made her move more slowly than she otherwise would.

She shifted back to her human form and carefully replaced the wood plank over the front door. When she walked into the bedroom, she sat down on the bed and immediately felt the presence of someone else in the room. "Who's there," she asked moving back toward the doorway.

"It's Aregund." He moved out of the corner of the room by the window. She recognized his voice even though she couldn't see him clearly.

"How did you get in here?" Aisne wasn't sure how to respond to him.

"…the window."

"Are you alone?" she asked.

"You should already know that. Aren't you a fairy?"

Aisne bloomed instantly and moved closer to him with her glowing hands outstretched. "You would be wise to answer my questions. I'm in no mood for games."

"I'm alone," he answered calmly. He suddenly realized how unsettled she was. He didn't know what she endured to get away from Tremeria on her own. "Are you alright?"

She lowered and hands and took a step back from him. "I'm quite well considering that I'm on the run. Why are the Garkin looking for me? Do you plan to take me back to Tremeria?"

Confident that the danger was over, Aregund walked over to the night table by the bed and turned on the lamp. "The Garkin soldiers are not after you, Aisne. They're searching for General Lok."

Aisne felt a rush of relief. "If the Garkin aren't looking for me, then why are you here?"

"They aren't looking for you but I am." His face suddenly turned more serious. "The queen wants you back."

"Is that so? Well, I hate to disappoint you but I have no intention of returning to Merovech either."

"What will you do then… go off on your own? Will you try to survive in the wilderness? That's no life for a princess."

"I am no princess! I am just a girl who was dragged into a game between two kingdoms. I've had enough."

Aregund watched her closely but he wasn't swayed by her words. "You are much more than that. I've watched you show the same courage that I see in Garkin soldiers. You are strong and fiercely loyal to those you care about. You defended Fyk and against your intended no less."

Aisne lowered her head. "I disappointed him. He practically told me so himself."

"No, you honored him. To risk your life in his defense…"

"I just couldn't stand there and let Rigunth treat Fyk so poorly. He risked his life to find King Tylwyth. And even after learning the truth of Tylwyth's deeds, Fyk did not speak ill of him. He is more than just a soldier. He is a man of great integrity."

Aregund looked at her and smiled. "I can't believe I never figured it out before. Fyk is the one who trained you… to fight Brous."

Aisne raised her head slightly. "Yes, he is. He saved me from a humiliating loss and possible injury. I promised myself that one day I would find a way to repay him."

"In doing so, you broke your engagement. You've weakened the stability of relations with the Garkin and Faeborn."

"You sound like Queen Nuestria." Aisne stiffened. "What else has she filled your head with?"

"A tribunal will take place. You must be in attendance."

"I will not go!"

"Then you risk everything that you fought so hard to preserve." Aregund turned his back to her.

"I have nothing left to preserve. You know that as well as I do."

Chapter 30

Aisne sat down on the bed and covered her face with her hands. The heated words they exchanged had not weakened her resolve but she was physically drained. "I need to rest." She spoke without looking at him. "Can I trust you to leave me unharmed?"

"I would no sooner hurt you than I would myself. You should know that by now."

Aisne swallowed hard as Aregund's words washed over her. She was instantly reminded of the last time they were in the cabin together. Their feelings for each had taken hold; neither of them could deny it. That seemed like a lifetime ago.

She no longer allowed herself to focus on the feelings she had for Aregund. The reality of who she was put a wedge between them that didn't seem movable. Even with Lena's demise and Rigunth's rejection of her, she and Aregund were worlds apart.

"No matter what we think or feel, the reality is the same. You are Garkin and I am not." She finally found her voice.

"We both have our duty, but duty cannot change the heart." He stood up to leave. "I'll let you get some rest."

Aisne knew that Aregund wanted to say more to her. There was more that she could have shared as well. In the end, their predicament would remain. Their words would only fill the air and then fade into nothing.

She'd spent so much time sacrificing of herself and now she was left with nothing. Aisne was more sure than ever about leaving Merovech for good. She couldn't stomach waiting around to see which Garkin woman Aregund would be promised to next.

Moments later, she heard a loud thump on the roof. She imagined that Aregund would become a fixed part of the cabin for the next few hours. There was no danger for him to watch for. It was more likely that he wanted to put some space between them.

In anticipation of the cold night air, Aisne lit a fire and sat down on the bed with her knapsack in hand. She thought it'd be a good idea to take inventory of her supplies. Other than the bread Emma had given her, Aisne packed some fruit she'd acquired in Ms. Miller's orchards. They wouldn't last her very long, but they were more edible than the beet roots she'd find along the rest of her journey.

At the bottom of the knapsack, Aisne discovered a silk pouch that covered the entire bottom of her bag. She opened the drawstring and pulled out a piece of silver fabric. She immediately recognized the dress that her mother had given her to wear months earlier. She couldn't' imagine why Emma would give it to her now.

Aisne took a bite of her banana loaf and sat staring at the garment. She remembered the night she wore it and how beautiful she felt. It seemed like a life time ago.

Before she could think too hard about it, Aisne was pulling off her pantaloons. What could it hurt for her to try the dress on one last time? She soon found herself twirling around the bedroom and laughing hysterically.

"Enjoying yourself?" Aregund asked from behind her.

Aisne whirled around to find Aregund in the doorway with his arms folded over his chest.

"I thought you were on the roof…" Aisne felt quite foolish. She had no idea how long he'd been standing there watching her. "Emma put this dress in my knapsack."

"I've seen that dress before," Aregund replied smiling. "You were wearing it the night of the ball; the night you rejected me and left me to dance alone."

"You mean the night you insulted me?" Aisne was able to manage a smile.

"Perhaps we can create a new memory." Aregund reached his hand out to her.

Aisne hesitated a moment before taking Aregund's hand. "What do you propose?" she asked nervously.

"Dance with me."

"There's no music."

"That didn't stop you from dancing before."

Aregund took Aisne in his arms and slowly swayed back and forth. He watched her with dark, brown eyes but she found it difficult to return his stare. He was completely open to her which made reading his emotions quite simple. But a part of her still feared that her own feelings might be clouding what she picked up from him… that is until he kissed her.

Aregund stopped dancing and rubbed his finger along Aisne's jaw. He gently tilted her back waiting for her to protest. When none came, he moved his lips against hers.

Every inch of her body tingled at the sensation of his mouth against hers. The way he held her was gentle but it was no less passionate. She wished that the moment would last forever but all too quickly Aregund pulled away from her.

"What's the matter?" she asked warily.

"You're glowing…" Aregund pulled at a strand of her hair that had fallen in her face.

"Maybe I want you to focus on me." Aisne waved her hand at the lantern devouring the only light other than the fireplace.

"I'm always focused on you, even when you're angry with me."

"I'm not angry now." Aisne smiled shyly. She had so little experience with men but Aregund always made her feel at ease. She wanted to be close to him in a way that she couldn't explain. "Will you stay with me tonight?"

"I'll do whatever you ask of me."

"Come." Aisne took his hand and led him over to the bed. She looked into his eyes as she unhooked the clasp that held the gown in place. She let go of the material and the gown fell to the floor around her feet. "I never imagined being with a man this way until I met you… and I don't know if I will ever feel this way again…" Her eyes filled with tears as she struggled to speak from her heart.

Without speaking a word, Aregund pulled her close to him. He kissed her more deeply than he ever had before. Every struggle that they'd faced and every harsh word they'd spoken to one another was torn away from memory. Only this moment mattered. It was all they cared about.

"I'll never love anyone but you," Aregund whispered.

"I love you too," she replied softly.

The little cabin was illuminated by the fireplace alone. Dancing on the wall, were two silhouettes that slowly blended into one.

Aisne woke to find Queen Nuestria sitting at the foot of the bed. The sight of her aunt filled her with fear. She'd never seen the queen outside of Merovech.

"Aregund…" Aisne uttered.

"He is unharmed," Nuestria assured her. "I had a task for him that was quite urgent."

"You came here in person to collect one of your soldiers?"

"Quite the contrary… I came here for you."

Aisne still felt panicked. "How did you know I'd be here?"

"Call it intuition but I knew it would only be a matter of time before you and Aregund returned to this place." Nuestria stared around the room showing her displeasure. "Merovech is a much more suitable place for you, Aisne."

"I've no interest in returning to Merovech and I'm sure you're already aware of that fact."

"But I need your help. We all do." Queen Nuestria stood up and walked over to the bedroom window. "The Faeborn are on their way to Merovech. They expect a Tribunal to take place soon after their arrival."

"I won't be a pawn between the Garkin and Faeborn anymore. You can settle your differences without me."

"Aisne, you must understand. When a king or queen dies, it upsets the balance of our world."

"What balance has there ever been? From the time Queen Harmonia went missing, you have been at odds."

"That is true. Tylwyth immediately requested a Tribunal. The Garkin lord at the time was my father, Gabon. He refused Tylwyth's request… not longer after that my father was poisoned. That started the war between the Garkin and Faeborn."

"But it was all a lie," Aisne added. "…Tylwyth's request for a tribunal, your father's murder and the deaths of so many others. All of these deaths lay at the feet of King Tylwyth and his queen."

Queen Nuestria turned around and stared at Aisne. "None of that can be discussed during the Tribunal."

"I don't understand…" Aisne replied. "You want me to lie?"

"If you tell the heads of the Faeborn, human and Garkin delegations that the Faeborn king was singularly responsible for the darkling attacks, there would be no way of avoiding an all-out war."

"But that is the truth. Everyone deserves to know it."

"So let's say went with your recommendation. The Faeborn queen would be held in a Tribunal and punishment would be sought from the human governor and my generals. If the Faeborn refused to give her up, and they would, war would soon follow."

Aisne knew that there was some measure of truth to her aunt's words but then there was always good reason for war. The kingdoms always discovered more motivation to be against each other than to be in agreement. "Very well, I will do what you ask. I won't speak of Tylwyth's treachery. But when I have done this, I ask that you leave me be. Once I leave Merovech, I won't return."

"Agreed." Queen Nuestria nodded her head and rose to her feet. "I'll be waiting for you outside."

Aisne dressed quickly and threw her knapsack over her shoulder. When she walked outside, she could hardly believe her eyes.

Other than the four Garkin who carried the Queen's mini carriage, there were thirty Garkin dressed in battle armor. Were the soldiers there for her benefit or for the queen's protection? She couldn't imagine that the Garkin had come to fear her so fully.

"Are you ready to leave, my dear?" the queen spoke from behind the blue silken curtain of her carriage.

Aisne nodded her head and started walking out of the clearing. Once the queen's caravan started moving away from the cabin, Aisne took one last look back at its quiet exterior. It was one of the few places in the world she experienced true happiness. The memory of that night with Aregund would stay with her forever.

The march toward Merovech was without incident but it was enlightening all the same. Even though Queen Nuestria needed Aisne's help to ease the tension with the Faeborn, it was obvious that the Garkin feared her. There could be no trust where there was fear and that left Aisne on her own when the Tribunal was over.

When they reached the front gates at Merovech, Aisne didn't feel the comfort that usually accompanied her visits to the Garkin fortress. Her feelings were similar to that of her time at Tremeria. Neither place could be home for her again.

When Aisne walked through the gate, Duran was waiting for her, smiling face and all.

"I was wondering when you'd get here," Duran gushed.

"It's good to see you too." Aisne didn't feel like smiling but she could spare a small one for the most cheerful Garkin she'd ever met.

"Duran, shouldn't you be attending to your duties?" Queen Nuestria stepped down from her carriage and stared at Duran in disapproval.

"Yes, Queen Nuestria." Duran bowed and turned to walk away but not before winking her eye at Aisne.

The soldiers on the fortress wall didn't seem to notice Aisne but that didn't mean she wasn't being watched.

"So will I be free to roam the fortress or should I expect a room in your dungeon as well?"

"Don't be so dramatic, Aisne. You aren't a prisoner here. You'll be staying in your old room."

"That's a relief." Aisne remained two steps behind Nuestria as they entered the main hall of the fortress.

Nuestria stopped just outside her throne room. "The Faeborn delegation should be here at first light. I'll send for you when the Tribunal is set to begin."

"Of course." Aisne bowed slightly and turned back toward the stone staircase.

Chapter 31

Aisne was led into the throne room which had been converted into the tribunal chamber. Overseeing the tribunal was the work of the magistrates of record. This three person panel would decide the fate of those they interviewed and as such their ruling was binding.

Queen Nuestria, Governor Pierce and Prince Rigunth sat on a raised platform at the front of the room. Having already interviewed and found innocent all of Aisne's companions, only her trial remained. To begin the final phase of the tribunal, Aisne was brought to a singular wooden bench at the center of the room.

In a monologue that seemed to go on without end, Aisne was advised of the tribunal proceedings and why she had been summoned. Every moment that Governor Pierce spent talking, was like torture for her. She felt the full weight of everyone's eyes locked on her as if she were nothing more than a common criminal. She made her best effort to ignore the throngs of soldiers and highborn spectators choosing instead to focus her attention on the Garkin crest hanging above the raised platform.

"Do you give your solemn promise to answer the questions asked of you to the best of your ability?"

"I will." Aisne glanced at the round faced governor and found an expression of sympathy. He probably wanted to be there as much as she did.

"Then let's begin," he said calmly before taking his seat next to Queen Nuestria.

Aisne sat up in her chair waiting for whatever verbal onslaught was to come. But when Kenbridge approached her with warm eyes and a sheepish grin, she instantly relaxed.

"Hello, Princess Aisne." He wrung his hands out in front of him and stared briefly in Governor Pierce's direction. "Peter has painted quite a picture of the danger you all encountered in Sjoborg. He testified that you risked your life to heal a soldiers. Is that accurate?"

"Yes, we faced many challenges."

"Can you elaborate?"

"We encountered a very powerful creature in the forest. I now believe that creature to be the Tempest Bloom."

There was a volley of whispers and heightened chatter that circled the room several times over. Kenbridge didn't bother trying to quiet the room. "Were you able to defeat the creature?"

"No, we weren't. But it was in our fortune that the creature was destroyed. I don't know what would've happened otherwise." Aisne lowered her head again as uncertainty crept in around her. She had no way of knowing how her admission would be perceived. There was also the matter of speaking too freely on events that she was forbidden to discuss.

"Do you feel responsible for the king's death?" Kenbridge's question brought some measure of quiet to the room.

"No, I don't." Aisne answered honestly.

"I have no further questions," Kenbridge announced before bowing to the magistrates.

In his haste to leave the floor, he dropped the parchments of paper he was carrying and they spread across the floor going this way and that. There was a bit of laughter in the room as he hurried to collect them. He'd just reached the final parchment when Aisne picked it up and handed it to him. He smiled kindly at her and shuffled noisily to his seat in the back of the room.

Aisne was soon joined near the center of the room by General Caldron. He was the newest member of Queen Nuestria's inner circle who had her ear in various matters of peace and war. He was a favored choice to fill the opening left by General Lok's disgraceful departure but he wasn't so easy on the eyes.

General Caldron had a deep scar that ran down the left side of his face. Wearing his long, dark hair pulled back in a braid was uncharacteristic for a male but it also served as a reminder to anyone who looked at him of just how virulent he was. He wore the wound with pride.

"Did you follow Legionnaire Fyk's orders at all times?" he asked the question as if he already knew the answer.

"Yes, I believe so…" Aisne wasn't sure how to answer him.

"Perhaps you should only respond when you're sure of your words, princess." Caldron slowly paced the floor in front of her as

THE TEMPEST BLOOM: RISE OF THE DARKLING

whispered conversations sprung up throughout the room.

"When you're in the field, life or death can be determined by the actions of one person. I know how to follow orders."

"Of course you do, princess." General Caldron smiled and then glanced over at the Garkin who had gathered in the room. Aisne was certain that Fyk was among them but she had no desire to search him out. Instead she focused on General Caldron and his quiet assault of her actions in the field.

He continued with a line of questioning that shed a positive light on Fyk, which pleased her. But his remarks also shifted the blame for the failed mission onto Aisne. It seemed odd that no one in the room, not even Queen Nuestria, inquired on his interview tactics. When Caldron was done, he clasped his hands together behind his back and took his seat within the benches most occupied by the Garkin. The room fell silent as everyone waited to see who'd take the floor next.

Aisne adjusted in her seat as she listened to the throne room doors open and close. Toben Marro walked to a point on the floor just a few feet in front of her but he faced the magistrates of record. He bowed in their direction before slowly turning around to face Aisne.

She remembered his blue eyes, his well groomed hair that was almost completely grey, and his slender fingers that he pressed against his lips. Aisne remembered how kindly he regarded her when first they met but now his face showed only disdain.

She suddenly remembered seeing him in the great room in Tremeria. He witnessed her assault on Prince Rigunth, an act he found unforgiveable. It didn't matter that Rigunth attacked an innocent man. He was the law in Tremeria and Aisne had violated that law.

"Princess Aisne, do you remember the events that led up to King Tylwyth's murder?"

Aisne was caught off guard by his candor. She expected him to drone on the way Governor Pierce had but nothing could have been further from the truth. "I remember everything that happened, my lord."

"Can you enlighten us, then? What were you doing while the king lay dying not far from where you stood?" Toben stared down his long nose at her.

"Well, everything happened so quickly. We were all fighting for our lives." Aisne found herself searching for a friendly face in the room. She found only the clusters of humans, Garkin and Faeborn seated around the room as if the sections were marked. "It was obvious the creature never intended to free the king. She only let him live to use him as bait."

"Bait for what, princess?" Toben smiled wide as he reacted to Aisne's admission.

"The creature wanted me to free her mother."

"And that's exactly what you did. Instead of freeing the king, you freed the very creature that created the darkling to begin with. Isn't that right, princess?"

"You don't understand... I didn't have a choice." Aisne moved forward in her chair. "The creature I freed saved us all. She took the darkling away!"

"But that wasn't your goal, was it? You were tasked with saving the king but you failed." Toben suddenly turned his back to her. "Your lack of action directly led to his death."

"That's not true!" Aisne shouted.

"I don't remember asking you a question, princess!" Toben turned toward her with his hands balled into fists at his side. "There will be justice for King Tylwyth and it will be swift. You can deny all you like!"

Aisne sat back in her chair and stared at the floor. No matter what she said, it was obvious that she was being blamed for the king's death. It was a weight she had no desire to carry.

Suddenly the door to the throne room swung open and landed hard against the wall. Everyone in the room turned to see what had caused the ruckus. Floating into the room as if on a tuft of clouds was Queen Harmonia herself.

Several of the Faeborn in attendance gasped in shock and bowed their heads as she moved deeper into the room. "I'd like to speak on this matter, Toben."

"Of course, my queen." Toben bowed his head and took two steps back.

Queen Harmonia smiled at Aisne before turning her attention toward the magistrates of record who until this point had been rather quiet. "I would like to speak to you now."

Queen Nuestria stood to her feet. "Queen Harmonia while it is a pleasure to see you well, this is an odd time for a visit. This tribunal has an urgent matter to contend with."

"I do not wish to disrupt this ceremony but as a witness to the events in question, I assumed my testimony would be welcome."

Queen Nuestria nodded her head slowly. "You are quite right. Please proceed with your recollection of the events."

Harmonia stepped closer to the raised platform before turning toward the room full of spectators. "My husband is a hero; brave and strong to the end."

"Go on, my queen…" Toben suddenly appeared at her side.

Queen Harmonia motioned for Aisne to stand up so that she could take her place on the bench at the center of the room. Aisne slowly stepped away from Harmonia and found an empty seat on the first row of visitor's benches.

Prince Rigunth shifted in his chair, quite discomforted by the sight of his mother being interviewed. This certainly wasn't what he had in mind when he requested the Tribunal. Should he protest now, the Tribunal would be cancelled and no justice would be found for his father.

"As the mayhem unfolded before me, I was too weak to assist Lord Fyk and the others. I watched the princess singlehandedly fighting off more than a dozen of the darkling." Harmonia paused as if she was reliving a painful memory. "In a desperate act, King Tylwyth decided to entertain the creature on his own. It was a costly mistake."

"What happened next, Queen Harmonia?" Governor Pierce asked moving to the edge of his seat.

"The creature easily overpowered him. It happened right in front of me." Harmonia lowered her head. "Lena killed my husband. There was nothing that anyone could have done to save him. As much as I would love to have someone to blame, I fear the only person to blame was Tylwyth himself."

The room grew quieter as Harmonia's body began to glow. Aisne stood to her feet and watched the Faeborn queen closely. Harmonia's show of anguish quenched the blood hunt that was evident just before her arrival.

"Thank you for your testimony, Queen Harmonia. We understand how very difficult this must be for you." Queen Nuestria stood up and addressed the room. "Now that we have heard from our witnesses, we will adjourn to make our decision."

Once the magistrates exited the room, many of those in attendance departed the room as well. However, they would all return for the final ruling. It was, after all, the only way to retain the fragile peace between the species.

Aisne sat in her room alone with her back to the door. She desired nothing more than to leave Merovech for good but she needed to wait on the ruling from the Tribunal. Only then would she be free to find a new life beyond the mountains.

A new life was what she wanted but Aregund was what she desired. Deep in her heart, she longed to be with him. But she knew that Queen Nuestria and the Garkin would never allow it. This quest he was on was no doubt a ruse to put distance between them.

Aregund was a fine soldier and the best tracker in all of Merovech. These things were also his identity. He'd never leave his home and she knew she couldn't stay. The night they spent together would certainly be their last.

There was a sudden knock at the door that surprised Aisne. "Come in," Aisne said weakly.

Queen Harmonia floated into the room and shut the door behind her. She sat down on the bed next to Aisne and smiled warmly. There was something about Harmonia that reminded her of Emma. "You've been cleared of any wrongdoing, princess."

"Has the tribunal reconvened?" Aisne asked with hope in her voice.

"No but I read Queen Nuestria's thoughts and my son's."

Aisne was surprised at how cavalier Harmonia was about reading others' emotions. It instantly reminded her of Rigunth. Even though Aisne shared this ability with them, she never felt that comfortable tapping into someone's innermost feelings. She was certain that most humans and Garkin would find this to be an intrusion.

"I certainly hope that's the case. The sooner I can leave Merovech, the better."

"Where will you go... to run and hide in shame?" Harmonia's tone was more deliberate than normal. "You have nothing to be ashamed of."

"I can't stay here." Aisne tried to keep her voice steady. "Even if I'm found innocent, there'll still be those who'd blame me for King Tylwyth's death."

Harmonia smiled. "Then they would be the fools. You saved us; you saved all of us."

"You really believe that?"

"Of course I do. Lena was evil to the core. She would have destroyed all of us to find her mother. Your act of freeing Ungotha gave her the strength to do what only she could do... only she could destroy her most powerful creation, Lena."

"She was very powerful. I could feel it..." Aisne was pulled into a memory of her own.

"She was powerful but not as powerful as you are. A Faeborn but with the heart of a Garkin.... you had the power to destroy and yet you showed mercy. You are the Tempest Bloom, Aisne."

"But I couldn't save the king," Aisne replied feeling warm tears on her face. "I'm so sorry."

Harmonia wrapped her arm around Aisne's shoulder. "Tylwyth sealed his fate long ago; we both did."

"What will you do now?" Aisne asked.

"I will have to live with what we did all those years ago. Rigunth will rule now but hopefully, I can guide him toward peace for all our sakes." Harmonia stood up quickly and approached the door.

"Be well, Queen Harmonia." Aisne stood up and bowed to her.

"And you as well, princess."

Chapter 32

Aisne stood in front of the three magistrates waiting to hear the findings from their deliberation. The rest of her team sat in the front row of seats closest to the raised platform. Queen Nuestria's words were brief but they were no less a relief to hear out loud.

"We have determined that King Tylwyth's death was the result of an ill-fated plot against Faeborn and Garkin alike. His death was meant to divide us further and to create a division between our people that would never be healed." Nuestria stepped closer to the edge of the platform. "But in actuality, these events have strengthened our resolve. Those who seek to destroy us will meet their own bitter end. Lena's fate is sealed and so will be that of her co-conspirator. I am confident that Lok will be brought to justice very soon!"

The room erupted in applause as Faeborn and Garkin soldiers alike clapped their hands and stomped their feet in approval. A few of them cheered loudly as Nuestria attempted to quiet them down. The noise in the room was louder than anything Aisne had heard before but of course this was her first Tribunal.

Aisne stared over at Fredegund who was standing near the front of the room. He nodded toward her in approval before turning back toward Dax who was standing next to him. She wondered if he'd heard news of Aregund but she wouldn't dare ask.

A swift knock at the door pulled everyone's attention. Peter Pierce strolled into the room and stopped a short distance from the raised platform. He bowed to Queen Nuestria who had taken her seat again. Although he kept his eyes locked on Nuestria, Prince Rigunth was the first to address him.

"Peter Pierce, the interviews are over and our pronouncement has been made. Why are you here?"

"Prince Rigunth, please forgive my intrusion but I have urgent business with this tribunal. I have presented the matter of the

Sjoborg settlement before the human court and I have been advised to speak to you all here."

"There is no settlement at Sjoborg," Queen Nuestria interjected. "Governor Pierce, what is this? Why is your son addressing this tribunal?"

Peter took another step closer to the raised platform. "I have petitioned the human court for the right to replace my brother as Governor of Sjoborg. I am addressing this tribunal today as a notification and a courtesy."

"On whose authority do you make this pronouncement?" Prince Rigunth had a hint of amusement in his voice.

"My own," Peter replied firmly. "We will invite no interference from the Faeborn or Garkin kingdoms. We will continue life in Sjoborg just as my brother started it... on our own."

"You seemed to have given this some thought," Queen Nuestria said leaning forward in her chair.

"Yes, I have Queen Nuestria. There are dozens of families that would like to return home and those are just the ones we know of. As word spreads that the darkling are gone, more people will return home." Peter smiled and glanced around the room. "We'll welcome everyone to Sjoborg; any walk of life and any family."

"That's a noble concept, Peter." Queen Nuestria seemed slightly amused. "But the law is the law."

"Your law, Queen Nuestria, isn't our law. I trust that you and the Faeborn will respect our right and desire to live without interference." Peter bowed slightly waiting for some response from the queen.

"Since Sjoborg is not recognized in any current agreement with these kingdoms, it is safe to assume that your goings-on do not affect us." Governor Pierce surprised everyone in the room when he rendered his opinion.

"Perhaps we can discuss this matter privately," Queen Nuestria said smiling. She waved her hand to quiet the room but it had little effect on the growing waves of low level banter.

"I thank you all for your attention." Peter bowed toward the magistrates before marching out of the room.

Queen Nuestria stood to her feet. "If no one else has any matters to discuss, I draw this Tribunal to a close." Queen Nuestria wore a smile on her face but it was obvious she was calculating something. She waved a hand at General Guntram and he started moving in her direction.

Aisne watched her aunt for a moment before a huge figure blocked her view. "I've been told that you intend to leave us..." Fyk said in his normal tone.

"This isn't my home anymore," Aisne replied as she stood to her feet. "I don't have one."

"Is that pity I hear in your voice? Pity is for the weak," he added firmly.

"Yes, I know." Aisne smiled at him and placed her right arm over her chest. "Be well, Fyk."

"Be well, princess." Fyk placed his arm over his chest and bowed slightly to her.

Before she let her emotions take hold, she moved away from the large Garkin and headed toward the door. She didn't want her last encounter with him be an emotional one.

The fortress gates creaked open and made a crashing sound against the stone walls. The sound seemed to drift into the background of Aisne's mind as she focused on putting one foot in front of the other. She thought about everyone she was leaving behind; Basina, Duran, Fyk and even Aregund. It made her chest heavy and her spirit dark but putting distance between herself and Merovech was what she needed to do.

With only her rucksack on her back, she made her way down the hill away from Merovech. The road she would take north toward the mountains was just out of view. Her new life was waiting for her.

She'd just passed a small group of red oak trees when she had the feeling of being watched. The thought made her smile.

"Don't you have some place to be, governor?" Aisne turned toward the oak tree that she'd just passed.

"Yes and so do you." Peter moved out from the shadow of the tree and leaned against it. "I'm afraid I can't allow you to leave."

"How do you plan to stop me?" she asked placing both hands on her hips.

"I told you she wouldn't convince easily," Duran stepped from behind Peter's tree.

"Duran!" What are you doing outside of Merovech?" Aisne was surprised and pleased to see the tiny Garkin.

"I'm going to help Peter." Duran kicked at a lump of grass on the ground in front of her. "I'm making a life for myself. Isn't that what you always told me to do?"

"Yes but I never expected you'd actually listen to me." Aisne answered calmly.

"Well, I did and now I want you to listen to us."

Peter stepped closer to Duran. "We need your help, Aisne."

"I know nothing of governing." Aisne shot back.

"But you do know how to protect people. That's why I want you to serve as the head of my security force."

"Me?"

"Why not a woman?" he asked coyly.

Aisne hesitated for a moment. She stared in the direction of the northbound road. She knew nothing of what lie beyond the mountains.

If she joined Peter, there were numerous possibilities. She'd be around friends, people she cared about. What could be better than that? "A woman indeed!" Aisne reached her arm out to Peter and he grasped it quickly.

"You won't regret this…" Peter smiled widely. "We will rebuild Sjoborg together!"

"Agreed!" Aisne replied happily.

In the days that followed, Peter moved into the First Residence and began the work of rebuilding Sjoborg one structure at a time. After repairing his own house, replacing the missing floor boards and broken windows, the new governor set about restoring the shops that formed the town square. Only then would the people have a place to return to that wasn't a reminder of the death and loss that once blanketed the town.

Aisne decided to take up residence in a cabin on the beach. It offered her some solitude when she could steal a few minutes to visit it. Otherwise, she was at Peter's side establishing a security force and interviewing everyone who desired to make Sjoborg their home.

Just as Peter suspected, word of his governorship spread quickly. Soon members from both Faeborn and Garkin kingdoms were converging on the city. The idea of living amongst other species was more desirable than Peter realized.

But the bulk of Sjoborg would again be made up of humans. The old shopkeepers, glass blowers and their families were overjoyed to be able to return home. Aisne finally began to imagine some sort of normalcy there.

On the twenty-eighth day following Peter's arrival in Sjoborg, a caravan ascended upon the city. There were two horse drawn carriages and a sizable foot escort approaching, a rarity in this part of the land.

Aisne and Peter were addressing three human recruits when the first carriage pulled up behind them. Aisne grabbed her staff and moved closer to Peter.

"What are they doing here?' he asked Aisne.

"I don't know but if they don't have a good answer for this surprise visit, it won't end well for them."

Several members of Aisne's security force, both human and otherwise, moved in behind her as they waited for the carriage door to open. The door slowly swung open and Princess Respa stepped out. Her carriage handler, Tevell, held her hand as she tipped down the carriage steps.

"Princess Aisne, it is a pleasure to see you again." Respa bowed slightly.

"There is no royalty in Sjoborg. There is only our community." Aisne relaxed her stance only slightly. "Why are you here?"

Respa took a deep breath and stepped forward. "We seek refuge. My husband and my sisters are with me. Patia and Raven are in the other carriage."

Aisne tried to hide her surprise at Respa's announcement. She didn't realize that Respa was engaged. But once she saw Respa's companion, she realized why they were here.

Soren stepped out of the carriage looking quite uncomfortable. He was dressed in fineries that divulged the newness of his wedding vows.

"This is a surprise, Respa. Does Rigunth know that you are married?" Aisne asked but not unkindly.

"I cannot concern myself with his opinions. I can only live my life." Respa took Soren's hand in hers.

Only then did Aisne understand the predicament they were in. Respa had married a man that her family would never accept. For their love, she fled her home to start anew.

Aisne felt a sort of connection with Respa but more than anything she worried if she could keep the princess safe. It wouldn't take Rigunth long to figure out where she'd gone and he'd certainly follow. They weren't prepared for a conflict with the Faeborn prince.

"Peter Pierce will decide if you can stay. After all, he is Governor of Sjoborg. I merely enforce his laws." Realizing that there was no danger, Aisne stepped back and stood next to Peter.

He immediately smiled at them. "You are most welcome. All of you are welcome here!"

Respa wrapped her hands around Peter's and held it firmly. "Thank you, governor. We are in your debt."

"We will find suitable accommodations for you." Peter turned toward Duran who'd suddenly appeared behind him. "Duran, will you show Respa and her family to the east road? There you'll find two newly repaired bungalows."

Duran raised her arm and said, "This way please. You must be weary from your journey, friends."

Soren raised an eyebrow at Duran but she hadn't notice. She was taking her new post very seriously.

Tevell helped Respa's sisters out of their carriage next. To Aisne's surprise, Laila stepped out of the carriage behind them. She didn't dare approach Soren's fairy mother for fear of showing favoritism. They did exchange a kind glance before Laila followed after Duran and the others.

"This may be a problem, governor." Aisne spoke to Peter over her shoulder. She usually called him *'Governor'* when she questioned a decision he'd made. It didn't happen often but he knew immediately when Aisne didn't agree with him.

"You fear some form of retribution from Rigunth? How would he even know that she's here?" Peter replied.

"Just like anything else, someone will tell him."

"Let's worry about it then, shall we?" Peter smiled at Aisne as they started back toward the square.

Sometime after midnight, Aisne was awakened by a loud crash. She hopped off the bed and landed in a defensive crouch on the floor. She waited for a few seconds before darting over to the front door.

"What in the heavens was that?" Duran asked from across the narrow hall. She and Aisne were sharing a cottage on the East road to make room for the ever growing number of families returning to Sjoborg.

"Stay here. I'm going to find out." Aisne bloomed and leapt through the open window. She landed on the ground and turned to find Soren walking toward her.

He motioned for her to wait before she took action. Of course she didn't listen. She had no idea how many intruders were lurking about but she didn't want them to reach the governor before she did. She flew up into the air and made a beeline toward the First Residence.

That was the moment she saw them; five Garkin standing at Peter's front door. One of them reached for the door knob and Aisne threw her lance through the air catching him in the back.

"I wouldn't do that if I were you," she said landing hard on the ground in front of them.

"That's going to leave a mark," Soren said from behind her.

"I've taken harder shots than that." Dax turned around and smiled at Aisne.

"Are you trying to get yourself killed?" Aisne moved out of her defensive position and walked over to greet him.

"Actually no… I had another idea."

Chapter 33

Aisne could hardly believe how much Sjoborg had changed since Peter petitioned the human council to become governor. The town, for the most part, had returned to its former glory as evidenced by the town square. It was fully populated with skilled craftsmen, food vendors and a full contingent of security who maintained order.

Once Dax, Roden, and other Garkin soldiers arrived, Aisne was more confident in their ability to protect themselves should they be attacked. But when Soren sent word they he and his new wife were safe and sound in Sjoborg, Faeborn cast outs began to arrive in greater numbers. The old issues between the species resurfaced.

As the security commander, Aisne was tasked with keeping the peace. She wanted to serve as an example for the settlements but how could she if she couldn't keep a few dozen Faeborn and Garkin from killing each other?

"The next person who strikes a blow will have me to deal with!" Aisne launched herself between two new arrivals. She waved her lance above her head and waited for someone to respond to her challenge. When no one did, she lowered her weapon and pushed passed the Faeborn who was holding a rock inside his fist.

"If you cannot get along with the team here, you will not be welcome to stay. Perhaps you should all think about that tonight. I won't make this request again."

"So what are you planning to do now, warrior princess? Will you beat them all into submission?" Peter teased Aisne as she escorted him around the square for his daily inspection. The shops were full of merchants ready to sell their wares in a completely open market. It was the first of its kind anywhere.

Peter didn't need to survey the area. No one would be foolish enough to get themselves uninvited from such a profitable situation.

He merely enjoyed Aisne's company and the chance to see how happy the people of Sjoborg were.

"Don't you have real work to do, *governor*?" Aisne shook her head as a boy offered her a chunk of mincemeat pie.

"Actually I do and I wanted to speak with you about it privately." Peter's expression suddenly turned serious.

"What is it this time... children skipping their studies?"

"Prince Rigunth has requested a meeting with me..."

"Absolutely not!" Aisne interrupted Peter mid-sentence. "He cannot be trusted."

"Do you presume to give me an order, constable?" Peter stopped walking and turned to face Aisne.

Aisne softened realizing that she had offended him. "Pete, you don't know him the way I do. He always has a hidden agenda."

"I knew you would protest. That's why I requested that he meet us here alone."

"And he agreed?"

"He did," Peter added nervously. "But with one small request..."

Aisne pulled at the neck line of the ridiculous gown she wore. It was covered in pink, ruffled tiers that reached the floor. "I can't believe Pete agreed to this. Rigunth will stop at nothing to mock me."

"At least Peter didn't request that you have dinner with them," Duran said softly. "Queen Harmonia would have enjoyed your company."

"It is for Harmonia that I am peaceable. Otherwise, I fear my lance would find its way into Rigunth's throat."

"You are such a charmer, Aisne. Did I ever tell you that?" Duran's laughter had become even higher pitched since she departed Merovech.

"I have no desire to charm that ridiculous prince." Aisne continued pulling at her collar. "As soon as I return, I will give you my blade so that you can cut me out of this thing."

Minutes later, Aisne walked into the sitting room at the First Residence to find Harmonia, Rigunth and Peter laughing and talking in hushed tones. She ignored the unease she felt and greeted Harmonia warmly before sitting down next to Peter on the narrow lounger. The nicest furniture Peter owned was in that room.

"I appreciate you both taking the time to meet with us this evening. It is an uncomfortable thing we're here to discuss." Rigunth kept his eyes locked on Peter but Aisne could sense his emotions. His presence there had nothing to do with the Governor of Sjoborg. There was deception within him and that gave Aisne cause for concern. "My sisters are here and we want them back." Rigunth became quite blunt when he realized Aisne was reading him.

"This is true, Rigunth." Peter was choosing his words carefully. "Your sisters are here of their own free will. They are productive citizens so I had no reason to turn them away."

Harmonia suddenly looked concerned. "Productive... what does that mean?"

"It means that my sisters are performing some sort of manual labor as if they were commoners." Rigunth's eyes turned a darker emerald shade. His attempt at civility had all but fallen away. "I would like to see Respa now!"

Aisne got to her feet. "That's not possible."

"Anything is possible, princess." Rigunth relaxed his tone and leaned back in his chair. "Is there somewhere that we can rest for the night? I'm afraid I've grown weary from our long journey."

"Of course," Peter interjected. "There's plenty of room here. I can show you to a quiet room upstairs."

"Excellent," Rigunth replied.

After completing her final patrol of the night, Aisne retired to the small bedroom next to Peter's office. The room was meant to be another sitting room but Aisne often used the room when she hadn't the motivation to return to her cottage. It also gave her the opportunity to guard Peter closely considering their Faeborn guests.

Aisne hadn't quite fallen asleep when she heard a scratching sound against her door. She rose off the bed and pulled a short blade from under her pillow. In one sweeping motion, she pulled the door open and launched herself into the hall. Everything was perfectly still in the house but she still felt uneasy.

She decided to check upstairs to make sure everyone was accounted for. Peter was fast asleep in his room as was Jenny Wright, who'd just signed on as Peter's new assistant. Harmonia hadn't completely closed her bedroom door so Aisne could see her lying across her bed.

But one person was clearly missing from the house and that was Rigunth. Although his dinner jacket was on the back of the chair, his bed hadn't been slept in. The window to his bedroom was wide open which probably served as his method of escape.

Aisne bloomed and launched herself out the window. She knew immediately where Rigunth would go. What she didn't know was what he was planning to accomplish in the middle of the night and without his soldiers to assist him.

When Aisne reached Soren's cottage, the front door was wide open. Rigunth was sitting comfortably on the couch in the front room with Patia seated next to him. Both Soren and Respa were standing on the other side of the room appearing entirely uncomfortable.

"Have I interrupted something?" Aisne smiled politely at Respa before turning her attention back to Rigunth.

"On the contrary," Rigunth replied. "I just wanted to visit with my sisters in private."

"Couldn't this have waited for the morning, dear brother?" Respa's countenance had changed from the last time Aisne saw her. Her sullen mood filled the room. She glanced from Rigunth to Aisne with a plea in her eyes that forced Aisne to take action.

"Rigunth, we do have rules for moving about after dark." Aisne stepped in front of Respa. "I'll have to ask that you come with me."

Rigunth slowly rose to his feet. "Is this how you treat your guests?"

"Yes… it is." Aisne motioned for him to walk outside.

"As you wish," he answered playfully.

Once outside, Rigunth's obnoxious grin quickly faded. There were a dozen members of the security force waiting to escort him back to the First Residence.

"This way," Heziel shouted toward Rigunth. He shifted to his Garkin form and shoved Rigunth harder than was necessary. It may have been a response to Rigunth's unauthorized nighttime stroll or maybe it was due to how much he disliked the prince. Either way, Rigunth knew that his fun was over.

"Another of your admirers, I see." Rigunth's tone was more sarcastic than normal. He walked into the house and Aisne shut the door behind him.

"What are you talking about?" Aisne was only mildly interested in his latest rant.

"The guard who first approached me... He's in love with you."

"Rigunth, I have no interest in your fantasies tonight."

"Ignore me if you must but I speak the truth." Rigunth walked toward the stairs. "Answer me this... is he one of the soldiers you healed?"

Aisne nodded her head. "What of it?"

"You must be careful who you heal, princess. A Garkin heart never forgets."

"Are you quite done?" she asked flatly.

"I am." Rigunth replied calmly. "So what do we do now?"

"Now you will return to your room and we will forget that any of this happened."

"If only you meant those words." Rigunth turned and climbed the stairs.

Aisne knew that Rigunth was not to be trusted and she had no desire to try and gain his trust. Before returning to her bedroom, she instructed Heziel to secure the ground around the governor's house using a memory stone. In that way, Rigunth would be unable to leave the First Residence should he desire to visit his sisters again.

The night progressed without incident or at least it seemed that way. Rigunth was asleep in his bed when Aisne performed an early morning inspection. And when he did wake, he made no mention of the extra precautions taken against him.

As Peter said his goodbyes to Harmonia, Aisne couldn't help feeling a bit of sadness. She had a strange feeling she wouldn't see Harmonia again and if she did, it wouldn't be on such good terms. Her daughter's departure and subsequent marriage must have been difficult to bare. Rigunth's antics certainly didn't make the situation more comfortable for anyone.

"I hope that he doesn't return with some other trickery. I would hate to have to kill him." Aisne adjusted the metal casing on her arm without noticing Peter's surprised expression.

"Could you really do it?"

"If he returns with his soldiers... it may not be avoidable." Aisne pasted a smile on her face. "Don't worry, *governor*. That's my concern."

"If you say so," Peter replied cautiously.

Aisne was relieved by Rigunth's departure. It allowed her to focus on what was important – training. She still needed time to convince her team of misfit soldiers that they could be a cohesive protection detail for everyone in Sjoborg. After all, that's what Peter promised everyone; a free and united city.

By the end of the day, Aisne was feeling slightly more optimistic. She hadn't had to break up a fight and the men were actually helping each other. They even practiced patrolling methods for those that were new to the team. She should've known that the calm wouldn't last.

"Aisne!" Duran's voice sounded in her ear like an alarm. "Come quickly, Peter needs you!"

She picked up her staff and hurried after the small Garkin. The only thing she could imagine was that Rigunth had doubled back or some other such horror. But when she reached the First Residence, she found nothing of the sort.

Peter was standing on the front porch with a blank expression on his face. "Come inside…" was all he said to her.

When Aisne walked into Peter's office, she was surprised to find one of the last people she expected to see standing with his back to her. "Leave us," he belted out and Peter quickly complied.

"Guntram, what brings you so far south?" Aisne asked trying to keep her voice steady.

"I needed to speak with you." When he turned around, she noticed for the first time how much Aregund resembled him. Their eyes were the same; their jaw lines quite similar as well. The major difference between them were the few creases on his face an obvious byproduct of keeping Queen Nuestria's counsel over the centuries. "Aregund has gone missing and I'd like you to find him."

"With all due respect, I'm not at the mercy of the queen any longer."

"I'm not here on Queen Nuestria's behalf. I'm asking you as a father to find my son." Guntram's rather personal request caught Aisne off guard as it was intended to do. "You are a Faeborn and the one he chose. You have the ability to find him… perhaps better than anyone."

"I don't understand…" Aisne could feel the tightness growing in her chest.

"I ordered Aregund to marry Lena and I still don't know if he would have gone through with it. You were his choice. Why do you think I ordered Fyk to train you?"

"That was you?" Aisne stared at him closely.

"Of course it was. I couldn't let my future daughter be injured by Brous, the happy houndsnout."

Aisne stood there for several moments staring out the window. "I appreciate you helping me before… but I've sworn to help Governor Peter Pierce. I can't leave now." Aisne took a step back from him.

"I told you she'd need more convincing." Basina suddenly appeared in the doorway.

This is a surprise," Aisne replied from over her shoulder.

"We need your help." Basina's tone softened. "You may not be a tracker but you do have gifts that you can use to find him."

"What does Fredegund say to all this?" Aisne asked. "Does he believe in my abilities as well as you both do?"

Basina swallowed hard. "He went searching for Aregund twelve days ago. No one has seen him since."

"I see." Aisne suddenly realized why Guntram had traveled so far to see her. Both of his sons were missing and he was desperate. Basina also suffered. She'd been separated from her husband with no sign of when he'd return. "I will go on the hunt for your husband and his brother but under one condition…"

"I'm listening," Basina answered sharply.

"…you're coming with me."

Basina hesitated for a moment before folding her arms over her chest. "Very well, when do we leave?"

Made in the USA
San Bernardino, CA
27 July 2016